"WHY ARE THE SIGNS IN ENGLISH?"
REMO ASKED.

"Mayana is an English-speaking country," Jiminez explained. "Many British citizens immigrated here."

"That is doubtless what attracted Smith's friend here," Chiun observed.

"Huh?" Remo asked.

"The one you and Smith were discussing," Chiun said. "The British enjoy their cults. If it is not Freemasons, it is Druids, if not Druids, Anglican Catholics."

"You're referring to the Jamestown tragedy," Jiminez said slowly, color rising in his cheeks. "Jack James was American, not British. And that's not a topic we like to discuss."

"Nice going, Little Father," Remo whispered. "Anyone else you want to tick off at us?"

"The day is young," Chiun replied ominously.

Created by Murphy & Sapir

THE Destroyer™

WASTE NOT, WANT NOT

A GOLD EAGLE BOOK FROM

WORLDWIDE®

TORONTO • NEW YORK • LONDON
AMSTERDAM • PARIS • SYDNEY • HAMBURG
STOCKHOLM • ATHENS • TOKYO • MILAN
MADRID • WARSAW • BUDAPEST • AUCKLAND

First edition January 2003

ISBN 0-373-63245-2

· Special thanks and acknowledgment to
James Mullaney for his contribution to this work.

WASTE NOT, WANT NOT

To Rick Drew, who has a Web site.
To Mike Harris, who finds unfindable things.
To John Cleese and Michael Palin, who once offered
kind encouragement to a very young writer.

And to the Glorious House of Sinanju,
e-mail: housinan@aol.com

PROLOGUE

She had lost faith in God even before the Almighty decided to slaughter his flock.

As she lay in the mud, she tried to remember when the loss of faith had happened. She supposed it came by degrees. She only remembered waking up in the jungles of South America one morning to the realization that the god she followed was a fraud. By then it was too late.

In the last few minutes before the bullet cracked her skull and pureed her brain, the thing that really vexed Jennifer Lonig's terrified mind was her own gullibility. He claimed to be *God,* for criminy's sake. Wasn't God supposed to be nice? Oh, sure, there was the occasional toad downpour or Mrs. Lot salt lick—but that was Old Testament God.

This was 1978. Smack-dab in the post-Watergate, free-loving, buy-the-world-a-Coke *New* Testament. All that everlasting-vengeance stuff had gone the way of burning bushes and *Ozzie and Harriet.* God was nice now. Everybody knew that. But it turned out the god Jennifer had chosen to worship was just a big old meanie.

"Check the ones at the back."

The voice came over the scratchy public-address system. The booming voice was calm, even as the world crashed down around his ears. The voice belonged to the man Jennifer now realized was not God.

Most of the others were already dead. They had lined up like good sheep at the big communal kettles. At their bad shepherd's command, the foolish righteous had dutifully drunk the tainted soft drink. As the first followers clutched bellies and throats, dropping lifeless to the muddy jungle floor, the rest continued to drink the poison.

They dared not defy God.

Jennifer had only pretended to drink. She found a nice spot in the mud and lay down, hoping—*praying*—to be lost in the crowd. Surely they wouldn't notice. There were hundreds of bodies—acres of dead.

Through barely open eyes she strained to see.

Jennifer was face-to-face with a glassy-eyed corpse. What was the woman's name? Tammy something. From Denver?

Greenish stomach bile dribbled down Tammy-from-Denver's pale cheek.

''The devil rides in on wind of fire,'' the man who wasn't God announced. ''The flock must perish to save the shepherd.''

Someone was coming to the camp. Government troops. Maybe even American Marines. Their imminent arrival had sparked panic among the camp's leadership. But they were an eternity away yet.

They'll be here soon, she told herself. *Soon.*

Jennifer just needed to hold on until the cavalry arrived. And they couldn't possibly check every corpse. If she could stay still, she might just survive.

The loud pop of a gunshot. Very nearby.

Jennifer almost jumped at the sound. By force of will she kept her body slack.

The gunshots had been coming sporadically over the past hour. It was clear that Jennifer was not the only one to fall from the faith. Others had refused the poisoned drink. Their eternal reward came at the end of a rifle barrel.

Another pop. Closer still.

Jennifer shivered in the humid afternoon sun. Shock numbed her senses. The world took on a hazy, unreal tone.

Tammy from Denver was smiling. Chin dripping black and green. Dead lips twisting over stained teeth.

Was she talking?

"He is not God, he is not God...."

The voice sounded familiar. But it couldn't be Tammy from Denver. Tammy was dead. See? There's a fly on her eyeball. Living people don't let flies land on their eyes. But if it wasn't Tammy speaking, who was it?

"He is not God."

Jennifer tried not to shiver.

The beatings, the forced labor, the stress and shock and horror. They had all taken their toll.

The sun was hot. So why was she so cold? And why wouldn't dead Tammy stop talking? Didn't she know? They would find her and kill her all over again if she didn't stop.

"Shh," Jennifer hissed. Her face was covered in a sheen of sweat.

A scuffling footstep. Somewhere nearby, a grunt.

"He is not God, he is not God...."

Wait. That voice. It wasn't Tammy. It was Jennifer. Her own lips were moving. She could see them puckering through her own half-opened eyes. And something else.

A shadow. Blocking Tammy's dead and grinning face. A pair of boots. Very close.

"I got another one," a man's voice called impatiently.

"The world will not be spared the wrath of God," called the voice over the PA system almost simultaneously.

But that wasn't right. The man making the announcement was not God. Jennifer was sure of it.

She almost said so yet again, but then she heard a sharp click behind her ear.

And then there was an explosion so loud and so close it was like the birth of the universe, but within the confines of her own skull.

The earthly Jennifer Lonig never even felt the bullet pierce her skull or the warm mud accept the twitching body that had been hers in life. The essence of what she was had already taken flight from her human shell.

She was swept up into the eternal hum of life that was something that had been beyond her understanding on Earth.

She saw brightness. Shadows of people that she knew in life but had lost. And something else. Something vast and warm and wondrous and everything else the man who had claimed to be God was not.

And in that moment of pure love and contentment, Jennifer Lonig was given a hint of something terrible. A vision of something that would not come to pass until two decades after her corpse had been flown back to the United States for burial. It was a glimpse of the vengeance that would be visited on those who had murdered her. A god from the East who wore the face of a man would visit the land of death. Where this man walked, the world would split, hurling blood and fire into the blazing sky.

And the false god of Earth who cowered in his path would tremble with fear.

1

They wanted garbage. Mountains of it. Piled high and reeking. They wanted much more than they could possibly produce themselves. For the volume of garbage they wanted, they'd had to advertise.

The call was heard around the world.

Household or industrial waste, it didn't matter. Coffee grounds and paper plates were the same as asbestos-lined pipes and dioxin drums. All was welcome.

Industrial sludge was shipped by the barrelful, rolled off boats on pallets by men in protective space-age suits with special breathing masks. It found a temporary home next to buckets of old paint, used-car batteries, rotting rubber tires and stacks of bundled newspapers oozing toxic ink.

When Carlos Whitehall toured New Briton Harbor in the small South American country of Mayana and saw the first of the scows festering at the docks, he allowed a tight smile.

"Beautiful," he said softly.

Oh, not in the conventional sense, of course.

The scows were practically overflowing. Men in masks raked the refuse as it smoldered in the hot sun.

The many seagulls flapping around the junk on the boats brought a sense of vitality, of *life,* to the trash heaps.

That's what this was all about—life.

The country of Mayana was coming to life. Finally claiming its place in the sun. And it would do so by making itself indispensable to the modern world.

The trash was coming in by the boatload.

Mounded in teetering piles, it was coming on slow-moving scows down through the Caribbean to Mayana. The first shipment had reached the port city capital of New Briton the previous evening. It was docked at pier 1.

As he walked, seagulls scattered and ran. Carlos Whitehall almost seemed pleased that the birds could share in his good fortune, in the good fortune of *all* Mayana.

Whitehall strode along the newly constructed docks amid a phalanx of his deputies of commerce. The men pressed white handkerchiefs firmly over their mouths to keep out the smell. Carlos Whitehall—Mayana's finance minister and direct adviser to President Blythe Curry-Hume—seemed to revel in the foul stench.

''There are eighteen scows so far, Minister,'' the young man nearest Whitehall said. George Jiminez was deputy finance minister and assistant director of the top secret Vaporizer Project. He puffed hard behind his handkerchief.

''When will the other bays be ready?'' Whitehall asked. He was a tall man with a deep, healthy tan.

Despite the surroundings, there wasn't a single spot or smudge on his light cotton suit.

"They tell me now it won't be until next Tuesday."

Whitehall stopped dead. The rest of his entourage stumbled to a stop.

"That's ridiculous," the finance minister snapped, eyes flashing with his trademark unpredictable anger.

Behind him, a scow loaded with rusted drums of human waste from a Mexican processing plant was baking in the hot South American sun. The smell failed to bother Whitehall.

"They've taken too much time already," he said, aiming an unwavering finger at Jiminez. "Tell them the president has authorized me to use whatever means necessary to have this up and running by Friday. I am not putting up with any more delays. After the conference Mayana's treasury will have more than enough to hire outside contractors."

"The people might not like that," George pointed out from under his sweaty hankie.

"The people won't care," Whitehall said. "This is going to make everyone in Mayana rich." He waved to the docked scows. "Now, Sears has a few trucks up there, but they'll need two more loads for the last tests." He pointed at the Mexican scow and the one beside it. "That one and that one."

"Maybe we shouldn't charge for these," Jiminez suggested. "A sample for new clients."

"Are either of them from the United States?"

"No," Jiminez replied. "If you'd prefer it, there

are at least two from New York out in the Caribbean.''

Whitehall shook his head firmly. ''The United States can afford to pay. This one is from Mexico?'' George Jiminez nodded. ''Okay, let them both have it on us.'' Through the swarming seagulls he read the markings on the next scow. ''Russian. There's some irony, I suppose,'' he muttered under his breath. ''They've got an environmental movement now. With the mess they've got they'll need our services.''

A half-dozen cell phones appeared from suit jackets. Arrangements were made to off-load the two scows.

Minister Carlos Whitehall spun on his heel. The tall man in the spotless beige suit began marching up the dock.

George Jiminez jogged to keep up. The wind was shifting out to sea. He came out from behind his handkerchief, testing the air. It was a little better.

''I've spoken with the president's office,'' Jiminez said, tucking his hankie back in his pocket. ''Everything's set.''

''Of course it is,'' Whitehall snapped unhappily. ''Our first-term executive president had to be dragged on board this project by me. He contributed nothing, George. Nothing. He only got elected at a propitious time.''

They were at the parking area beyond the docks. Whitehall's driver ran around his limousine to open the back door for the finance minister.

George Jiminez knew this was a touchy subject. There was animosity between the finance minister and the executive president's office. Still, they would all be able to bury their differences soon. Today Mayana would take the first step to becoming the richest country in South America.

As Minister Whitehall climbed into the car, Jiminez glanced back over his shoulder.

A few of the men were coming out to the parking lot, clicking shut cell phones. They got into government cars.

The harbor teemed with seagulls. They filled sky and land. In the far distance, another scow piled high with teetering garbage was making its lazy way in from the sea.

The wind shifted suddenly. The fresh stench nearly caused George Jiminez to vomit his breakfast. He fumbled in his pocket for his handkerchief.

"See Mayana and lose your lunch," he coughed as he climbed into the back seat of the air-conditioned limo.

As the finance minister's limousine sped up into the Mayana hills, George Jiminez wondered briefly how that slogan would look on a T-shirt, perhaps spelled out with rotting banana peels. He made a mental note to bring it up at the afternoon public-relations meeting.

THE VAPORIZER WAS a square pit the size of two Olympic-size swimming pools. The interior was lined with a frictionless black substance that seemed to absorb light. A black hole, plucked from the depths of space and pressed into the virgin Mayanan hills.

Spaced down along the walls of the device, thousands of black-coated nozzles aimed across the vast pit. The tips of the nozzles glowed dull orange.

A black patio rimmed the pit, surrounded around by an eight-foot-high wall. Both deck and wall were coated in the same material as the Vaporizer. Carlos Whitehall noted the drabness of the device as he and his entourage entered the Vaporizer deck through a silent sliding door.

"I still think they could have done something better with the color," the finance minister complained. As usual, he tried to see to the bottom of the pit. As usual, the severe black made it impossible for his eyes to find focus.

"Dr. Sears says the black is necessary," George Jiminez replied. "Whatever's in the nonreflective coating wouldn't work with another color."

Whitehall snorted derisively. "Dr. Sears is hardly the expert I'd quote on any of this," he grumbled.

A group of men waited at the far corner of the deck. Leading the way, Whitehall marched over to them.

His feet made not a scuff nor a sound. Before entering through the sliding door, Whitehall and the rest had pulled special clear boots over their shoes. The booties were required as a precaution to keep visitors from losing their footing on the slippery surface of the deck.

Even wearing the special shoes, Whitehall felt uneasy stepping along the deck. He had been present for some of the more recent tests. Although a chain-link fence had been set up around the very edge of the pit to prevent anyone from falling in, it didn't help him forget the very near danger. Whenever he ventured out on the deck, he felt as if he were climbing down into a massive garbage disposal unit to retrieve a wayward spoon that had fallen down the drain.

The waiting men gave only quick glances as Whitehall and his entourage approached. While irritating, their lack of deference wasn't a surprise. There was already a preening rooster in the henhouse.

Executive President Blythe Curry-Hume stood at the center of the crowd of men at the edge of the pit. If his close proximity to the Vaporizer caused him any concern, it didn't show. His blandly handsome face was drawn into something that might have been a smile or a grimace of pain.

The president of Mayana seemed to have only one facial expression. For the hundredth time since election day, Carlos Whitehall strained to see a hint of the alleged magnetism that had propelled this political neophyte to his nation's top elected office. As always in Whitehall's critical eye, Executive President Curry-Hume came up lacking.

"I'm glad you could finally make it," the president said thinly as Whitehall stopped before him.

"Yes, Mr. President," Whitehall said tightly. "You do understand that we are not scheduled to begin until two." He made a show of checking his watch. It was barely past ten.

"The world waits. If we are ready, why not go ahead? We *are* ready, aren't we?"

Whitehall's lips tightened. "I'll need a few minutes to line everything up," he replied, biting off each word.

The two groups went into huddles. Whitehall's men got back on their phones, barking orders down to the docks. At one point an exasperated Carlos Whitehall glanced over at the president.

Executive President Curry-Hume stood with hands planted on his hips as he stared into the Vaporizer pit. His sharp eyes had taken on a dreamlike quality. This was one of the things that had appealed to Mayana's female voters: the president's soulful eyes.

One of the executive president's security men stepped up to whisper something to Curry-Hume. The security agents were always around. About a dozen of them had been brought into government with the current president, supplanting the normal presidential security force. The silent men had a habit of making everyone around them feel uncomfortable.

Frowning, Finance Minister Whitehall turned away.

"We're ready," George Jiminez was saying. "The first two trucks are here."

Nodding sharply, Carlos Whitehall went to inform the president. The call went down the line as men snapped into action. The gates were opened. Reporters who had been waiting impatiently outside swarmed onto the deck, all outfitted in slip-resistant boots.

Finance Minister Whitehall had seen some press when he arrived half an hour earlier. There were many more now.

Many were already there to cover the Globe Summit, the world environmental meeting which was being hosted by Mayana and was scheduled to begin later in the week. But they had no idea why they had been called out here to the hills above New Briton. Some wondered if it had something to do with the Mayana government's call for trash from around the world. Many suspected the call for trash was a PR trap set up by environmental groups to be sprung on the world leaders who would be flying in for the conference.

The president worked the crowd, answering questions in an impromptu news conference. As he watched with growing jealousy, Finance Minister Whitehall clenched his teeth until the enamel squeaked. Barely controlling his anger, he whipped out his phone to call up to the control booth.

"Yes, that is true," Executive President Curry-Hume was saying to a reporter from the *Washington Times*. "This demonstration is of global significance. Its reach is so great it is only fitting that it take place now, the week of the Globe Summit. Mayana is about to change the world for the better. I won't spoil the surprise that my people have worked so hard to get ready for you. I think we should stand back and let them show us what they've done for us all."

He was backing into his entourage, ready to permit the demonstration to commence, when a final question was shouted from the gaggle of reporters.

"Isn't this near the site where the Jamestown tragedy took place?" a reporter for the *Boston Blade* called.

On his cell phone, Carlos Whitehall froze.

This was the one question he had feared more than any other. The finance minister had yelled, bargained and begged not to build here. But the land was government owned and ideally located. Whitehall had been outvoted.

The finance minister held his breath, awaiting the president's response.

The executive president nodded soberly to the now silent crowd. "As you say, Jamestown was a terrible tragedy," Curry-Hume said, voice rich with sadness. "But we are not here to focus on the past. We are here to celebrate the future. A better, cleaner future for the entire planet." He turned his back on the reporters. "Gentlemen, if you please."

Carlos Whitehall released a secret sigh. "Begin," he barked into his cell phone. Turning expectantly, he handed the phone off to George Jiminez.

Immediately, a large set of double doors at the far end of the long pit yawned open. Like the smaller door through which the reporters had come, the double doors had been invisible when closed, blending in with the smooth wall.

All eyes turned. Cameras rolled.

Something big crawled up an unseen ramp. When it stopped, everyone there briefly wondered why they were looking at the back end of a dump truck. The truck was dwarfed by the vast black pit.

The truck was overflowing with garbage. Heaps of torn plastic bags spilled their contents. A few seagulls had flown up from the bay. They swooped lazily in the warm air around the truck.

Even the breeze was cooperating. The wind blew away from the press, toward the truck.

At a nod from Carlos Whitehall, George Jiminez spoke in hushed tones into the phone. An instant later, the nozzles lining the black pit glowed brighter. They went from orange to brilliant white.

Through their special boots, the gathered men and women felt a growing hum beneath their feet.

Across the pit, the back of the dump truck slowly began to rise. The maw swung open and the truck's contents slid down into the black pit.

The trash never reached the bottom.

As it passed by the array of white-tipped nozzles, there came a series of sharp flashes from all around the pit. And like popping soap bubbles, the bags of trash began to vanish.

There was a shocked intake of air all around. Reporters ran to the chain-link fence that surrounded the pit.

"Not too close!" Finance Minister Whitehall called.

He nudged himself cautiously to the edge, careful to keep at least a foot away from the fence at all times.

The falling trash continued to vanish. The reporters blinked as if witnessing some sleight of hand in a sidewalk shell game.

Another door opened above the pit. A second truck was already in position. Bags and steel drums of solid waste were dumped into the deep hole. When they passed by the glowing nozzles, they began winking out, piece by piece.

The backs of both trucks tipped nearly vertical, loosing the last of their cargo. Not a single piece of trash made it to the bottom of the deep pit.

The final floating scraps of paper and plastic caught the dying breeze on their way into the pit. They went the way of the larger trash bundles— erased from the air by some invisible force as they passed the glowing nozzles.

The dump trucks drove away, the doors slid closed once more and the hum of energy faded to silence. As it diminished, so, too, went the nozzle lights. The brilliant white dulled to yellow, then orange.

Sensing their meal had gone, the circling seagulls swooped curiously once more high overhead before heading back down toward the harbor.

The reporters stood in shocked silence, staring down onto the empty black floor of the pit. A floor that should have been lined with trash.

"Where did it *go?*" one small voice finally asked.

President Blythe Curry-Hume stepped forward.

"It went where it can never harm the environment again. It went where no beaches are despoiled by medical waste and no neighborhood is poisoned by seeping toxic chemicals. It went where the air is clean and the water is pure.

"Ladies and gentlemen," the leader of Mayana called, "I give you the hope of a cleaner future for all the world. I present to the world its own salvation. The Vaporizer." His grimacing smile of triumph was a little too tight near his ears.

2

His name was Remo and he was Master of all he surveyed.

The thought came to him as he stood on a rocky bluff that jutted over the cold waters of the West Korea Bay.

Remo. Master of all he surveyed. Him. Remo Williams. *Master* Remo Williams. It was a strange feeling and, at the same time, so very, very right.

It had been a long time coming. Days spreading to decades. At times it seemed as if it would never happen. Now? The wink of an eye. Master of all he surveyed.

Remo looked out over his domain.

The tiny North Korean fishing village of Sinanju had been settled among craggy rock and sunken mud flats five thousand years before. It looked as if it hadn't seen a lick of paint or a single straight nail hammered since then.

The crummy little shanty homes of tumbledown wood and moldy thatch were clustered together against the elements. The dilapidated shacks looked like something out of *The Grapes of Wrath* without the cheery Steinbeck optimism.

With the melting winter snow came the annual rising tide of mud. Thick goop like brown oatmeal filled the crooked little streets and clogged the main town square.

The Mission San Juan Capistrano had the annual tradition of its returning swallows. Sinanju had a similar event, but with a non-avian twist. When the ground thawed, the sleeping snakes of Sinanju percolated to the surface. Remo had seen the first million serpents of spring slithering through the ugly brown weeds the previous week. There seemed to be a lot more with every passing year. The exhausted female snakes of Sinanju apparently spent the long winter months unsuccessfully fending off the amorous advances of hissing, horny paramours.

Remo would have thought the men of Sinanju were slipping the snakes Viagra for laughs if not for two things. First, the men of Sinanju were far too lazy to bother with the effort. Second, if they did have access to the drug, they'd need all they could spare for themselves.

Which brought him to the people of his dominion.

The women of Sinanju were shapeless lumps with manhole-flat faces that looked like the south end of a northbound mule. The chronically unemployed men had raised indolence to Olympian heights. With a village stocked to its rotting rafters with ugly women and lazy men, the only good to come from the arrangement was an exceedingly low birthrate.

Not that a larger population couldn't have been cared for. Oh, not by the villagers. As a fishing village, Sinanju had always been a failure. The waters of the West Korea Bay supported little marine life. If there had been fish there at one time, the bay had long since been fished out. The surrounding plains were bad for farming, not that the villagers had ever shown much of an aptitude for agriculture. There were no minerals to mine, no crafts with which to barter. There was nothing really that the people of Sinanju had to offer.

At least not on the surface.

That's where Remo came in.

Sinanju had one great asset, one shining jewel amid the cold and mud that made it far greater than it appeared.

The tiny, seemingly inconsequential village was home to the Masters of Sinanju. The most ancient and deadly martial art had been born on these inhospitable shores. Death was the brush of the Masters of Sinanju; the world their canvas.

If all the other, lesser martial arts were rays, Sinanju was the sun source. The rest had splintered from it. And, being but imitations, they were all inferior. Sinanju was the pure source, the essence of what could be for men in complete control of mind and body.

Since the start, the Masters of Sinanju had used their skills as assassins. And they excelled at their craft. Scalpels employed to take the place of clumsy armies, the Korean assassins were capable of feats that would seem superhuman to the average man.

There were only two Masters of Sinanju in a generation, teacher and pupil. But that was more than enough. The people of Sinanju need never work, for the efforts of the Masters of Sinanju kept them fed and warm.

Since before the time of the pharaohs, emissaries had come to the village to retain the services of the famed Sinanju assassins. And for aeons empires flourished or fell thanks to the secret services of the men from Sinanju.

The dawn of a new century had brought a new beginning to the venerable House of Sinanju.

Remo—a white American—had recently become the first non-Korean Reigning Master, accepting the title and all the responsibilities that came with it. But in his heart he knew that his skin color didn't really matter. In truth he knew that he was just the latest in an unbroken line stretching back through time to that long-ago, forgotten day when the first crooked beam was set upon the first mossy stone to form the first pathetic hovel from which would grow the village over which he now stood as Reigning Master.

Taking it all in on the lonely bluff above the village—the history, the surroundings, the wind, sea and air; allowing the salty mist to sting his exposed flesh—a newfound poetic sense swelled deep in the spirit of Remo Williams. And the newest Reigning Master of Sinanju did give word to his innermost feelings. And that word did roll off his tongue, loudly proclaimed for all around to hear.

And that word was, ''Yuck.''

Thus spake Remo Williams, newly invested Reigning Master of the House of Sinanju.

He might have gotten in trouble for saying it aloud, especially if it fell on a particular pair of sensitive ears. Fortunately for Remo, only one person was nearby.

"Excuse me, Master of Sinanju?"

Though Korean, the groveling man's English was very good.

The man in the North Korean general's uniform was not of Sinanju. General Kye Pun was head of the People's Bureau of Revolutionary Struggle. He had recently been given a temporary assignment by North Korean Premier Kim Jong-Il. Kye Pun was to personally act as liaison between the new Master of Sinanju and the Communist government in Pyongyang.

A few months before, there had been a power struggle in the village. A man had come to the ancient seat of the Masters of Sinanju to claim the title of Reigning Master for himself. At the time it was not absolutely certain who would be the victor. But the premier had a history with the white Master of Sinanju. The truth was, the crazy American scared him silly. Kim Jong-Il had thrown his support behind Remo.

When the dust settled, the premier was relieved to find that he had chosen wisely. Still, he wanted to be sure that the brave but dangerous Master Remo knew that he had the continued full backing of the leadership in Pyongyang.

General Kye Pun had been put at the disposal of the new Reigning Master by Kim Jong-Il as a show of support. At the moment Kye Pun seemed confused by Remo's spoken thought.

"What?" Remo asked, annoyed. Annoyance came

easy to him lately. He had spent most of his days in Sinanju annoyed. As time went on, he had only grown increasingly annoyed.

"I do not understand this word 'yuck,'" Kye Pun said.

"Oh." Remo nodded. "Yuck," he repeated slowly. "As in 'Yuck, this place is a shithole, I want to go home.'"

"Ah," said Kye Pun. "Home."

The general looked over his shoulder at the lone house that sat across the bluff on which they stood.

It was an eyesore, but of a different kind than the shacks of Sinanju. The big house looked to have been contracted out to a hundred blind architects who had each graduated last in his class. Dozens of architectural styles from countless centuries had been forced together in a clash of rocks, marble, granite and wood that made the sensitive eye ache just looking at it. Sitting on the roof was a gleaming satellite dish. The newly mounted eyesore-on-an-eyesore was aimed up at the heavens.

The building had become Remo's official residence when he assumed the mantle of Reigning Master.

"There is mud on the path to your home," Kye Pun said. "Allow your unworthy servant."

The general began to lie down in the mud to form a human bridge so that Remo's Italian loafers would remain unsoiled.

At any other time this would have been far too great an indignity for Kye Pun to bear. Not any longer. At least, not for this particular man.

Four months ago, when this young Master of Sinanju had arrived by jet in the capital of Pyongyang, Kye Pun met him at the airport. Kye Pun's personal bodyguard was present. The bodyguard was a massive, muscled mountain of flesh who could have wrestled a live ox through a meat grinder one-handed. He was assigned to kill the white Master of Sinanju. The young white Master of Sinanju swatted the behemoth bodyguard's head from his shoulders with a single slap. The head lodged in a jet engine.

After that incident, Kye Pun decided that there was nothing that he would not do to make the white Master of Sinanju happy. If that meant lying on his belly in the mud, he would wallow like a pig in a pen with a song in his heart.

The Korean general had barely gotten to his knees when he felt a strong hand on his shoulder.

"Hey, Sir Walter Dingbat, I'm not talking about that dump," Remo said, lifting the general from the ground and setting him back to the path. "I meant America."

Kye Pun felt his breath catch. He could scarcely believe what he was hearing. "You will return to the bourgeois land of the capitalist oppressors?" he sang.

"I prefer to think of it as the good ol' U.S. of A.," Remo said thinly.

"Of course," Kye Pun said quickly. He pumped a clenched hand in the air. "Go, Dallas Cowboys, John Wayne and Mickey Mouse." He pitched his voice low. "You know, I have always secretly been a great fan of the exploitation of the workers by the power elite," he confided.

"As a card-carrying Commie, you'd have to be," Remo said dryly. The sarcasm was lost on the North Korean general.

"How soon will you leave?" Kye Pun asked excitedly. "Do you wish for me to make the travel arrangements? They are still repairing the engine of the Iraqi jet you came in. Shan Duk's accursed skull caused much damage." He spit angrily on the ground. "Or I am certain the premier himself will gladly loan you his plane, as he has in the past."

"Hold your horses," Remo said. "First, are you absolutely sure we're all through here?"

The general looked at the clipboard in his gloved hand.

A stack of papers had been snapped to the board. Lines of neat text were written in English for the benefit of the new Reigning Master of Sinanju. Across the top of each page, columns were labeled National Leader, Assassin's Name, Method/Date of Shipment, Time of Contact/Name of Caller. To the left were lined up the names of countries, one atop another. To the far right were boxes to be checked off when a line was full. All of the boxes on the first page had received a tidy red check mark.

Most of the paperwork had been filled in four months before. The Contact/Caller column and the checks had been slowly filling up as the months wore on.

General Kye Pun licked the tip of his black-gloved thumb as he rattled through the paperwork.

"Yes, yes, ye-es," he said, nodding as he went. "As I mentioned when I arrived, it appears to be finished. Norway and some of the African nations took a long time to get back to us. But the last was Morocco, and that call came today. That is why I came here. Not that I would not trade my eyes for another glimpse of this, the Pearl of the Orient.''

He waved a hand to grandly encompass the mud pit and decaying shantytown that was Sinanju. At the same moment, the shifting wind brought a fresh gulp of putrescence from the thawing public outhouses.

''Beautiful,'' Kye Pun enthused even as he turned to vomit down the side of the bluff.

''Thanks a lot,'' Remo groused. ''That was the one spot in town that didn't have something disgusting dripping off it.''

Kye Pun apologized profusely. The general was climbing down, handkerchief in hand to clean off the rocks even as Remo turned on his heel and headed down the path.

Remo's gait was easy as he headed into the village proper. More a steady glide than a walk. The villagers he passed seemed delighted to see him. They offered reverent bows as he strode through their midst. In Korean, they offered what sounded like words of praise.

''I will never get used to those eyes,'' one said, bowing deeply to the new Reigning Master.

''Yes, they are homely things,'' agreed another. ''Still, they are better than that ghost-belly white skin.''

Remo—who was fluent in Korean—pretended he didn't understand a word they were saying.

It was a little game he had been playing to pass

the time. He had come to Sinanju many times over the past few decades. While there, some had heard him speak Korean. This visit, he wondered how easy it would be to convince the populace that he had only ever spoken words and phrases by rote, and that he didn't understand the language at all.

He was stunned to find the people of Sinanju were even dumber than they were lazy. A few helpless shrugs and loud "whats?" during conversations, and all of them were convinced he couldn't speak a word of their language.

Through feigned ignorance he was finding that he was having to knock the bottom out of his already low opinion of the ungrateful inhabitants of Sinanju.

"Woe are we to live in this time," a man said. "To have the greatness of Sinanju squandered on this white."

"Yes," lamented a decrepit old woman as Remo passed out of the square. "If that is our future, it almost makes me wish the old one was back as Reigning Master."

These last words stung Remo.

Not for himself. He could take whatever barbs the people of Sinanju hurled at him. His troubled thoughts were of another.

He had come to Sinanju four months previous as part of the Sinanju Time of Succession, the final rite of passage before his ascension to full Reigning Master. And now that it was finally time to leave, he was afraid he would be going alone.

He followed the path to where it veered away from the shore. The hills rose above the West Korea Bay.

A pair of tall rocks in the shape of curving horns framed the sparkling water. Climbing past the artificial rock formation, Remo found himself on a wide plateau.

The mouth of a deep cave yawned wide at the back of the hilltop. A wizened figure fussed near the opening.

The old man's skin was like leather left to bleach in the desert sun for a hundred years. It was as delicate as rice paper, pulled taut over an egg-shaped scalp. Above each shell-like ear, soft tufts of yellow-white hair danced in the breeze. A thread of beard touched his sharp chin.

Chiun, former Reigning Master of the House of Sinanju, wore a striking kelly-green kimono. Across the back, mirror-image dragons of bright red reared, their embroidered tails extending down the billowing sleeves. The piping at the neck and hems was spun gold. The robe's colors made the old man look like an ancient Christmas present, forgotten and left unopened for more than a century.

The kimono danced around the elderly Korean's ankles as he breezed around the cave's entrance. He fussed at the tiny copse of three trees that grew at the mouth of the cave.

Near the old man, a peculiar little animal stood on stumpy legs. It was no more than three feet tall, with a long body that looked like a blend of cow and camel. The sad-eyed creature chewed languidly on a pile of straw.

As Remo approached, Chiun's face remained bland. He didn't lift his head from his work.

"And to what do I owe this honor, that the Reigning Master would deign to visit this lowly villager?"

"Ha, ha," Remo said. "That's almost as funny as it was last night at supper, not to mention the thousand times before that."

With fingernails like curving daggers, Chiun snipped a dead branch from the hearty pine tree at which he worked.

"If my mean utterances do somehow bring offense to the delicate ears of the Reigning Master, I beg his forgiveness," he intoned seriously. "Now, if the most gracious and honored Reigning Master would kindly move his giant clubbed white feet, his servant would be most grateful."

Frowning, Remo moved and Chiun slipped by, humming happily to himself as he went.

"You know, if your attitude fell somewhere between the sarcastic ass-kissing and the full-out insults, that'd be okay with me."

Chiun paused in clipping another dead branch. The old man cast a dull eye on the Master who had succeeded him.

Remo sighed. "Just a thought," he said.

"Our new Reigning Master is truly compassionate. How kind of you to postpone this new flirtation with thinking until spring. It would have been cruel to force the mice who lodge in your brain out into the snow."

"Yeah, I'm in real tight with the North Korean SPCA," Remo said dryly. "Speaking of animals, are you sure it's safe to drag that thing around with you?'' He aimed his chin at the strange creature near the cave.

The old man glanced at the sad-eyed animal.

''I appreciate the company,'' Chiun replied. ''It is an improvement over what I am used to.''

''I'll buy you a dog,'' Remo said. ''That thing was built out of genetically engineered spare parts by a certifiable psycho. It's probably hatching diseases that don't even have names yet. Plus it's ugly as all hell.''

''Do not say such things about Remo,'' Chiun scolded.

Remo frowned. ''And that's another thing. I don't appreciate you giving it my name.''

''I meant no disrespect,'' Chiun replied. ''I only wished to honor our village's newest Reigning Master.''

When he looked up at his former pupil, Remo noted the old man's eyes. He had been doing that a lot lately.

Chiun's hazel eyes had always been much younger than his years. For a time there had been a growing weariness in them. Remo hadn't even noticed until the weariness was gone. It had disappeared four months before. Of late, there seemed a spark of renewed vigor in his teacher's eyes.

It was a thing Remo was not allowed to mention.

During the Time of Succession, Remo and Chiun had been separated. While Remo was elsewhere in the world, Chiun had come back to Sinanju alone.

Something had happened to his teacher while they were apart. Something had restored the old man's fresh, youthful outlook. But whatever it was, Chiun was not yet ready to share. Remo had asked a few times.

"When I understand," was all Chiun would say, his voice mysterious. And that ended discussion on the subject.

Remo was understandably curious, but he respected his teacher's privacy. As the old man pruned the trees, Remo wondered again what had happened with Chiun. He had the distinct impression it was something big.

Chiun seemed to sense his pupil's unspoken thought.

Papery lips puckered as he worked his way around the far side of the pine. "How do you feel?" Chiun asked, preemptively changing the subject.

"Not sprouting any extra arms or eyes, if that's what you mean," Remo said. "I'm one hundred percent me."

"You say that like it is a good thing," Chiun said.

"From where I was four months ago, you better believe it is. Don't get me wrong. It was good those couple of days. You know, to see. That's still with me. But as for being something other than Remo Williams, not anymore."

Briefly during his Time of Succession ordeal, Remo had been given a glimpse of something larger than himself. For years Chiun had maintained that his pupil was the fulfillment of an ancient Sinanju prophecy. The old man claimed that Remo was the avatar of Shiva, the Hindu god of destruction. There had been moments in Remo's life that appeared to confirm this. Whenever some strange occurrence during their association arose to bolster Chiun's claim, Remo turned a blind eye. For years it was the eight-hundred-pound gorilla sitting in the corner of his life that he studiously ignored.

There was a reason why he chose to ignore it. In his secret heart, Remo was afraid. Afraid that if it were true, that if some ancient force dwelled within him, his own days as an individual were numbered. For if he was merely a vessel, Shiva was simply awaiting the day to spring forth and consume him utterly. And when that day finally came, the god would win and there would be no more of Remo Williams.

It was a fear he had lived with for as long as he had quietly believed the truth of Chiun's words.

All that was different now. For a little while, Remo had seen what his future would be.

It was impossible to put into words. He had tried to explain it to Chiun several times. It was a feeling of...*completeness* like he had never before experienced. The world and everything in it—including Remo Williams—finally made sense. When Remo had told Chiun this last part, the old man strongly disputed the possibility that Remo could ever make sense. Remo had dropped the matter.

The god was gone and the man remained, but Remo no longer had the fear that he would be whisked into the ether, a forgotten soul, cast into eternal nothingness.

Reflecting on the experience, Remo felt another momentary shudder of peace. He watched quietly as

Chiun stooped to collect the twigs he had trimmed from the trees.

"Kye Pun's here," Remo said all at once. "He heard back from the last Time of Succession country. The last body has been shipped and acknowledged. The new Reigning Master of the House of Sinanju has now been officially introduced to all the important courts of the world."

At this, Chiun only grunted.

There was a long moment during which neither man said a word. Chiun finished gathering his sticks. On shuffling feet, he carried them to the open mouth of the cave. As he laid them carefully inside, Remo finally broke the silence.

"I'm going back, Chiun," he announced all at once.

The old man turned slowly. His expression was unreadable. "How soon?"

"Soon. I haven't checked in with Upstairs in ages. Smitty's probably wondering if I'm dead again." A thought occurred. He turned from his teacher, cupping his hands to his mouth. "Hey, Pun!" he hollered in the direction of the village. "You nimrods get the phone working yet?"

Although he should have been too far away for anyone other than Chiun to hear him, his words carried easily across the village far below. Somehow the sound avoided the ears of the people, who were busily engaged in their daily business of hanging around doing nothing. Like a vocal dagger it landed only on the ears to which it was directed, those of the North Korean general, who was still using his hankie to polish rocks over on the bluff near the House of Many Woods.

Far, far on the other side of the village, Kye Pun scrambled to his feet. There was panic on his face. He twisted left and right, looking for ghosts.

"Over here, you doof!" Remo yelled.

Kye Pun's eyes were drawn to the source of the voice. Squinting, he saw the impossibly tiny speck of Remo standing way off in the distance, on the flat hill in the shadow of one of the Horns of Welcome.

"The phone!" Remo yelled. "Is it working?"

Kye Pun took in a deep breath. "The work was completed this morning, Master!" he screamed at the top of his lungs.

More than a few heads in the village turned his way. The villagers had no idea why the North Korean general was standing up on the bluff with a dripping hankie and shouting like a lunatic to himself.

Across the village, Remo turned to his teacher. "Phone works. I guess I can finally call Smitty."

"You need not have waited four months," Chiun said. "You could have phoned your emperor from Pyongyang."

With some sadness, Remo noted the "your" emperor.

"I don't like Pyongyang. Too many Pyongyangers for one thing. Plus I have it on good authority that a young man puts his virtue at risk just walking down the street there."

"And so you remained here," Chiun said. "Which I suppose means that you now like Sinanju?"

"Parts of it," Remo said. He looked around. Below, the morning sun was burning steam off the thatched roofs and mud streets. With the rising steam came the rising stink. "*A* part of it," he admitted. "Pretty much just the you part."

Chiun could feel the sympathetic waves emanating from his pupil. He turned his weathered face to Remo. "And so you thought to extend your time here. Why? To watch your poor old Master in his dotage? To mope around and stare me to an early grave? I told you before. I have a future."

Remo released months of frustration in an exhale of angry air.

"Of what?" he asked. "Really, Chiun. What? Pruning hedges? Taking care of Flossie over there?" He waved a hand at the homely little animal. "You're retired, Little Father. And I know the rules. First I become Reigning Master. At some point after that, I get a pupil of my own. As soon as I do that, the retired ex-Reigning Master is required by tradition to climb into that cave over there like Punxsatawney Phil, and we all pretend you're dead."

"That has been the tradition for many years," Chiun admitted, nodding agreement.

"Well, it's stupid. But you're this big stickler for tradition, so I know one morning I'm going to turn around and you're gonna be squirreled away in the back of that cave. I say screw it. You're better than a freaking hole in the ground. You're not ready for retirement."

Chiun considered his words thoughtfully.

"No," the Korean said eventually, the light of wisdom dawning in his young eyes. "You are right."

Remo felt a tingle of hope in his chest.

"Yes, Remo, you are correct," Chiun insisted firmly. "I am ready for something else."

"Yeah?" Remo asked, a hint of relief in his voice.

The old man's jaw was firmly set. "I am ready for breakfast," he announced with certainty.

Unhooking the leash from the rock, he led the strange little animal past his pupil.

"Come, Remo," the wizened Korean said to the creature. The animal struggled on short legs to follow. Beast in tow, Chiun headed back down the rocky path to the village.

"On the other hand, I could always toss you in there myself and roll a rock in front of the door," Remo called after his retreating back.

"If that is the wish of our beneficent new Reigning Master, this humble retired villager would have no choice but to obey," Chiun called back. "*After* breakfast."

And he was gone.

Alone on the bluff, Remo glanced at the dark mouth of the cave. Only a few months before, he had seen a hint of his own future. Now, looking into that cave was like staring into the future of his teacher. Cold and unavoidable.

A dark chill gripped his heart.

Turning his back on the cave, Remo headed down the rock-lined path to Sinanju.

3

Captain Frederick Lenn had sailed his ship beneath the proud shadow of Lady Liberty in New York Harbor and down the Eastern Seaboard of the United States.

He had been blessed with calm seas and good weather, something for which Captain Lenn was grateful. The Caribbean Sea was a sheet of glass. He could have skipped a flat stone all the way to Puerto Rico. The perfect blue water sparkled as he dropped anchor, barely making a splash or ripple.

It was truly a beautiful day. Unfortunately, Captain Lenn was too busy to enjoy it.

Lenn had spent his life on or near the ocean. He had enlisted in the Navy at nineteen, a few years before Vietnam began to ooze up into the nation's consciousness. When the war was over and his hitch was up, he drifted from job to job. Somehow he always wound up near water.

He repaired fishing nets in Nova Scotia, worked as a night watchman at a cranberry bog on Cape Cod and even opened an unsuccessful fried-fish restaurant near the U.S. Naval Academy in Annapolis.

A stint in the merchant marines led to a long career

with a passenger cruise line. He retired from that job two years earlier with a captain's rank, a nice pension and—still fit at the age of sixty-two—the promise of a long and healthy life of shuffleboard and Thursday-night bingo.

After two weeks of sunny retirement, Frederick Lenn was going out of his bird. Within three weeks he had a new job.

It was not a luxury cruise liner this time. But he was a captain again. And with the command of his own vessel and a rolling deck beneath his feet, there was nothing that could destroy the romantic allure the ocean had for Captain Frederick Lenn.

Sure, other ships had names that challenged the human spirit like *Endeavor* or *Enterprise.* Or called to mind great historical figures like Washington, Grant and Nimitz, or places like Alabama, Maine and Virginia. But a rose was still a rose no matter what you called it.

So Captain Lenn's ship was called *12-B37.* It was a serviceable name. It might not inspire poets or bal-ladeers, but then Samuel Coleridge and Gordon Lightfoot probably had a bugaboo about garbage scows.

So what if *12-B37* hauled trash around the high seas? It was still Captain Frederick Lenn's boat and he treated her with the love and tenderness he had failed to show either of his two ex-wives and his three estranged children.

On the bridge of his ship, Captain Lenn looked back across the mountain of trash that was mounded behind him. The scow was like a long flat pan floating in the sparkling sea. The bridge sat at one end, a rusted rectangular box. The windows were weathered, filled with pits and scratches.

The smell was strong, even in the closed-off bridge. This was New York City trash. The worst of what the Rome or Athens of the modern world considered junk. Seagulls flapped all around the massive pile, leaving blobs of white everywhere they went.

"How is it they crap more than they eat?" asked Lenn's first officer.

Lenn glanced at the young man who was peering out the window beside his captain. Besides Frederick Lenn and his first officer there were only two other crewmen that served aboard *12-B37*.

"How long till Briton Bay flags us in?" Captain Lenn asked, ignoring the man's question.

"Nothing is moving from the docks. They're saying now it could be days."

"That damn Globe Summit," Lenn complained. "They've got politicians from around the world in there. *And* their state departments and security. Why they couldn't put us off for another week I'll never know."

"They wanted to make sure they've got enough shit to dump in that machine of theirs," the first officer replied.

They had seen the Vaporizer unveiling on the news from their cramped crew quarters.

Lenn sighed. "I guess we get paid no matter what."

Lenn rubbed his fingers through his shock of gray hair. It felt dirty. It would have been nice to take a few days in Mayana, maybe a night or two in a hotel. Time away always made his return to his boat that much sweeter. But there was no way that was happening now. The whole of New Briton was booked solid. And now, as the country that was going to solve the world's waste disposal problem, things were going to get even more insane.

"I just hope we have enough provisions if they keep us stuck out here." Lenn scooped up a pair of binoculars.

There were many other scows in the same metaphorical boat as his. So many, the crews had come up with a name. "Garbage City" was rapidly filling this part of the Caribbean to capacity, with more scows on the way.

"It's getting pretty tight out there," Lenn commented as he passed his binoculars to starboard, aft. As he spoke, something caught his eye. He almost missed it through the flocks of crazed seagulls.

Another scow—this one from Mexico—was anchored nearby. When he trained his binoculars fully, he saw a thin line of black smoke curling up from the far side of the ship.

"Have we gotten any radio messages from next door?" Lenn asked his first officer.

The younger man had left the window. "No, why?" he asked absently, not looking up.

Lenn held his binoculars steady.

"They're in some kind of trouble," he said with a frown. "Looks like a fire. Radio over. Ask if they need help."

"Aye, sir," the first officer said. As he reached for

the radio, Captain Lenn continued to monitor the other scow.

It was still smoking. Could be an engine fire. But who knew what they were hauling? Depending on what was on board, a small fire could send a scow up in flames in seconds.

"I can't raise them, Fred," the first officer said. "Could be they have their hands full."

"Hmm," Lenn said, lowering his binoculars as the first officer came up beside him. "You and Bob better take the little boat over. See if they—"

"Holy shit!" the first officer interrupted. He was staring out the window.

Lenn wheeled just in time to see the other scow's nose lift out of the water. He whipped his binoculars back up.

A huge fissure ripped the side of the scow. Streams of garbage slurped overboard as the ship listed to one side. As Lenn watched in horror, the bridge windows shattered. Flames began pouring out into the clear blue sky.

Lenn spun. "Weigh anchor," he ordered.

"Sir?" the helmsman asked.

"Do it! Get us out of here, best possible speed!"

"What is it, Captain?" asked the suddenly worried first officer. "What's wrong?"

"Get on the radio to Mayana," Lenn snapped. "Tell them we're under attack."

"Attack?"

"*Now!*" Lenn twisted back to the grimy window.

The scow was already slipping under the waves. All that remained was a thick oil slick and bits of floating garbage. He searched desperately for survivors in the widening debris field.

The first officer had raised Mayana.

"They want to know if this is some kind of joke," he said, holding out the microphone.

"Give it here," Lenn commanded.

He took a step. But only one.

The scow lurched suddenly. Lenn had to grab the navigation station to keep from being hurled to the deck.

"Dammit!"

He scrambled to his feet and ran to the bridge window. The sea was still calm. Not a cloud in the sky. They hadn't been hit by a sudden squall. Lenn's stomach sank, growing cold as the ocean deep.

"Captain?" the first officer asked. He was steadying himself on the back of a chair.

Lenn's voice was flat. He had known it as soon as he'd seen the other scow's damage. Hoped to hell he was wrong.

"Torpedo," Captain Frederick Lenn replied, voice hollow.

The instant he spoke, a second explosion rocked the scow. Lenn felt the rolling impact through the metal deck.

The men were thrown from their stations.

As Frederick Lenn watched, the rear of his boat split apart. The bridge twisted as the massive weight of garbage shifted and began vomiting into the sea.

"Abandon ship!" Lenn shouted.

The bridge was angling into the water. As the ship

listed, the men stumbled and crawled across the slanted floor and out the door.

The deck was slick. Greasy water attacked their ankles. When his helmsman slipped and fell against the rail, Captain Lenn dragged the kid back to his feet by his shirt collar.

A lifeboat hung behind the bridge. Holding on to chain railings, the men scurried back to it. As they reached for the metal hooks, there came a sudden painful groan.

Captain Lenn stopped dead. "My God," he whispered.

And the ship bucked beneath his feet and split cleanly into two halves.

The bulk of the cargo dumped into the sea, the bridge pitched forward and a pile of front-loaded garbage came toward them in an avalanche.

Eighty thousand pounds of trash barreled across the cabin and slammed full force into the struggling crew. Captain Lenn caught a mouthful of rotting garbage before he and his panicked crew were swept into the churning sea.

With more groaning and spilling greasy mounds of trash, the little scow from New York joined its proud captain and crew in a watery grave.

Seagulls pecked away at the lazily scattering trash.

And far off, the single eye of a periscope watched in silent satisfaction. Sun glinted off glass as it dipped below the waves. And was gone.

4

It was awful. Just so sad and scary at the same time. And they didn't really care. They were doing it just to shock. It was like all those TV programs now. Those ones where men would jump out of airplanes with rubber bands around their legs or practically set themselves on fire for money. Or worse, the ones where women with tattoos and no self-respect cavorted around like little tramps with men to whom they weren't even engaged, let alone lawfully married.

One thing was certain—years ago they never would have allowed such things on television. This was just the latest example of the sorry state of the media. In fact, this was worse than all those other shows combined.

All these thoughts passed through the empathetic brain of Eileen Mikulka as she sipped fretfully at her morning coffee in front of the fifteen-year-old TV in the warm and tidy living room of her small home in Rye, New York.

''How long has it been going on?'' the matronly woman asked, her sympathetic eyes glued to the screen.

The steam from her World's Greatest Grandma mug curled up around her blue-tinted perm.

"About one last night. I can't believe they're wasting all this time on it. They should just let them drown."

It was just like Kieran Mikulka to say something horrible like that. Eileen's youngest seemed fond of shocking his mother with such thoughtless statements.

The boy was in his mid-thirties and without a job. He did little but sit around and watch television all day. They said that TV viewing desensitized the young to violence. If Kieran Mikulka was any example, that was certainly true.

"Kieran, that's a terrible thing to say," Mrs. Mikulka scolded as she put down her mug. She was careful to use one of the cute little froggy coasters she'd picked up twenty-seven years ago on a Jersey shore vacation with her late husband, God rest his soul. The frog was mostly worn-out now, but you could still see his faded green eyes.

Of course it was terrible. That should have gone without saying. Anyone with an ounce of heart would think the same thing. On the screen the image played again.

Fire and rescue personnel stood on the street. Beyond them a crowd of onlookers—some still in pajamas and nightgowns—stood anxiously. All around, raging water from a fierce overnight rainstorm rolled furiously down the gutter, cascading into a culvert at the end of the road. The water crashed white around the boots of the burly men.

The storm drain was barely visible, so deep was the river. The men stooped and dug with their gloved hands. Tree branches and clumps of wet leaves were pulled out. Once they were removed, some of the raging water rolled into the drain. With shouts from the men, a tiny camera no bigger than a wire was slipped down through the metal grate.

Eileen Mikulka had seen the footage three times. She held her breath as she watched the tiny camera snake its way through the water and into the dark cavern below the street.

She didn't know how far down it went. It seemed to go on a very long time. At the last moment, it twisted....

And there they were. All wet and frightened.

The three kittens sat meowing on a slippery ledge. Mrs. Mikulka's heart broke when she saw them.

"No one knows how they got here or what happened to their mother," a reporter said, voice as serious as if she were reporting on an attempted presidential assassination. "But the three kittens—dubbed Muffy, Tuffy and Sam by the children who first heard their pitiful cries—have so far evaded all attempts by rescue workers to save their lives."

"It's terrible," Mrs. Mikulka said, eyes sad as she watched the drama on the flickering TV screen.

"It's ridiculous, Ma," Kieran insisted. "Lookit." With the remote, he flipped from channel to channel. All the networks were carrying the same story. "It's been going on like this all night. Three mangy cats were stupid enough to fall in a hole and they're treating it like a dead Lady Di, for Christ's sake. Who the hell cares?''

"Language," Mrs. Mikulka scolded. "And *I* care. You should, too. Remember Mr. Tiddles?"

Mr. Tiddles had been the Mikulka family cat until an unfortunate encounter with Mr. Phillips's Oldsmobile had sent him prematurely to kitty Heaven. His earthly remains were buried in an old Buster Brown box out behind the toolshed.

When she thought of her beloved cat—gone ten years come June—Eileen Mikulka made a mental note to do a little weeding when the ground dried out later that spring.

"They're just strays, Ma," Kieran insisted morosely. "Who'd notice if they all died?"

Eileen Mikulka stood. She fixed her son with a hard look. "*God* would notice," she said firmly. "He has a place for all his creatures, whether they know it or not."

She had been saying that a lot lately. Eileen was a Presbyterian with a churchgoing record that could charitably be described as spotty. But the more it became evident that Kieran intended to waste his life on the couch, the more she had been speaking about God's great plan for everyone. She had said it so much Kieran didn't even roll his eyes anymore. With a grunt, he flipped over to *Barney* on PBS.

Frowning, Mrs. Mikulka glanced at her watch.

"Oh, dear," she clucked.

She didn't have more time to lecture her son or to fret about those poor, poor kittens on television.

Gathering up her coffee cup, she hurried into the

kitchen. It was immaculate, just as she liked it. It was getting harder and harder to keep it that way. By the time she came home in the evening there would be dirty dishes, crumbs and empty cracker boxes all over.

She rinsed out her coffee mug and put it in the dishwasher. Her handbag was near the refrigerator. This was where she'd kept it for years, ever since the children were little. But for a while recently she had started keeping it in her bedroom. Ever since that time a few months back when she started to notice bills disappearing from her wallet. But she had started leaving it out again now that she was keeping enough money for lunch locked in her desk at work.

"I should be home at the usual time, dear," she called into the living room. "Don't lean on the door to the fridge when you look in, and don't hold it open too long."

This time there wasn't even a grunt.

Purse in hand, Eileen Mikulka hurried out to her car.

She seemed to be having a harder time getting to work on time these days. She used to come in much earlier than eight o'clock. But her employer had lately cut her back to a strict forty-hour work week, insisting that it was for her own good. After all, she wasn't getting any younger.

It seemed to be harder for her these days. She now had too much time in the morning to get ready. As she drove up the lonely wooded road she wondered if she could start sneaking in earlier again. Probably not. Other bosses might not notice that she had started coming in at the old, early time. Maybe they would even applaud her diligence. Not her employer. When he said 8:00 a.m., he meant 8:00 a.m.

In fact, this was one of the traits she admired in him. Unlike a lot of men these days, her boss meant what he said. He was also serious and strict and punctilious. He liked order to his world. Her employer was very much of the old school, which was just fine with Eileen Mikulka.

A high wall rose beside her car. As she rounded a bend, she noted a lighter spot in the rough shape of an arch. The wall had been damaged more than a year earlier and had only recently been repaired. Mrs. Mikulka assumed it would take many years for that one spot to fade in with the rest of the wall. She doubted she would be around to see that far-off day when the wall finally matched once more.

Her thoughts turned once more to Kieran, sitting on the couch in the living room, day after day. Wondering who would take care of her poor lost son on that day, Mrs. Mikulka drove the rest of the short way to work.

The wall led to a gate. Mrs. Mikulka steered her car under the watchful gaze of two granite lions and headed up the gravel drive to Folcroft Sanitarium.

The big brick building was coming to life in the warm smile of early spring sunlight. The crawling ivy that clung to its sides had lately darkened and was ready to bud. Beyond the sanitarium, Long Island Sound invited morning pleasure boaters to enjoy the unseasonable warmth.

Mrs. Mikulka watched the crisp white sail of one

boat close to shore as she walked from the parking lot to the side door of the building. It was so nice to see people enjoying themselves. Kieran didn't seem to have that anymore.

When she thought of her son, she immediately thought of the poor kittens trapped in the storm drain. They were so pathetic. Dripping wet and meowing pitifully. You just wanted to take them and cuddle the daylights out of them.

How her son could say something so awful about those cute little creatures was beyond her. Maybe it was the lack of a male role model. His father passed on when Kieran was still in his twenties. He had already been a handful at the time. He'd only gotten worse in the past decade.

She shook her head as she pushed open the fire door.

It was cool inside the stairwell. Mrs. Mikulka climbed up to the second floor.

It was dark in her office. A flick of a switch and the overhead lights hummed to life. As she did every morning, Mrs. Mikulka went to her desk and locked her handbag in the bottom drawer. Getting back up, she carefully smoothed the wrinkles from her skirt.

She cast a glance at the inner office door. A brass nameplate read ''Dr. Harold Smith, Director.''

Not a sound issued from inside. Still, Mrs. Mikulka knew that her employer was already on the other side of that door, toiling away. Dr. Smith rarely missed a day, and only then because he was away on business of some sort. It made her feel good that there was still someone in this crazy world who treated his work as seriously as Dr. Harold Smith.

Mrs. Mikulka ran some water in her little sink, starting the coffeepot in the corner.

There was an empty can in a cupboard that she had decorated with a piece of old wallpaper. It was for the office coffee fund. When she picked it up, the change inside rattled. She shook it out into her palm. She didn't bother to count it. There was always the right amount.

As part of her duties every morning, Mrs. Mikulka got her employer a little something from the cafeteria. It was not something he had requested. Dr. Smith's wife was a notoriously bad cook and, well, Eileen Mikulka had decided to see to it that the poor man had something to keep his strength up. He worked so hard.

The first time she had done it, she paid out of her own pocket. The first time was also the last time. Dr. Smith liked to pay his own way. On the second day the change had appeared in the coffee-fund can. It was always the exact right amount, down to the penny.

The coffeemaker was just beginning to gurgle as Mrs. Mikulka left the office.

She headed down to the cafeteria, which was at the tail end of the breakfast rush. Individual trays were being prepared and loaded on carts for Folcroft's patients. A few doctors and nurses sat scattered at the cheap tables around the room.

Mrs. Mikulka took a tray from a stack and went

to the serving line. There was only one person in front of her, a lean young man in a blue suit.

A woman in a starched white uniform and red-checkered apron was ringing up the man's order.

"Good morning, Eileen," the cafeteria worker said as she worked the old-fashioned register.

"Good morning, Helen."

The young man glanced back over his shoulder.

"Oh, morning, Mrs. M.," he said, offering a pleasant smile. "I didn't realize it was you sneaking up on me."

Mrs. Mikulka returned the young man's smile. "Good morning, Mr. Howard," she said.

Assistant Director Mark Howard was a new addition to the Folcroft family. He was such a nice young man. Always so cheerful. Although lately he seemed a bit more careworn than when he'd first arrived at Folcroft two years earlier. That was no doubt due to his great responsibilities. Folcroft administered to the needs of many elderly and invalid patients. Mr. Howard took that duty very seriously. So nice for a man his age to treat his job with such sobriety.

Mrs. Mikulka wondered briefly how old he was. Probably about thirty. Younger than Kieran and already in a position of authority.

"You're a little late getting down here today, aren't you?" Mark Howard asked Mrs. Mikulka as he paid for his food.

"A little," she admitted. "I was still on time for work," she added hastily. "It was just something I saw on the television this morning slowed me down.''

"Not those poor kittens?" the cafeteria worker asked as she prepared Dr. Smith's usual breakfast. Two halves of toast. Dry. No butter, no jelly.

"You saw?" Mrs. Mikulka asked. "My Kieran showed it to me. Wasn't it terrible? The poor dears."

"They say it might be *hours* before they get them out," the cafeteria worker said knowingly.

With a bemused smirk, Mark Howard extricated himself from the conversation. "I'll see you in a bit, Mrs. M.," he said softly, not wanting to interrupt.

Still grinning, he carried his tray with its bowl of cornflakes, carton of milk and glass of orange juice out the side door and was gone.

Mrs. Mikulka felt her face flush. She didn't know what was wrong with her this morning. She certainly hadn't wanted to seem like a gossip in front of Mr. Howard.

Paying hastily for her breakfast tray with the change picked from the coffee-fund can, she hustled upstairs.

The coffee was ready. She filled a mug from the pot and placed it on the tray beside the plate of toast.

She walked to the inner office door and rapped a soft knuckle beneath the nameplate even as she pushed the door open.

The room beyond was cheerlessly functional. Everything was bland and colorless, including the gaunt man who sat behind the big desk across the room.

"Good morning, Dr. Smith," Mrs. Mikulka said

as she brought the tray over. She set down coffee and toast. ''Is there anything else you need?''

''No,'' replied Director Smith, in a voice as tart as unsweetened lemonade. ''Thank you, Mrs. Mikulka, that will be all.''

She nodded efficiently. Cafeteria tray in hand, she left the drab office to begin her day's work.

When the door clicked shut behind Mrs. Mikulka's ample form, Dr. Harold W. Smith checked his Timex.

One minute after eight. Mrs. Mikulka was a minute later than usual this morning.

Frowning at what he hoped was not the start of a trend for which he would have to discipline his normally punctual secretary, he turned his attention to his desk's surface.

The gleaming onyx desk was a high-tech departure from the rest of the decidedly low-tech office. Beneath the surface was a computer monitor, canted so that it was visible only to whoever sat behind the desk.

With eyes of flint gray, Harold Smith watched the monitor. Every now and then, long fingers swollen at the joints with arthritis tapped at the edge of the desk. Where fingertips pressed, luminescent keys of a touch-sensitive keyboard lit like sparks of amber lightning.

Relentless streams of data rolled past, reflected in the owlish glasses perched on Smith's patrician nose.

Though Smith had been in this same position since coming to work at 6:00 a.m., there was no strain in his back or on his face. He had spent the better part of his life like this, staring into the electronic abyss.

The information that rolled past had nothing to do with operating a small, private hospital.

Here there was a report of a corrupt judge in Ohio; there was damning data on a crooked mayor in Massachusetts. A major drug shipment was due in the country that night, flying from Haiti into Louisiana.

In each of these cases, Smith merely watched. A program he had written took the necessary action.

State police and the FBI were informed of the problems in Ohio and Massachusetts. The DEA was told about the drugs. Orders were issued surreptitiously. Through untraceable means they were sent back along invisible tendrils to the persons and agencies who would need to look into each event.

It was all handled in seconds. Quietly and efficiently, and in such a way that no one would know of the involvement of the dull little man in a drab, three-piece gray suit sitting in a sedate, ivy-covered brick building on the shores of Long Island Sound.

Such was the life's work of Harold Smith.

Eileen Mikulka knew her employer only as Dr. Harold W. Smith, director of Folcroft Sanitarium for the past forty years, and her employer for just over thirty of those years. She and the rest of the regular sanitarium staff would have been surprised to find that penny-pinching and time-clock-watching Dr. Smith held another post, vastly more powerful than that of Folcroft's director.

Harold Smith was also secret director of CURE.

CURE was the dream of an American President,

long dead. The agency was created to work outside the Constitution in order to preserve that most sacred document. Harold Smith was CURE's first and only director. For forty years he had come to that same office every day, doing his small part to see to it that the greatest experiment in democracy survived for another generation of Americans.

So engrossed was he in his work, Smith scarcely noticed the toast and coffee Mrs. Mikulka had brought him.

An electronic beep sounded from within his desk. As it did so, a new window opened on his monitor.

It was an interoffice communication. There was only one other person on Earth with access to the CURE system.

Smith scanned the information forwarded him by Mark Howard—his assistant both at Folcroft and with CURE.

It was the latest information on the expanding list of dignitaries who intended to visit the small nation of Mayana for the Globe Summit later in the week. Smith frowned when he saw additions to the Cuban and Iraqi delegations.

Mark had denoted each of the add-ons. With no trouble Smith was able to find summaries of all available background information on each of the men. None were diplomats. Most were members of security or armed forces.

Smith shook his head. "It would be safer for him to not attend," he muttered to his empty office.

Worry etched deep in his frown lines, he closed out the window and returned to his other work.

He didn't realize he had worked for nearly a full hour until there came a knock on his door.

"Come in," he called tartly.

As Mark Howard entered the office, Smith noted the time. Precisely 9:00 a.m. The CURE director met with his assistant at the same time every morning. This day as every day, Smith was quietly pleased that good fortune had blessed him with such a conscientious young man for an assistant.

"Did you have a chance to read the stuff I sent you?" Howard asked as he took his familiar plain wooden seat before the CURE director's desk.

"Yes," Smith said. "And there is virtually no way the Secret Service or FBI can weed through all of the data. Not on this timetable. It's a security nightmare. And I have just read an account of an incident in the Caribbean. Apparently two garbage scows have sunk."

"I saw that," Mark Howard said. "There was an open radio. They heard the captain yell something about a torpedo before the boat went down. Mayana's dismissing it all as an accident. You think the guy was for real?"

"I'm not sure," Smith said. "If so, it is something outside the ordinary purview of the Secret Service." An uncomfortable expression passed over his gray face. "Mark, you have no, er, sense that something is wrong, do you?"

Howard shook his head. "Sorry, no."

It was a subject neither man was comfortable discussing. Mark Howard's unexplained sixth sense for danger had come in handy for CURE in the past.

Wordlessly Smith pursed his lips, lost in thought.

"If you're worried, Dr. Smith, you should talk to the President again," Mark suggested.

Smith shook his head. "It would do no good. The President has stated in no uncertain terms publicly and privately his intention to attend the Globe Summit."

"But doesn't that vaporizing thing of theirs change things? In the past three days, the Caribbean has been piling up with garbage scows. They're leaking oil, trailing trash in the water. There are a half-dozen countries in the region with environmental complaints already. It's a bigger zoo down there than anyone thought it would be, even for an environmental conference the size of the Globe Summit."

"Yes," Smith agreed, his voice grave. "And perhaps someone sees Mayana's new technology as a threat. Or views the Globe Summit itself as an inviting target."

"You think there's really a sub loose down there?"

"Perhaps," Smith said. Tapping a finger on his desk, he considered for a thoughtful moment. "If someone is creating mischief, the risk is greater than to just the President of the United States. By week's end, most of the other leaders of the world will be there, as well. It might be wise to investigate."

"In that case, I might have some good news," the assistant CURE director said. "I've had the mainframes checking the Sinanju 800 line repeatedly for the past few months, like you asked. It's working again."

Smith's eyes widened slightly behind his rimless glasses. "When?" he asked with more interest than he normally would exhibit.

"Just before I came up here. They've gotten it working a couple of times before, but it's fritzed out. But it looks like it's going to hold this time. If you think you need them, you can call Remo and Chiun back to work."

Smith's frown deepened.

The phone line to Sinanju had been cut months earlier. Threats from Chiun had encouraged the North Korean government to make repairs a priority. Unfortunately the Communist government's talent for dispatching telephone linemen was on a par with its skills at solving the perpetual famine that plagued their country. During the previous winter, under the watchful eye of the People's government, North Korea's population had continued to starve and the phone line to Sinanju had persisted in stubbornly not working.

"Very well," Smith said. "I'll recall Remo. His injuries should be healed by this time. Knowing the way he feels about Sinanju, he is probably anxious to leave by now. However, I'm still not certain how Master Chiun sees his status with us. The last contract we signed was hastily drawn up *before* Remo took over officially as Reigning Master. It is possible that Chiun may decide to remain in Sinanju."

"You think he'd do that?"

"I'm not sure. This is unprecedented for us. Technically Remo has always been CURE's lone enforcement arm. The Master of Sinanju only ever accompanied him on assignments to protect the investment he had made in Remo's training. But now that Remo is Reigning Master, Chiun is officially retired. He could opt to stay home. The contract does provide such an escape clause.''

Smith and his assistant had been present in Sinanju for the ceremony that had seen Remo elevated to Reigning Master and Chiun step down from the post that he had held for the better part of a century. Briefly Smith wondered if CURE had lost one of its most valuable assets.

''I will not press the issue,'' the older man decided finally. ''Not now. Besides, this might be nothing. And we don't need both of them for such a simple matter. I will phone once we are finished here.''

The decision was made. Putting thoughts of Mayana from their minds for the moment, the two CURE men turned their attention to the other problems of the day that might require the intervention of America's best-kept secret.

5

After breakfast, the former Reigning Master of Sinanju padded off to a back room in the House of Many Woods.

Most of the Master's House was crammed full of treasure—generations of tribute to the Korean assassins. For years this back room alone had been kept bare. With just a few candles and reed mats scattered on the wooden floor, it was traditionally a place of spiritual contemplation.

There had been a recent addition to the room, a gift from North Korean Premier Kim Jung-Il.

Chiun sat cross-legged on a simple mat before a magnificent, fifty-one-inch high-definition Panasonic television. The set was turned up full blast. Speakers from the new Sony surround sound system, which had been placed carefully around the room, rattled the rafters.

The new satellite dish on the roof picked up shows from all over the world. When Remo entered the room he found Chiun watching a Mexican soap opera. Women with too much makeup and men with too-white teeth squinted and sneered at one another in extreme close-ups, just like their American counterparts. It occurred to Remo recently that soap operas might be the first hint that world peace was just around the corner. If—thanks to modern technology—lousy entertainment was proving to people across borders that things weren't so different on the other side, surely peace, love and understanding among all nations couldn't be far behind.

This day, Remo wasn't thinking about world peace.

Chiun had the volume turned up so loud the house shook.

"I think you're causing structural damage with that thing," Remo said, eyeing the ceiling worriedly.

"Repairs are no longer my problem," Chiun replied, eyes glued to the set. On the screen, a man who was evil because the music said he was squinted in extreme close-up. Thanks to the big screen, his nostrils looked like open manholes.

Remo tore his eyes from the rattling ceiling. The old Korean was still staring in rapt attention at the TV.

"You sit too close to that thing. You're probably getting dosed by a trillion rads of radiation. And you don't have to listen to it so loud. There's nothing wrong with your hearing. I wanted to call Smith."

"Do your complaints never end? Can you not just go outside and enjoy the beauty of spring in Sinanju?"

"What spring? There's two seasons in Sinanju, winter and mud."

"You are the American Reigning Master. If I bother you so much, do what Americans do. Build an apartment for your unwanted father and his meager belongings over the garage. Do not trust the Carthaginians for the labor, however. They pad their bills.''

"*A*, we don't have a garage. *B*, that junk must've cost more than four bills. It's not meager. And not to split hairs, but it's mine, not yours. Kim sent all this garbage to me as a Reigning Master coming-out present."

"Do you want it?"

"You know I don't watch much TV."

"Then I lay claim to it. Now leave an old man in peace and answer the phone."

Remo hadn't heard it ring. He was surprised when it suddenly jangled to life. When he glanced at his teacher, there was a look of soft satisfaction on the old man's face.

Eyes narrowing, Remo scooped up the phone.

"Captain Clyde's Clam Shack," he announced. "All-you-can-eat buffet now guaranteed eighty percent ptomaine-free."

"Remo, Smith."

Remo was surprised how good it was to hear the CURE director's lemony voice. From what he *could* hear of it. The music from the TV had risen to ear-splitting levels.

"Hey, Smitty. I was just gonna call you. Just a sec."

He held the phone to his chest. "Chiun, could you, please?"

The old man's show had come to an end. As the music fed into a commercial, a bony hand reached for the remote. The screen collapsed to a dot and the walls stopped shaking.

"Thanks, Little Father," Remo said, turning back to the phone.

"I'm glad you called, Smitty. I'm ready to get back to work. I've cooled my heels here for so long I've got moss growing on my rust."

"If Chiun thinks you are ready, I may have an assignment for you," Smith said.

"My opinion no longer matters, Emperor Smith," Chiun called. "Remo is now Reigning Master of Sinanju. Ask *him* if he is ready, not me. Go ahead, ask him."

"Er, are you well enough, Remo?" Smith asked.

"I'm all healed up, Smitty," Remo promised.

"See?" Chiun called. "He can speak for himself. And it is important that Remo feel fine, for he is Reigning Master. You do not have to waste breath to ask how I am, Emperor. I am only the one who has taken mud and transformed it into diamonds, who has made a thing of greatness from a pale piece of a pig's ear. I am Chiun, the human alchemist who raised a worthless white foundling to the loftiest peak of perfection. Do not ask me how I am, for I am but a servant. And a retired one at that."

"I think he wants you to ask him how he's doing, Smitty," Remo said.

Smith had gotten the hint. "How are you, Master Chiun?"

"Don't ask," Chiun replied.

"Okay, that was fun," Remo said. "Now, where's

this assignment? Preferably it's someplace where I can get a really bad sunburn.''

''Then this is an ideal situation,'' Smith replied.

He spoke too quickly for Remo's liking.

''What do you mean?'' Remo asked, suddenly suspicious.

''I realize you are isolated, but have you heard any press reports out of Mayana?''

''Just on CBS, NBC, ABC, CNN, MSNBC, Fox, Lifetime, Telemundo and the freaking Food Network. That Don King–headed dipweed Kim Jong-Il wired up Chiun's house for cable.''

''It is not my home any longer,'' Chiun interjected. ''I abide here only through the kindness of the Reigning Master.''

Remo cupped the mouthpiece. ''Knock that off, will you?'' To Smith he said, ''Mayana. They've got some newfangled garbage disposal or something, right?''

''If they are to be believed, it is much more than that,'' Smith replied. ''It is an amazing technology. According to Mayanan government fact sheets, it was developed by one Mike Sears, who until 1991 was a developmental scientist with the aerospace industry in California.''

''So this guy sold American technology to another country and you want me to zap him.''

''No,'' Smith replied. ''Actually the device is a distraction in what might be a larger problem. In fact, it might be the greatest contribution to modern civilization since the start of the Industrial Age.''

''The Industrial Age is overrated. The Han Dynasty in China, now that was a good age. Profitable for the House. We hooked them up for trade with the Roman Empire, you know.''

Across the room, Chiun gave a faint smile of approval.

''Be that as it may,'' Smith said, steering them back to the topic at hand. ''Everything is composed of atoms. Atomic mass gives density to all matter. The Mayana device allegedly breaks the bond at the atomic level. Substantive objects are broken up into their most elemental forms. They are literally disintegrated.''

''Okay, I'm no good with this science mumbo jumbo. Are you saying it turns something into nothing?''

''Not exactly,'' Smith said. ''More accurately, it transforms something you can see into something too minute to see. Allegedly,'' he added.

''There's that skepticism again,'' Remo said. ''It sounds like you don't believe them.''

''I have my reasons to doubt their claims,'' Smith said. ''Dr. Sears has had an unremarkable career. It is unlikely in the extreme that he could have developed the device on his own, as they claim. Mayana's own scientific community is unspectacular at best. He did not receive help there. It is almost a certainty that aid in development came from outside the country. That is, assuming it works at all.''

''I saw it on TV, Smitty. It looked real to me.''

''Much can be rigged these days. I am having Mark delve more deeply into the matter. If there is something amiss here, I have confidence he will find it.''

Remo grunted acceptance.

When Mark Howard first came aboard CURE, Remo was skeptical of the young man's worth to the organization. The assistant CURE director had drained little of that doubt away as time wore on. But the bulk of Remo's disapproval had gone out the window four months before when Mark Howard had proved brave and selfless in a crisis, aiding Remo during battle with his greatest adversary. Remo hated to admit it, but the kid had something.

"So you don't want me to knock off the guy who built it," he said. "It sounds like you don't want me to pull the plug. What is it you want me to do?"

"That is the thing. This so-called Vaporizer of theirs has complicated an existing problem. You have heard of the Globe Summit later this week?"

"Sure," Remo said. "That's when the world gets together in the nicest slum of some stink-ass rathole of a country and berates the United States for drilling holes in the ozone, torching the polar ice caps and leaving the rest of the environmental toilet seat up so the rest of the planet falls in when it has to take a whiz in the middle of the night."

"Yes," Smith said slowly, not disagreeing. "The President has confirmed that he will be attending."

"Brilliant," Remo said. "No fun flinging mud at America if you can't get some in the top dog's eye. Doesn't he know the bad guys are trying to kill us more than usual lately?"

"Which is one of my concerns," Smith said.

"There is a troubling report that two of the garbage scows waiting to be brought into Briton Bay may have been sunk by torpedo."

"Why would someone want to do that?"

"I don't know for certain. To foment chaos and fear, perhaps." Smith sighed. "Not that there is not already a large enough problem to worry about. Heaven only knows what is being shipped in on those scows."

"Smitty, I am not going down there to frisk garbage heaps for Shining Path whack-jobs."

"Neither am I," Chiun chimed in. "I spent enough years pawing through white garbage. I am not starting over again."

"I thought you were retired," Remo said.

"My work status is in flux," Chiun sniffed.

Smith seemed cheered by the old man's words. "Obviously Master Chiun is welcome to join you. In fact, the last contract—"

"It would be my joy to accompany Remo, Emperor Smith!" Chiun interrupted hastily. "Though but a humble citizen of Sinanju now, if by some modest contribution to his great work I might bring further glory to your crown, I would consider myself honored."

Remo's eyes narrowed suspiciously. "What's all this about?" he asked Chiun in Korean.

"How should I know?" Chiun sniffed in the same language. "When you and Smith talk, it is all garbage to me." He focused a little too much innocent attention on the TV.

"That thing's more interesting when it's actually

turned on," Remo said in English, nodding to the black screen. To Smith he said, "I don't suppose you'd care to fill me in on what his game is, Smitty?"

"Er," Smith said hesitantly.

"Remo, do not press your Emperor," Chiun insisted. "Have I taught you nothing?"

"As usual, Remo's in the dark," Remo grumbled. "Now I've got something else to worry about while I'm doing the Secret Service's job."

"Then you will go," Smith said. "Do I need to make arrangements for you to leave North Korea?"

"Nah. Kim's got us covered. He'll be relieved to get us out of here."

"Good. Because of the Globe Summit, Mayana is limiting the movement within the country of those not with foreign delegations. To make things easier, I have placed you on the American delegation. As a cover, you and Chiun will be Interior Department scientists who study waste disposal. I will have Mark overnight credentials to New Briton. They will be waiting at the airport when you arrive."

"What do you mean, study waste disposal?" Remo asked.

"There are scientists who have made a career of studying human trash," Smith explained.

"I take it they do more than snap on *Jerry Springer*?" Remo said dryly.

"Much of the work is done in garbage dumps," the CURE director said. "Decades' worth of trash can be drilled through and drawn up, presenting snapshots in time, like rock strata. Scientists are able to study decay rates, soil contamination and a host of other refuse-related topics.''

''You've gotta be pulling my lariat,'' Remo said. ''Are my tax dollars paying for that?''

''You do not pay taxes.''

''Glad I don't. I'd feel a real urge to toss something more than tea into Boston Harbor if my hard-earned money was going to study snotty Kleenex. I'd probably start with my congressman.''

''Be that as it may,'' Smith said blandly, ''you will be Dr. Henell. Chiun will be your assistant.''

Across the room, Chiun's eyes opened wide. ''I will not be Remo's assistant,'' the old Korean snapped.

Remo was cringing even before Smith had finished. ''Chiun won't play second fiddle to me,'' he told Smith.

''It will only be for a day or two,'' Smith said. ''I assumed that with your new status as Reigning Master—''

''It's not a problem with me, Smitty,'' Remo whispered.

''It is with me,'' Chiun called. ''I may have surrendered my honorific here in Sinanju, but in this case I must remain senior to Remo, for I am the far greater expert on garbage. Remo has only had the mirror to study, lo these many years. I have had all of Remo, all the time.''

''Ha, ha,'' Remo said. ''And I thought being Reigning Master was supposed to bring me a little more respect.''

''If you believe a title alone confers respect, Remo

Williams, then I have wasted the past thirty years of my life," Chiun replied, tone serious.

"Very well, Master Chiun," Smith said. "You and Remo may be partners."

"Partners, Little Father?" Remo asked hopefully.

The old Korean's leathery face drew into a scowl. "I will accept this as the latest episode in a long history of abuse. But I am the more senior partner," he added quickly.

"We're a go, Smitty," Remo said into the phone. "Let's just hope Chiun and I don't end up bamboozled into some cyanide-swilling cult. Mayana's got a history in that department."

"It would be best if you did not mention Jamestown while you are there," Smith said. "Jack James and his followers are still a sore subject as I understand it. The Mayanans are resentful that an American cult became so infamous on their shores. Now, if there is nothing else, I will make the arrangements with Mark for your identification."

He broke the connection.

Remo hung up the old-fashioned phone. "You want to tell me what that stuff was about the contract?" he asked Chiun.

The old Korean was rising to his feet like a puff of soft steam. He turned in a swirl of kimono silk.

"You have never before been interested in the business affairs of our profession," the old man said dismissively as he breezed past his pupil. "Why break a perfect record of ignorance?"

The wizened Asian hustled from the room to pack.

"Because maybe I have a feeling I'm being

hosed?'' Remo hollered at the old man's disappearing back.

His answer was a self-satisfied cackle from somewhere in the depths of the House of Many Woods.

6

The normally sedate international press was gathered with giddy excitement on the hot tarmac at Mayana's New Briton International Airport. When the portly man finally stepped from the Learjet onto the air stairs, an enthusiastic cheer rose from the crowd of ecstatic newspeople.

It was unusual in the extreme for the press to display anything but cynical disdain for Western leaders. The farther west, the more disdain. But this was a special case.

The dumpy little man offered a melancholy smile.

Nikolai Garbegtrov, the last premier of the old Soviet Union, had shed his usual heavy wool overcoat in favor of a light French-tailored suit.

The sun was hot on his pale face. As he climbed down the steps, he waved politely to the crowd of reporters. His tired eyes scanned for Mayanan government officials. Any dignitaries at all who might have come out to welcome the arrival of the man who had once had at his fingertips control of one of the world's greatest nuclear arsenals. He saw only press.

"Mr. Garbegtrov, why are you in Mayana?"

"Mr. Garbegtrov, could you sign this? It's for my son."

"Mr. Garbegtrov, I just *loved* you in Reykjavik."

He knew why they were called the press. They swarmed him, pressing in. Scarcely allowing him room to breathe.

It was always this way. For the Western press—particularly that of America—Nikolai Garbegtrov was like the Beatles landing in New York.

As usual, he politely shook hands and signed a few autographs as he made his way through the crowd.

His bald scalp itched under his golfer's cap, which he wore pulled down tight to his eyes. Beads of sweat rolled from the band down the back of his neck. He wanted more than anything to scratch his head. He fought the urge.

"Mr. Garbegtrov, Mr. Garbegtrov, I have a question," a reporter said, muscling in. "Why do you wear a hat in public all the time these days?"

He had gotten as used to hearing the question as he had to ignoring it.

Garbegtrov moved with the surging crowd to his waiting sedan. As the reporters clawed at him, desperate to touch his greatness, he fell through the door, collapsing exhausted onto the rear seat. His driver slammed the door on the shouting crowd and in a minute they were speeding away from the plane, away from his adoring public. The same public that would turn on him in a heartbeat if they learned his secret shame.

Garbegtrov was a bland little man in his seventies. A nondescript apparatchik who had risen up the ranks of the Soviet political system in the dying days of the failing Russian Communist empire. Everything about him was bland, from his physical appearance to his demeanor. His one great distinguishing physical characteristic was the large birthmark that was splotched on the front of his bald head.

The birthmark was his most famous feature. It had also not been seen in public for over two years.

His great, secret shame.

Alone in the back seat of the speeding car—behind tinted windows through which no eye or camera lens could see, beyond a panel that separated him from the driver—Nikolai Garbegtrov finally, gratefully, tugged off his hat. Desperate fingers scratched away at his bald scalp.

It was always itchy these days. Ever since that dark night two years ago.

As he scratched, he leaned over to get a glimpse of his reflection in the chrome lid of the armrest ashtray.

There it was. As big as life. The reason he could no longer show his head in public.

U.S.A. #1

The logo was plastered around his bald pate, put there as a twisted joke by vandals while he slept. They had used his birthmark as a jumping-off point.

He had tried everything to get rid of it. Lotions, chemical peels, laser removal. Nothing worked. Whatever process had been used to tattoo the slogan there kept bleeding it back to the surface. The doctors finally gave up, and Nikolai Garbegtrov was forced to put a hat on or face the wrath of those who professed to love him most.

The press had always been his most devoted fans. Short of diddling Lenin's corpse in Red Square on May Day, there was little he could do to make them turn on him. But tattooing a pro-American slogan on his head was one thing a rabidly anti-American press corps would never stand for.

And the worst thing—the absolute *worst*—was the itch.

As he dug away at his scalp with his pudgy fingers, he pondered anew what would happen if the world found out.

Garbegtrov had always had the press. Without them, he truly would be a man without a country.

The metaphor stirred old embers in the former Communist leader's heart. He stopped scratching. Hat in his hands, he sank back tiredly in the seat of his speeding car.

It was his fault. All of it. And it was all a horrible, horrible mistake. He never intended for the Iron Curtain to fall. As premier, he initiated reforms, but they were never meant to go so far. The dissolution of the Soviet Empire was all a terrible accident.

Western commentators at the time insisted that he would not be able to put the toothpaste back in the tube. But he had always assumed that, were it to become necessary, he would be able to cram it back in somehow.

When he declared himself to be the first Russian president, he didn't leave the Communist Party. Yet another mistake. The Communist Party was now openly despised, thanks to Garbegtrov's misfiring reforms. When the party was thrown out of power, Garbegtrov was thrown out, as well.

With the dawn of a new, freer age, there was no longer anything for him at home. He wandered the world for a time. A speech at a press gathering here, another at a university there. Always well received, of course. But for a man who had helped run the world, it was never enough.

His whole life changed because of his blundering. He thought he could never find anything to compare with the clumsy, iron-fisted, pigheaded Soviet Communist system.

Then he went to San Francisco.

Nikolai Garbegtrov's spirits were at their absolute lowest when he was called to make a speech before something called Green Earth, an organization devoted to environmental concerns of global scope.

He assumed he was being hired as a whipping boy. Since the Green Earth people were supposedly concerned with the environment and since the USSR had been the most notorious environmental offender in the history of civilization, Garbegtrov naturally assumed they would hammer him with accusations concerning Russia's dismal record. He would willingly suffer the slings and arrows of these self-loathing products of capitalist wealth. All for a big, fat paycheck.

But at the meeting something strange happened.

During the question-and-answer period he brought up the Chernobyl disaster. The Green Earthers dismissed it as nothing. They wanted to talk about Three Mile Island.

"But Chernobyl was catastrophe," Garbegtrov said. "Many have died. Many more will die. Poison cloud of radioactive material spread across Europe. Chernobyl was disaster on scale that still cannot be calculated. Your Three Mile Island was—how you say?—like X ray at dentist."

But try as he might, they would not let go of Three Mile Island, a twenty-year-old accident that did little more than prove that American safety procedures worked.

Changing focus, he mentioned Russian dumping of nuclear waste and reactor cores into the Arctic Sea, poisoning coastal land and water for hundreds of miles. They talked about Meryl Streep and Alar on apples. Wasn't she great in *The China Syndrome?* That was Jane Fonda. Oh.

Garbegtrov talked about draining Lake Aral, which devastated the center of Russia and destroyed the largest body of fresh water within the former Soviet Union's borders.

They finally grew suspicious, asking if he was really *the* Nikolai Garbegtrov and demanding he show them his driver's license.

After his talk was through, Garbegtrov stayed behind to speak with members of the environmental group. Something about their attitude struck him as familiar.

He quickly learned that their faith in the dire pronouncements of dubiously accredited doomsayers was unshakable, even with mountains of evidence to the contrary. There was not an ozone hole that was not man-made nor a polar ice cap that was not melting because someone somewhere liked to squirt cheese on his crackers.

If saving an endangered rat in a California farmer's field threw hundreds of human families into chaos, so be it. Everyone knew animals were intrinsically good and humans were, by nature, evil. After all, the only rat on the bridge of the Exxon *Valdez* was the human kind.

No matter the motives, no matter the bad science, no matter the downright dangerous silliness, they accepted the words of their leaders with pure, blind faith. In short, they were better Communists than any the old Soviet system had ever produced.

On that day, after years of dispirited wandering, Nikolai Garbegtrov finally found his new home. After joining the international environmental movement, Garbegtrov quickly became the poster boy of Green Earth. He traveled the world—lecturing, hectoring. He liked the West especially. He could always be guaranteed a warm greeting by a fawning press. For the ex-Communist premier who had lost an empire, it was *almost* like the good old days.

The traffic grew heavier as his car drove into the heart of New Briton. Despite the air-conditioning, his head was sweating. The itch began anew. He did his best to ignore it, pulling his golf hat back on.

His car dropped him off in front of the Chamberlain Hotel in the center of New Briton. He was met by a fresh crush of reporters.

Green Earth handlers hustled the former premier

up the sidewalk, beneath the gilded canopy and into the hotel lobby.

After a brief exchange of pleasantries with some of the Green Earth leadership, he was led into the grand ballroom and herded onto the dais amid a flurry of flashbulbs and shouted questions. Someone handed him a few 3 x 5 note cards. On them, carefully typed lines had been written out phonetically. Behind the podium, he perched a pair of bifocals on the end of his nose.

The ballroom noise swelled, then subsided.

Garbegtrov didn't smile to the crowd as he read Green Earth's statement. He spoke in heavily accented English.

"Ladies and gentlemen." His words echoed out across the ballroom. "The eyes of world are directed here this week. People of good conscience are about to come together in this small country to confront serious, devastating environmental havoc that the West continues to wreak on rest of globe. Now, during this time when environmental misdeeds of the West should be on trial, Mayana has chosen to reveal its new technology for the disposal of waste. We at Green Earth are skeptical of this device. Is it smoke screen to provide cover for polluting America? If it works, what is cost to precious environment? Will release of atoms destabilize ecosystem?

"These are questions for vigilant press to ask. I would caution other leaders of world as they convene here in days that follow to not forget the environmental horrors the United States and others—but mostly United States—have visited on planet. Green Earth remains vigilant.''

He tapped his note cards back together. A few reporters shouted from the hall. Garbegtrov held up a staying hand.

''There will be no questions now. I, like you, seek answers. Donations may be sent to Green Earth world headquarters in San Francisco. Is your planet, people.''

And with that, Nikolai Garbegtrov walked offstage. He left behind the growing murmur of the dispersing press corps.

Backstage, Garbegtrov's brow was furrowed beneath the brim of his hat. Members of his Green Earth entourage hurried up to meet him.

''Sock it to 'em, comrade,'' said an intense, bearded man in a hemp suit. He was just the sort of political agitator Garbegtrov would have sent to a gulag back when the Western media used to ignore the fact that Garbegtrov's gulags were standing room only. ''Show them the power of Mother Earth.''

The former Soviet leader's eyes were flat. This idiot—indeed all of the dolts in Green Earth—had no idea what real power was like. Or, worse, what it was like to lose it.

''Is my room ready?'' Garbegtrov grumbled morosely. His head was itching like mad.

''Oh, yeah. Sorry.'' The man clapped his hands.

Garbegtrov's entourage reassembled around the former Soviet premier. Like a sad little tyrant prince surrounded by his pathetic court of sycophants, Nikolai Garbegtrov—itchy tattoo and all—trudged from the shabby backstage.

7

Petrovina Bulganin steered her cute little 2002 Ford Thunderbird convertible through the sharp twists and turns of Moscow's narrow old streets. In the urban valleys the growling engine was a nasty rumble that rattled dirty windows high up in ugly Communist-era tenements.

Petrovina didn't pay much attention to the engine sound. She was too busy reapplying lipstick in the rearview mirror.

Barely nudging the steering wheel, she flew around a corner. A big truck blocked her side of the street. Two men lugged a ratty sofa down the back ramp.

Petrovina noted the workers with bland impatience. She flew up to them without slowing, cutting sharply at the last moment and zipping around the truck, her rear wheels just nipping the corner of the ramp. The sports car bounced and the men dropped their sofa. They were cursing and raising their fists at her even as she zoomed off down the street.

Petrovina waved a dainty hand back at them.

Petrovina Bulganin was in a hurry. And when Petrovina Bulganin was in a hurry, she slowed for neither pedestrians nor other vehicles.

A dumpy old woman in a tattered babushka was crossing the street. Petrovina had finished checking her makeup. She frowned as the woman grew larger. Laying on the horn, Petrovina raced straight up to the horrified crone, zooming neatly around her at the last possible moment.

She watched in the mirror. When the woman twirled and fell, it was from shock. Petrovina knew she hadn't hit her. The car handled like a dream.

The Thunderbird was a gift from a French government official. Petrovina had gotten it for a weekend of passion in his family villa outside Paris. The deal was a simple one. The Frenchman got the lovely Petrovina Bulganin, warm and without reservation. She got her new Thunderbird, along with the latest detailed intelligence on the whens, wheres and hows of NATO's integration with the former Soviet republics of Western Europe. The latter included up-to-date espionage and government contacts—payrolls, codes and time schedules—within four countries. The former included fully independent suspension and an overhead-cam V8.

Petrovina loved her little Thunderbird. She was so glad that Ford had decided to make them again. It was a beautiful little joy, sleek and dangerous at the same time. Much like Petrovina Bulganin.

Petrovina was part of the new wave of Russian espionage agents. Brash, young, good at their game—none of whom had ever set foot inside KGB headquarters. Not that they had not been in the actual

building. But by the time this generation came
around, the KGB was the SVR. Many in their field
had never even known life in the old KGB.

There was a time not too long before when that
would have been unthinkable. But ten years was an
eternity in the espionage business. The old KGB men
were retiring out of the service or moving up to desk
jobs. The void was now being filled by young agents
for whom the old Soviet system was something that
had been dismantled while they were still laughing
as children on playgrounds. Those same children—
now grown—had known adulthood only in the new
Russia.

Petrovina had not been groomed for the espionage
business from early childhood or plucked out of
school by a keen-eyed KGB scout. When she completed her studies, she entered the job market like
anyone else. Her language skills and intelligence
quickly landed her a dull desk job with the SVR. She
might have stayed for years in that dreary little out-
of-the-way position if her personnel file hadn't found
its way into a special set of hands.

It had all started nineteen months before.

The events unfolded so quickly Petrovina was
fuzzy on all the details. She was working at her desk
one Friday morning translating English-language in-
tercepts from Kosovo when her supervisor came to
collect her.

Petrovina wasn't sure what was going on. The man
brought her to the back of the building, to a corridor
and elevator that she hadn't known existed. Two
minutes later she was stunned when she found herself

being ushered into the office of Pavel Zatsyrko, the head of the SVR.

As a lowly language clerk toiling away in the basement, she had never had cause to catch the eye of someone so important. Briefly she wondered if she was being fired.

Zatsyrko did not offer her a chair. He sat behind his desk, the slats of the blinds closed on the morning sun.

"You have been reassigned," the SVR head announced dully. He didn't look her in the eye. He was looking down at the file on his desk.

"Sir?" Petrovina questioned.

"Here."

He slid her the file. Hesitantly—for she still did not know what was going on—she picked it up. She was surprised to see the file was her own. All of her employment records, all of the data that had been collected on her when she joined the SVR, her entire life—*everything* was in the file.

"Bring this with you to your new assignment. Your desk has already been emptied. Collect the box with your personal belongings on your way out. If you are asked, you never worked here. The rest will be explained when you get there."

Confused, Petrovina asked where "there" was.

Pavel Zatsyrko offered her a withering look and pointed to the file before turning his attention to his desktop and other, more important matters of his workday.

Petrovina found a small scrap of paper in the back

of her personnel file. A pink Post-it note with an address.

She took the bus—back then she could only afford public transportation—as far as it would go, then walked the rest of the way. She found the building in an out-of-the-way corner of a bustling Moscow district. It was an impossibly huge slab of concrete that occupied an entire city block.

As she drove her Thunderbird up to the building this day, she thought of herself nineteen months ago.

This day she had the top down on her car. Her tousled mane of glorious hair blew wild in the cold, its raven hue matching the twinkling cunning of her coal black eyes.

Back then she was a timid mouse, hair pulled back into a sensible ponytail. When she was ushered through the gate back then, she didn't know what to think. It felt as if she were walking inside a prison.

But that was ages ago. Another lifetime. A different Petrovina Bulganin.

She stopped the Thunderbird at the gate. Her pass card got her through. She waved to the woman at the security window as she drove into the first-floor garage.

There were a few other cars inside. Not very many for a building this size.

The size of the building did strike Petrovina as odd. There never seemed to be very many people there. On that first day more than a year and a half earlier, she had not asked why so large a building was needed for so small a staff. She was too busy absorbing new information.

On that day she had been ushered into a basement office. A honey-blond-haired woman of about forty sat waiting patiently behind a small desk. The woman's name, Petrovina learned, was Anna Chutesov. She was director of an agency so secret that few outside a tight circle knew of its existence.

"We are called the Institute," Director Chutesov had explained. "I act as an adviser to our president. But I am understaffed." She seemed puzzled at the admission. As if she had worked there for many years, never having noticed that she was alone in the drafty concrete building. "There have been a few instances during my tenure here where simple advising has not been sufficient. But I have no field agents. That has changed. I have recently gotten permission and funding to increase Institute staff."

"So I am to be transferred from the SVR?" Petrovina asked, confused. She was a nervous little thing back then. So timid, so fearful. The big building was cold. She hugged herself for warmth.

"You have already been transferred," Director Chutesov had said blandly. "You work for the Institute now. For me. Give me your personnel file."

Petrovina still held the manila folder she had been given back at Pavel Zatsyrko's office. Her clenching hand had made a wet imprint on the light cardboard. She gave the file to Director Anna Chutesov.

The Institute head opened the file and began feeding it piece by piece through the shredder beside her desk. The confetti curls of Petrovina Bulganin's life whirred out the far end.

"You are dead to the SVR," Director Chutesov

said. ''They have expunged your files. You never worked for them. Nor do you work for me. At least as far as the world knows.'' She offered a mirthless smile. ''Welcome to the world of espionage, Agent Dvah.''

In Russian, *dvah* was *two; adeen* was *one*. Bewildered, Petrovina asked if Director Chutesov was Agent Adeen.

''No,'' Director Chutesov had replied. ''And never ask that question again.''

Petrovina thought there was some sort of dreadful mistake. She was not a spy. Even when she began her training, she expressed doubts to all her instructors.

No one listened to her protests. Eventually, as the months wore on, she stopped protesting, due mainly to the fact that the training began to draw out elements of her personality that she had not even known existed.

Marksmanship and limited martial-arts training weren't a problem. Petrovina had taken several self-defense courses while at the SVR. A single girl in Moscow couldn't be too careful. She had a good eye with weapons and had always had an athletic bent. So said her SVR file.

But as her skills increased, so, too, did her coldness. A veneer of icy confidence slowly emerged from the shell of the timid little language expert. By the end, Petrovina was the ugly duckling that became the beautiful, deadly swan.

In under a year's time Agent Dvah was on assignment, becoming the Institute's first official field agent, answerable only to Director Chutesov herself.

It was a life Petrovina Bulganin had been born to live and that, but for the intervention of the Institute's director, she would never have discovered.

Now, months since that first assignment and already in her mind a seasoned pro, Petrovina danced through the labyrinthine hallways of the Institute building.

The scattered workers she passed were all women. There was not a single male face among them.

She found her way downstairs to the special room in the private corridor. There was no secretary.

She knocked on the door. Petrovina heard the sound of a bolt clicking back. She pushed the door open.

Director Chutesov sat behind her desk. There was a computer monitor sitting on the corner near the shredder. Her vacant ice-blue eyes watched the pulses of the screen without really seeing them. She said not a word as her finger retreated from the switch that had unlocked the door.

After an awkward moment, Agent Bulganin cleared her throat. "I came as quickly as I could."

Director Chutesov didn't stir from her trance. She continued to stare at the monitor. One hand rose above desk level, waving Petrovina to a chair.

Petrovina watched the director of the Institute, unsure if she should speak again.

"This building is an odd thing, Petrovina," Director Chutesov said after another long moment. "You thought so yourself many months ago. It is large, isn't it? Too large, it seems, for the needs of the Institute.''

Director Chutesov looked up from her monitor. There was a glint of deep intelligence in her blue eyes.

''There are rumors that ghosts once lived here,'' she continued. ''The people in the area swear this building was haunted. Do you believe in ghosts, Agent Bulganin?''

Petrovina admitted that she did not. ''I believe in what I can see, Director,'' she said.

''As you are, I once was. And yet there are things that neither you nor I can see. For instance, why would an individual empty a building of furniture—give every last scrap of it away—and then forget they had done so?''

It was an odd question. Director Chutesov seemed very serious asking it. As if she desperately wanted an answer.

''Madness?'' Petrovina suggested. ''Drugs or alcohol?''

''I do not take drugs. I drink alcohol rarely, and then only lightly. And I am not mad.''

Petrovina blinked. She hadn't realized they were discussing Director Chutesov herself.

''There are outdoor markets near here,'' Director Chutesov explained. ''Perhaps you've been to them. No? Well, I have. A few months ago I went one afternoon looking for antiques.'' She dropped her voice knowingly. ''Some of these sellers are idiots. They would not know good furniture if it fell on their heads. The parents or grandparents die, and the children immediately race off to sell hundred-year-old antiques for kopecks at market. As I was looking for bargains at a particular stall, I caught the eye of the seller. Before I knew what was happening, he began to argue with me. He told me that I had given everything to him fair and square and that I could not have it back.''

Petrovina frowned. ''Did you know this man?''

''No. He was a complete stranger to me.''

''Then I do not understand.''

''Nor did I. Nor do I still. But he was adamant that the items for sale at his stand were from me. He claimed that I had allowed him and others like him into this very building. They are the ones who emptied it of furnishings.''

''He mistook you for someone else,'' Petrovina said. ''That is, assuming you did not give away Institute furniture.'' She laughed a tinkling little laugh.

Director Chutesov's face was deadly serious.

''I did not. Not that I can remember. But there were a few others at the market who made the same claim. I could not believe that they were all insane. When I pressed them, they were able to give a fairly detailed description of the interior of this supposedly secret building.''

Petrovina was intrigued. ''Thieves,'' she said. ''They somehow got in here and stole whatever they were selling. What is it they had for sale, by the way?''

''Blankets, cots, storage bins. The Institute was apparently home to some secret garrison. And, no, Petrovina, they were not simple thieves. If there was a break-in, I would have known of it. Or should have. No, the likeliest, if most disturbing conclusion to be reached is that I did indeed open the doors of the Institute and allowed strangers inside to empty it out.''

Petrovina was at a loss. ''Forgive me, Director Chutesov, but what does it mean?''

Anna Chutesov tapped a slender finger to her own forehead. There were care lines in the perfect porcelain skin. They had appeared only recently.

''I think, Agent Bulganin, that there is a piece of something missing,'' Director Chutesov said. ''Up here. One day I will find out what was taken and how. And when that day comes, woe to the man who took it from me.''

Petrovina understood. Director Chutesov believed that some invisible someone had stolen parts of her memory. That it was a man was a given. Agent Bulganin had learned early on that her superior at the Institute was a staunch feminist. This was why no men worked in the big concrete building.

''That is why you called me here,'' Petrovina said confidently. ''To look into this matter.''

Director Chutesov shook her head. ''There is not enough information at the moment. I will continue to investigate this myself. We will address it when the time comes. You are here for another reason. The *usual* reason, in my experience. To clean up a mess the men have left for us.''

The Institute director reached inside her top drawer. She tossed a file across her desk.

Petrovina noted that there were old Red Army

codes on the flap. Inside was data on a shipyard in Latvia, as well as detailed personnel information on several former Russian navy men. Agent Dvah scanned the old photograph of a Captain Gennady Zhilnikov. The picture was ten years out of date.

"The Institute is a clearinghouse for information," Director Chutesov explained. "From that raw data I have identified something that might be a problem, if it is true." She pointed to the file. "That will be your primary assignment. Have you seen the news today?"

Before becoming a spy, Petrovina had watched the news faithfully. She watched less these days. The only story she had seen that morning was about three kittens trapped in a storm drain in California. Russia had pledged equipment and manpower to help rescue the trapped animals.

"No, I have not," Petrovina admitted.

"There is also a device in Mayana that the SVR has been assigned to look into. A machine that destroys trash. There is a team of SVR agents that, like you, will officially be part of our Globe Summit delegation. As long as you are there, you will handle that task, as well. It is only simple reconnaissance. It will not take you long away from your main mission. That was my excuse for getting you in the country. And as simple as it is, I would not trust the men of the SVR to not bungle the assignment. You may sign for the equipment downstairs. For now, read that file. Save your questions until you are through."

Petrovina Bulganin nodded, pulling open the file.

Director Chutesov exhaled, turning attention back to her computer. The Institute head muttered as she poked lifelessly at the keys.

"And if we are very lucky, Agent Bulganin, perhaps I am wrong for the first time in my life and the idiots who run this country have not given the world yet another reason to think us a dangerous laughingstock." Disgusted, she pulled up her solitaire program. "Men," Anna Chutesov swore.

8

Traditionally a Master of Sinanju departed the village to much fanfare. Remo didn't like fanfare. Preferring not to make a big scene, he suggested that he and Chiun slip out of town quietly.

Chiun wouldn't have it. A newly invested Reigning Master of the House of Sinanju could not sneak out of his village like a common thief. What would the villagers think?

Remo pointed out that they'd probably be pretty okay with it, since they spent their entire lives from cradle to grave with their hands stuffed in someone else's back pocket.

"I'll toss my Visa card in the mud on the way out the door," Remo said. "They'll be so busy massaging the cramps from forging my name they won't even know I've left."

"Do you want to break with five thousand years of tradition? Is that what you want?" Chiun demanded.

"I'm down with that," Remo replied.

Chiun tried a different approach. "Do you want to spend the entire trip to South America listening to why you have shamed me yet again in front of my ancestors?''

The entire population of Sinanju was gathered in the main square of the village to bid farewell to the new Reigning Master. General Kye Pun was allowed to witness the Rite of Departure. He was swept along behind Remo and Chiun by the mass of humanity.

Remo was ushered uncomfortably through the multitude to the edge of the village. Men and women who had spent the past four months bad-mouthing him wore phony smiles as they sang him on his way.

"Hail, Master of Sinanju, who sustains the village and keeps the code faithfully," they shouted, their voices raised as one. "Our hearts cry with joy and pain at your departure. Joy that you undertake this journey for the sake of we, the unworthy beneficiaries of your generosity. And pain that your toils take your beauteous aspect from our midst. May the spirits of your ancestors journey safe with you who graciously throttles the universe."

Remo was tapping his toe impatiently on the wellworn path as they recited. When they were finished, he pointed at several random villagers.

"Up yours, yours, yours and yours," he said in English. He said it with a smile, as if conferring a blessing.

There were happy smiles all around.

"And I think I hate you most of all," Remo added, pointing to a woman with a particularly nasty tongue and only three teeth. She seemed delighted to have been singled out by the new young Reigning Master.

She sneered through her jack-o'-lantern dental work at the rest of the villagers.

"Now beat it," Remo said, motioning with both hands like a farmer scattering chickens. "If I have to look at your ugly faces for two more seconds, I'll have to start drinking again." As the villagers turned back to the center of town to resume their long-standing tradition of doing absolutely nothing, Remo wandered over to Chiun. "Can we go now?"

The old Korean was conversing with an elderly woman who had stood separate from the other villagers. She was nodding intently as she listened to his instructions.

"In case of emergency, you may use the telephone in the Master's House to reach the Emperor of America," the old man was saying. "He will locate me."

"I understand," the woman replied.

"She already knows about the phone, Little Father," Remo said. Kye Pun waited near him. "Let's shake a leg."

Chiun ignored him. "And the burner in the basement," he told the woman. "It must be checked every day."

"As you wish, I will do," she said.

"Little Father?" Remo insisted, touching the old man on the elbow. "She knows the drill. It's time to go."

The old man's frown lines deepened. At last he nodded. He offered the crone a bow. She gave one to both Chiun and Remo in turn before turning back for the village.

General Kye Pun hurried up the weed-lined path before the two men.

"You don't have to worry. Hyunsil will do fine," Remo said as they walked along behind the North Korean general. "She already knew most of the stuff from Pullyang."

Chiun nodded. "Her father taught her many of his duties before he passed on. However, it is important that she make no mistakes, for she is the first female entrusted with the duties of caretaker."

"Gotta break that glass ceiling sometime," Remo said.

The long path led to a wide, four-lane highway. The strip of blacktop seemed as out of place in the Korean countryside as a yellow racing stripe up a pig's back.

A car waited for them on the road. Kye Pun held the door, ushering the two Sinanju Masters into the back before sliding in behind the wheel. In another minute they were speeding down the empty highway.

When they got to the airport in Pyongyang, Remo was surprised by the crowds. There were soldiers lined up as if for review, as well as many government officials.

Remo assumed they had driven into the middle of some big Commie block party commemorating the invention of the airplane by Karl Marx. His eyes grew flat when he saw Leader-for-Life Kim Jong-Il on the reviewing stand in the middle of the crowd. The North Korean leader was smiling nervously as Remo's car drove through the parting throng.

"Holy cripes," Remo complained. "It's for me."

"Take it while you can," Chiun advised from the seat beside his pupil. "As the new Reigning Master this is likely the only time you will be heralded on your way like this."

"New Reigning Master, my foot. Kim is just happy to get me out of the country. This is his party, not mine."

The car stopped between the reviewing stand and the waiting North Korean plane. It was the premier's own plane, not the Iraqi jet on which Remo had flown to Korea four months earlier. His stolen plane was still being repaired. From what he'd seen of the technical skills of the North Korean people, he'd give them another million years to fix the broken jet engine, give or take a hundred thousand.

Kye Pun raced around to open Remo's door. Schoolchildren threw flower petals from woven baskets onto the red velvet carpet at Remo's feet.

"I'm surprised they don't have a goddamn brass band," Remo groused to Chiun as they stepped up the carpet.

The minute the words were out, a brass band marched around the side of the terminal playing something that sounded like John Philip Sousa being sucked up a tin whistle.

On the platform, Kim Jong-Il's anxious smile stretched wider. The shock of hair bestowed on him by cruel nature and crueler genetics stuck straight up in the air. Sweat beaded on his broad forehead. He waved a frantic pudgy hand for the band to cut the music. The reedy tootling petered out.

"Your unworthy cousins bid farewell to the new

Reigning Master of the House of Sinanju,'' Kim Jong-Il announced. ''Would that you could stay with us forever, but we understand that your awesome responsibilities must take you from our midst. Any words that the Reigning Master would bestow on us in departure would be drops of honey on our unworthy ears.''

Remo looked up at the Korean leader. His eyes settled blandly on the fat man's standing-up hair.

''Buy an effing comb,'' Remo said.

He made a beeline for his plane.

Kye Pun's worried eyes darted wide apology to the North Korean premier as he ushered Chiun to the waiting jet.

Their flight to the South had already been cleared. It was a short hop across the thirty-eighth parallel. At the airport in Seoul, General Kye Pun got them to the gate of their commercial flight and waved them gladly on their way.

From the plane's window, Remo saw the general weeping tears of joy as the plane taxied from the terminal.

When they were airborne, the Korean peninsula slipping in the wake of the rising plane, Remo snapped his fingers.

''I should have told them to make sure they keep my Iraqi jet hangared for me,'' he said. ''Just because I'm not in town anymore doesn't mean I want them stripping it for spare parts or boiling the seats for soup.''

''They will not damage your plane,'' Chiun replied. "They would not dare. You are the Reigning Master of Sinanju."

This time, almost for the first time, he said it without sarcasm. Chiun was sitting by the window, careful eyes trained on the gently shuddering left wing. Remo smiled at the back of his teacher's age-speckled head.

He felt good. Here he was, sitting beside his teacher on a plane while Chiun studied the wing to make sure it didn't fall off during takeoff. It was business as usual. He had spent the past four months worrying for nothing. Things hadn't changed as much as he had feared.

When the plane leveled off at cruising altitude, Chiun turned from the window.

"Move your feet," he insisted. The old man scampered around his pupil, forcing Remo to vacate his seat.

They switched places, Remo settling in by the window, Chiun taking the aisle seat. It was a familiar drill that Remo normally found annoying. This day it made him smile.

"What are you grinning at, imbecile?"

"Nothing. This is just nice is all, Little Father."

Chiun's hazel eyes narrowed. "What is?"

"Me, you. Together again. Just like old times."

"When you are my age you may think wistfully of old times. Only dying insects wax nostalgic for last week."

"Don't rain on my parade. Which, by the by, Kim Jong-Il nearly threw for me back there. Everything's coming up Remo. I feel so good I don't even care about whatever's up with Smitty and you and that contract stuff you won't tell me about.'' He raised a brow. ''You want to tell me about it?''

''No.''

''Okay by me,'' Remo said sincerely. ''I'm just glad things are finally getting back to normal. You're here, the world's back in order, God's in his heaven and everything's just hunky-dory with me.''

Chiun fixed his level gaze on his pupil. ''Only the white parts of the world are ever in disorder,'' he droned. ''And do not drag in whatever god it is you people bend your knees to this week. As for me, where else would I be? I cannot be allowed comfortable retirement when I am needed so desperately. You might be the Master of Sinanju, Remo Williams, but *I* am the Master of Garbage.''

He grabbed a passing male flight attendant. ''You,'' he demanded. ''Go and inform the inebriate who pilots this air carriage to take care, for he has some very important cargo.''

''Sir?'' the young Korean asked, confused.

''You're not going to sour my mood, Little Father,'' Remo warned, ''so you might as well give it a rest.''

The old man ignored him. ''I am a famous scientist of garbage,'' he confided to the flight attendant. ''En route to an important conference.''

The young flight attendant's face lit up. ''Are you going to the Globe Summit in Mayana?'' he asked.

''Is that the ugly name of the place we are going?'' Chiun asked Remo over his shoulder, face puckering in displeasure.

"Not helping you out," Remo said. In his seat pocket he had found a magazine that he was pretending to read.

"The name does not matter," Chiun said to the flight attendant. "The only thing that matters is that I go there to unveil my prize specimen of garbage to a horrified world. And there it sits." He held out a bony hand to Remo. "I call it 'Hamburger in White.' Do not get your hands too close to its ravenous mouth," he cautioned.

"Oh," the young Korean said, the light of understanding dawning. He offered the sort of smile flight attendants were trained to give to senile old passengers. "How nice. If you will excuse me, I have to help get the meals ready."

He slipped cautiously away from the strange little man.

"If you're trying to get my goat, it won't work," Remo said once the young man was gone. "I'm happy and that's that." He contentedly rattled his magazine.

Their plane brought them to Mexico City. From there a connecting flight took them across the Gulf of Mexico to the Caribbean Sea and the tiny South American country of Mayana.

For both flights, Chiun grabbed random flight attendants and lavatory-bound fellow passengers to inform one and all that he was a noted garbage scientist. When asked what this entailed, he confided that he mostly studied Remo. Remo did his best to ignore the old man's stage whisper. In his head he kept repeating to himself that this was better than the alternative.

Remo had hoped the old Korean would have exhausted his little joke by the time they landed at Mayana's New Briton International Airport. His hopes were dashed when they entered the terminal and Chiun raised his pipe-cleaner arms high into the air.

"I am Chiun, noted garbageologist!" he announced to the throngs of harried travelers. "Behold! My lab specimen!" He stepped aside to allow Remo into the terminal.

"Okay, okay, you've had your yucks," Remo snarled. "Now do us all a favor and cram it."

A thin smile of satisfaction toyed with the corners of Chiun's papery lips.

Chiun stayed in the main concourse while Remo went off in search of their false identifications.

He had spoken to Smith for instructions once in the air. He found an airport storage locker, located the counter to get the right key, then broke the key off in the lock and had to rip the door off the locker. There was a sealed shipping envelope inside. Tearing it open, Remo dropped both envelope and locker door in the trash before rejoining Chiun.

Hands tucked deep in his kimono sleeves, the old Korean was standing at the edge of a small crowd that had gathered near the terminal doors. He and the rest of the group were listening to a young man in a business suit.

"What are you doing?" Remo asked as he came up beside his teacher.

"Working," the old man replied. "Hush."

The man at the front of the crowd noticed Remo. "Oh," he said. "I assume you're Dr. Chiun's associate. I'm George Jiminez, deputy finance minister."

Jiminez checked Remo's and Chiun's identification. Satisfied, he wrote their names in felt-tipped pen on two sticky name tags, which he handed to them just as he had to the others in the group. Remo stuck his on a potted plant. Chiun stuck his to the side of a passing woman's American Tourister suitcase.

At the front of the group, Jiminez was entering their cover names into his pocket organizer. With a satisfied smile, he slipped the small computer into his pocket.

"If that's everyone, we can begin our tour of the Vaporizer site," he said.

He led the group outside to a waiting bus.

"This is just a cover," Remo whispered as the rest were getting on the bus. "Do we really want the nickel tour?" He noted that most of the others looked like nerdy scientists.

"If there is a charge, you pay it," Chiun replied. "I forgot my purse in Sinanju." Hiking up his kimono skirts, he climbed aboard the bus.

The front seats had already filled up. The only ones open were in the rear. Chiun stopped dead near the empty driver's seat, a flat look on his leathery face. Remo didn't have to ask what he was thinking.

"The cool kids always sit in the back," Remo suggested tactfully.

Chiun gave him a baleful look. With swats and

shoves, he promptly expelled the seated men from the front, bullying them down the aisle and into the back.

When George Jiminez boarded the bus a minute later, he found most of the tour group cowering in fear in the back of the bus. Chiun sat directly behind the driver's seat, his face a mask of pure innocence. Remo had reluctantly taken the seat next to him.

The confused deputy finance minister got behind the wheel. Pulling away from the curb, the bus headed off into the hills above New Briton.

Remo glanced toward the back of the bus, where the group of wheezing scientists were reliving junior high. A few were sucking on asthma inhalers.

"Why didn't you shake them down for their milk money while you were at it?" he whispered.

"They should thank me for building strength of character," Chiun sniffed.

"Yeah, I'm sure they'll do that right after they finish pissing their snow pants." He was watching the scientists through narrowed eyes. There appeared to be faces from around the world in the group. "They've got a regular League of Geek Nations going on here," he commented.

"That would explain the stink," Chiun replied.

Remo knew what he meant, although the men on the bus were not the source. The smell had been strong ever since they left the airport terminal. It was the combined stench of hundreds of garbage scows moored just offshore. They had seen the boats from the window of their plane.

A major highway out of the city took them into the sloping hills above the bay. New Briton Harbor sparkled in the brilliant white sun. A finger of land formed a seawall at the mouth of the wide bay. In the Caribbean Remo could see the eyesore of Garbage City—scows as far as the eye could see waiting to be called to land.

And then they were gone. Boats, sea and harbor vanished behind thickening jungle foliage. Signs along the road warned that they were entering a restricted area.

"We're nearly there," George Jiminez promised over his shoulder.

"Why are the signs in English?" Remo asked.

"Mayana is an English-speaking country," Jiminez explained. "We were a British protectorate until the 1950s. Many British citizens emigrated here."

"That is doubtless what attracted Smith's friend here," Chiun observed. He had a sharp eye directed on the men in the back. One had strayed over an invisible line. The old Korean scowled him back over it.

"Huh?" Remo asked.

"The one you and Smith were discussing," Chiun said. "The British enjoy their cults. If it is not Freemasons, it is Druids—if not Druids, Anglican Catholics. Smith's friend must have felt right at home here."

"Ye-es," George Jiminez said slowly, color rising in his cheeks. "You're referring to the Jamestown tragedy. Jack James was American, not British. And I'm sorry, but that's not a topic we like to discuss." Jaw clenching, he turned full attention on the road.

"Nice going, Little Father," Remo whispered. "Anyone else you want to tick off at us?"

The old man's hazel eyes were still trained on the back of the bus. He was watching one man in particular—a nervous-looking Asian.

"The day is young," Chiun replied ominously. His suspicious gaze never wavered.

9

Mike Sears was not good under pressure.

He should have been able to keep up a confident front. After all, as the official mind behind the Vaporizer, the world now considered him a genius. But he just didn't seem to have the confidence to pull it off.

Not that he was an intellectual slouch. His credentials were top-notch. He had been hired as a developmental scientist for Lockheed after graduating from Massachusetts Institute of Technology in the early 1980s. He had worked on some of the new tiles, as well as the remodeled booster system for the space shuttle after the *Challenger* disaster. From there he had gone on to help develop new titanium Mach shields for the Air Force's top secret Aurora Project.

Such important work should have given him at least some grace under fire. But the stress of the Vaporizer project, getting the device up and running, and now the busloads of experts and foreign officials who were being hauled hourly up to the site for demonstrations—it was all becoming too much for him to handle.

Mike Sears felt a grumble of nervous bile in the pit of his empty stomach as he stood in the cramped room.

"Grid four, section thirteen," Sears said into a microphone. The words echoed across the Vaporizer pit.

Sears was in the control booth above the Vaporizer. The booth was nestled in a niche carved into a small hill. On a monitor screen he watched a man in a white lab coat scurry over the removable scaffolding on the unit's black wall.

"Four, thirteen," the man responded.

The speaker next to Sears crackled with static. A residual effect of proximity to the device.

"D-four," Sears said.

Through a remote camera, Sears watched his assistant as he worked on the Vaporizer. The man was Japanese. His dark black hair shone in the sun.

Toshimi Yakamoto had been uncomfortable going into the machine ever since it had gone online. His face betrayed his anxiety as he inched along the interior wall.

Yakamoto found the problem nozzle and went to work on it with a tool that resembled a pair of tiny forceps.

Sears spun in his chair. Sharp green images on another computer screen offered a three-dimensional image created by sensors buried in the frictionless black walls.

"Careful," Sears warned into the microphone. "You've gone too far."

Yakamoto readjusted the nozzle again. Even on

camera, beads of sweat were visible on his broad forehead. They rolled down his anxious face.

"Is better now?" he asked hopefully.

In the control booth the computer image showed the problem nozzle in perfect alignment.

"That got it," Sears said. "Lock it down and get back up here. We've got company."

On the security camera he saw Deputy Minister Jiminez's bus coming through the front gate.

The bus was loaded with thirty more scientists. Thirty more chances that Sears's secret might become known.

"Play it cool, Mike," he muttered to himself.

Leaving the booth, he went down the fence-lined path to the parking lot. The visitors were already getting off the bus. Two men had gotten off first—a young Caucasian and a very old Asian. The rest seemed to be avoiding these two. They stumbled off almost desperately, forming a fearful group away from the first pair.

George Jiminez was the last one off.

"Ah, Dr. Sears," the deputy finance minister said. "Are you ready to dazzle your latest guests?"

"Of course," Mike Sears said, a nervous smile plastered across his face. He turned to the group of scientists. "Welcome to the future, gentlemen. I'm sure your governments will be fascinated by your reports. If you'll come this way." He and Jiminez began herding the scientists into the Vaporizer compound.

Remo and Chiun brought up the rear. Remo was sniffing the air. "It stinks worse here than it did back in the city,'' he complained. ''You'd think they'd figure out a way to zap the stink when they zap the garbage.''

When he got no reply, he glanced at his teacher.

Chiun was still studying the Asian man he had singled out on the bus. The man was Japanese. His name tag identified him as Dr. Hiro Taki. Dr. Taki seemed nervous and jumpy. Remo assumed it had to do with first being assaulted on the bus, then drawing the exclusive attention of his assaulter.

''Remember, the war's over, Chiun,'' Remo warned.

''I am not an American who thinks it is high-minded to turn a blind eye to human nature,'' the old Korean replied. ''That man is up to no good.''

''Could be,'' Remo said. ''Or it could be he senses he's being targeted by a known Japanese basher.''

''Is it bashing to point out that all Japanese are liars and thieves?''

''Yes,'' Remo said. ''Especially when there's actual bashing involved, which there most times is. And while we're at it, wasn't the guy who founded Sinanju Japanese?''

Chiun tore his eyes from Hiro Taki's back. ''Why do I even talk to you?''

Quickening his pace, he shuffled ahead of his pupil.

A hurricane fence surrounded the area. Beyond was the exterior wall of the Vaporizer.

Special reusable boots were issued to the group from a large bin inside the fence.

''These will keep you from losing your footing

inside," Mike Sears explained, forcing a smile as the men slipped the boots over their shoes. "I doubt any of you want to fall in."

Wearing the protective boots, the group stepped through the gap in the outer wall and out onto the deck of the Vaporizer. The black pit yawned before them.

"You'll notice that the walls around us are of the same material as the Vaporizer itself," Sears said. "This upper level will eventually be part of the unit, almost doubling capacity. For tests until now we have dumped single loads into the device. That's good for demonstration and experimentation, but isn't cost-effective. When we settle into daily use, the main pit and upper level will be filled to capacity before the unit is activated. Hundreds of tons of waste will be removed in the wink of an eye."

Some members of the group were touching the walls. Their faces grew surprised. Remo and Chiun tried it, as well.

There was barely any sense of anything at all. The strange coating seemed to dissipate Remo's touch across the surface. It was almost like touching air.

"It's a kind of rubberized tile," Sears explained. "We use some of the same principles used by defense departments, NASA, the computer industry. The walls were tricky. We had to design them so that the process itself didn't swallow up the unit. If we got it wrong, when we switched it on, it would theoretically destroy itself along with most of the hill we're standing on."

Some of the braver men edged toward the fence

that surrounded the pit. The capped nozzles in the black walls glinted in the sunlight.

Workmen were in the Vaporizer pit. An Asian scientist was just climbing out. His face glistened sweat. Other men drew up the scaffolding he had been working from.

"Dr. Yakamoto was just making some minor adjustments," Mike Sears explained. "I think he's all set now."

Yakamoto nodded.

"Great," Sears said. "Maybe you'd like to see a demonstration before we get into Q and A. Please come this way."

Sears and Jiminez began to herd the crowd back to the door. Dr. Hiro Taki lagged at the back of the group, as did Dr. Yakamoto. The men didn't seem to know each other. In fact, they seemed to make a point of not knowing each other. It was a subtle nuance that would have gone unnoticed by anyone other than Remo and Chiun.

Remo didn't know how he knew the men were acquainted. It was something instinctive. His suspicions were confirmed when the men—just for a moment—locked eyes. Dr. Taki offered a single nod. Yakamoto's face showed a flash of horror before turning away.

"See?" Chiun said. "Do you see why my father always said never trust a son of Nippon?"

"Was he trying out for the role of Korean Archie Bunker?" Remo said dryly.

Unseen by the Mayanans, Remo had kicked off one shoe to test the surface underfoot. It was as frictionless as the walls. Without their special boots, even he and Chiun might have fallen. He slipped his loafer with its boot back on.

When he glanced up he saw that Chiun had padded farther ahead. The old man had caught up to Toshimi Yakamoto. Leaning in, he whispered something to the Japanese scientist.

Yakamoto responded with shock. The color drained from his sweating face. He hustled away from the wizened Korean, forcing his way through the group of visitors and out the gate.

"Do I want to know?" Remo asked once he caught up to his teacher.

"It was nothing that you do not already know," Chiun replied. "I told him that the Japanese as a people cannot be trusted and that I know he is up to no good. And look, see how he runs like a frightened rabbit when confronted by the truth. Pitiful. The one thing these Japanese had was pigheaded bravery, and Western subversion has robbed them even of that. I blame the French."

Leaving his pupil on the Vaporizer deck, he flounced out of the gate to remove the special boots from his sandals.

Remo tipped his head, considering. "Now, *there's* some racism I can finally support," he said, nodding.

He followed the others out the gate.

10

Toshimi Yakamoto ran.

Fear slowed his legs. His lungs burned, his brain sang a symphony of panic.

The old man *knew*. Somehow he knew.

He hadn't been specific. But those penetrating hazel eyes said all that was unspoken. He knew the truth.

The Korean had spoken Japanese. It was unlikely that anyone would have understood had they even heard, but the fact was, Yakamoto had been found out.

It was no wonder.

Toshimi Yakamoto had no business being here. He was a scientist, not a spy. But he was a scientist who had been there at the start. The *real* start, not this bastardized Mayanan version of it. He understood the nuts and bolts of what needed to be done and so—despite his protestations—had been drafted kicking and screaming into this project.

But now it was done. He had been found out.

Mind swirling, he ran out of the Vaporizer compound and through the hurricane fence.

He passed colleagues whom he had worked with

for nearly a year, as well as other workmen from the project. He ignored all their smiles and hellos, shoving through them.

Another tour bus was coming up the road from New Briton. The driver had to lay on the horn as Yakamoto darted out in front of it. The bumper nearly nicked him. He felt the exhaust breeze as he made it to the other side of the road.

Passengers watched the little man in the white lab coat running like a maniac from the Vaporizer site.

The bus continued up toward the cluster of buildings as Yakamoto ran down into the lower parking lot.

He found his Toyota, fumbling his keys from his pocket. He dropped them to the gravel drive, knocked them behind a tire and scraped his palm clawing them back out. Keys rattling, he unlocked his car and fell inside.

He hunkered down in the back seat. His injured hand found his cell phone in his coat pocket. With shaking hands he pressed out the special number.

The phone was answered on the first half ring.

"What is it?" the deep voice demanded in Japanese. A demon's voice, rumbling up from some low circle of Hell.

"I have been discovered!" Yakamoto blurted. As he spoke, he glanced in fright around the parking area. There was no one else there. He expected them to come any moment. He sank farther in on himself, trying to melt into the seat.

"Explain," demanded the man on the phone.

In a voice bordering on hysterical, Yakamoto

whimpered out the details of his brief confrontation with the visiting Korean scientist.

"What exactly did he say?" the man on the phone demanded once Toshimi Yakamoto was finished.

"He said I was untrustworthy and that I was up to no good," Yakamoto pleaded.

There was a pause. "And?" the voice asked.

Yakamoto felt his breathing coming under control. His head was clearing. Somehow actually repeating the words of his accuser out loud made them sound not quite so damning.

"He said Japanese eyes were funny," Yakamoto said.

"In other words, he said nothing specific except to insult your nationality?"

Yakamoto was thinking much more clearly now. His brow furrowed deeply. "I suppose not. No, he did not."

"You became panicked for nothing," the man on the phone said. "This Korean merely saw a Japanese and automatically became envious. It is not uncommon. After all, Koreans spring from a pool of envy. It is in their nature, for they all wish they were Japanese. Who can blame them?"

Yakamoto was feeling much better. He wiped some sweat from his face with the cuff of his white lab coat. "Do you really think so?" he asked hopefully.

"Of course. From what you say, he did not accuse you of anything specific, nor did he speak to your supervisor. He did not even threaten to do so or to go to the Mayanan government. You misinterpreted this Korean. That is easy enough to do. Their mouths form words funny.''

Dr. Yakamoto didn't mention that the old Korean spoke flawless Japanese. He was just relieved that the man on the phone was not yelling at him for wasting his time.

"I am sorry to have panicked," Yakamoto apologized.

"Never mind," the deep voice said. "This is not your field. As long as you have called, have you spoken with Dr. Taki yet? We have gotten him in as consultant to the prime minister. It was the best way to get him into Mayana without arousing suspicion. He should be in New Briton by now."

"No," Yakamoto admitted. "He must have just arrived. He was in the group that just came up from the airport. The same group with the old Korean."

A sharp intake of angry air. "What do you mean, the group that just came from the airport? Your confrontation with this Korean, when did all this happen?"

Yakamoto felt the fear rising again. Different now than the fear of discovery. It was fear of a man who held the power to hire and fire.

"Less than five minutes ago," he admitted guiltily.

The low voice rumbled deeper. "You are not calling from a secure location?" the man demanded.

This was one of the most important security details that had been drilled into Toshimi Yakamoto. He was to find call-in sites where he was least likely to be monitored. Public places were not perfect but were preferable. Parks and the rest rooms of restaurants and bars were good. Not his car and not his apartment, since they could be bugged. And the one place over all others where he was never, ever to call from was the Vaporizer site itself.

"I am...that is— The Korean frightened me."

"Tell me, Toshimi Yakamoto, that you are not at the site of the Mayanan device," the deep voice said.

"There is no one else around," Yakamoto blurted. "The parking lot is empty. And the people who saw me run down here did not know why I was running."

There came a few seconds of angry snorting on the other end of the line, like a bull getting ready to charge. When the voice spoke once more, it was a growl of barely controlled fury.

"Get back to work," the man snarled. "If anyone asks, tell them you were running because you thought you left the lights on in your car. Have your scheduled meeting with Dr. Taki in the city. You said you required help. He will help you. And when you call to report this evening, Toshimi Yakamoto, you had better do so from a secure location. If not, I will personally wring your idiot neck."

The phone went dead in Yakamoto's hand.

Clicking it shut, he slipped it back into his pocket.

He had never heard his employer so angry. Far more frightening than his trademark outbursts of temper was this quiet, controlled rage.

Yakamoto had made a mistake. It was not his fault, since this was not his field of expertise, but that obviously didn't matter. It was clear that this incident would not be forgotten. One more misstep like this one and he would be out of a job. His only hope now was to impress the higher-ups by completing this mission successfully.

It was humid in the car. Yakamoto mopped the sweat from his glistening face with the tails of his lab coat before opening the door.

He thought he had left the lights on. A plausible excuse. He came in early enough in the morning that he might have had them on. People would believe that.

He climbed out of the car, careful to lock it up tight.

Yes, the lights. They hadn't been on, of course, he would say. But he was afraid he *might* have left them on.

"I left my lights on, I left my lights on, I left my lights on...." He repeated it many times just to be sure.

The perfect excuse.

Straightening his shoulders, the little scientist pressed his black hair back carefully with both hands. With a deep breath, he marched back up to the Vaporizer site.

Above, the parking lot security camera recorded his every move. And, unknown to Toshimi Yakamoto, in the coil of a spring under the front passenger seat of his Toyota, a hidden listening device had picked up his every word.

"I LIGHTS my left on," Toshimi Yakamoto announced with great confidence to the roomful of men.

No one paid the Japanese scientist any attention when he marched into the control booth. The tour group—which included the old Korean and his young associate—was at the window. Below them was the Vaporizer. Deputy Minister Jiminez was nowhere to be seen.

"I mean, I left my left on. My *lights*. On. But lights were not on, were off. But I was afraid lights were on."

The Japanese scientist's babbling finally drew someone's attention.

"Oh, Toshimi, you're here," Mike Sears said. "Can you give me a hand setting up this test?"

"I did not leave lights on in car," Yakamoto promised.

Mike Sears was no longer paying attention. He was fussing at a computer keyboard.

Yakamoto felt a wash of great relief. It was clear he had barely been missed. His employer—his *true* employer—had been correct. And Dr. Taki was not looking his way. He was staring out the window, back rigid.

Things were fine. He had panicked for nothing.

Careful to keep out of the way of the envious old Korean who wished he was Japanese, Toshimi Yakamoto hurried over to assist Mike Sears.

At the window, Remo glanced back at Yakamoto. The Japanese scientist's confrontation with Chiun was already forgotten. Yakamoto was engrossed in his work.

"I'm surprised he came back," Remo commented

to Chiun in Korean. "The way you spooked him out, I figured he'd be dog-paddling back to Tokyo."

"Doubtless he remembered there were more rolls of toilet paper to steal from the lavatory," Chiun droned. He didn't turn to watch Yakamoto working. The old man's button nose was pressed against the window.

Two trucks piled high with teetering stacks of garbage had been lined up on ramps at the edge of the Vaporizer pit.

"Probably just an industrial spy," Remo said. "The Japanese'll steal the design of this thing and start cranking them out like toasters. Still, whatever you said to him, it probably wasn't very nice. You know, Little Father, it wouldn't hurt to tone down the racist stuff."

"Bah," Chiun grunted. "I am not racist. The aberration of you as Reigning Master notwithstanding, true Masters of Sinanju have always been Korean for a reason. The only good race is Korean. In fact, to accuse me of racism is to slander the most perfect specimen of Koreanness. Me. I refuse to speak to one who is so racist."

Eyes narrowing to razor-thin slits, he stared out the window.

Mike Sears talked the group through the process. It was exactly as Remo had seen it on television.

The nozzle tips buried in the black walls of the deep pit glowed a brilliant white. The trucks tipped their loads into the pit, and the trash winked out of existence in star flashes, piece by piece.

Remo tried to track some individual pieces of garbage. In the microsecond before they disappeared, they seemed to elongate. No human eye save those of the two Masters of Sinanju could have seen it. The trash stretched, then seemed to explode in bursts of brilliant white.

With flashbulb pops that were blinding in their speed, the two loads of trash vanished, absorbed back into the ether as scattering molecules.

"So much for Smith's doubts," Remo said.

He glanced at his teacher. Chiun had been looking for a trick. Anything that might have gone unnoticed by the rest of the world. But, like Remo, he saw none.

Bearing witness to such new, powerful technology, the former Reigning Master of Sinanju's face became a mask of stony silence.

George Jiminez had slipped into the room for the end of the test. The deputy finance minister had been out greeting the next bus of guests.

"If you'd like to come to our visitors' center, Dr. Sears will answer your questions now," Jiminez announced.

While the group filed out, Sears gave instructions to Yakamoto to check another misaligned nozzle before the next test. Grateful for the opportunity to keep busy, Yakamoto hurried downstairs. The American scientist left the room, as well, making a detour down to the Vaporizer deck.

"We better skip out on the spiel, Chiun," Remo whispered. "It's getting late and I want to get a decent night's sleep before I check out those sunk scows tomorrow."

He slipped out the door with the crowd.

Chiun gave a single backward glance at the Vaporizer.

The next tour group had donned the special boots and was now coming out onto the deck. Near the open gate, Dr. Sears was in whispered conversation with a janitor. The man wore coveralls and leaned against a push broom.

Out on the deck, a beautiful woman with long black hair pulled up in a bun mingled with the rest of the new group. Every now and then, her long fingers brushed the broach that was pinned to her sensible white blouse.

She was subtle, for a white woman. Her mannerisms were not broad enough to give her away. Chiun alone knew the woman was taking pictures with a miniature camera.

Aiming her broach at the gate, the woman snapped a photo of Mike Sears and the janitor.

The old Korean quickly lost interest. Turning from the window, he followed the others out the door of the Vaporizer control room.

11

In the bowels of the Institute building in Moscow, Anna Chutesov sat behind her tidy desk.

The head of Russia's secret Institute was bathed in the glow of her desktop monitor. The only sound over the soft hum of her computer was the regular click of her mouse.

Through careful eyes she studied the photographs e-mailed to her by Petrovina Bulganin.

Most of the pictures were of little interest to Anna. They depicted, from different angles, shots of the Vaporizer unit. The Institute wasn't interested in the technology. She would forward those photos to the proper scientific directorate.

Anna doubted anything could be learned from them. A photograph of an automobile didn't tell one what was under the hood. Still, she had usurped the investigation of the Vaporizer from the SVR in order to get her agent into Mayana. The time Agent Dvah wasted on the pictures was necessary.

Originally reconnoitering the device was going to be the SVR's responsibility. But at a security meeting with the president and other high-ranking officials at the Kremlin three days before, Anna had argued that the assignment required subtlety—a trait sorely lacking among most of the KGB throwbacks who filled the ranks of the SVR.

"Give this job to the SVR and they will kill, drug and blackmail everyone in Mayana," Anna had said. "And they will still find a way to come back empty-handed."

"This is outrageous," Pavel Zatsyrko, the head of the SVR, spluttered to the president of the Russian Federation. "This woman is a menace and her agency is a joke. The SVR has handled far more serious tasks. And, I might add, so has the KGB, which she is so quick to dismiss."

The president—a former KGB man himself—turned his watery eyes to the head of the Institute.

"Why are you even interested in this, Anna Chutesov?" he asked, suspicion on his bland face.

Anna shrugged. "My field agents need experience," she replied simply.

"My agents *have* experience," Zatsyrko interjected.

"Yes," Anna said. "But why trust a tank when you have a scalpel?"

A few of the other men laughed. Even the president cleared his throat, covering a smirk behind a small hand.

Pavel Zatsyrko was outraged. Even more so when the president handed the assignment over to the Institute.

Anna could not have cared less about the victory. The truth was, she wasn't interested in the Vaporizer. But with the delegations of each nation to Mayana being limited, thanks to the Globe Summit, she couldn't very well say she wanted to assign one of her agents there based on suspicion alone.

Once Petrovina was done at the Vaporizer, she could begin her true assignment.

The thought troubled Anna Chutesov.

Out of necessity, Anna had been forced to entrust her Agent Dvah to a team of SVR men who had been assigned to Mayana. Anna was reluctant to recruit assistance from the SVR, but she had no other choice. She had won a victory with the president for one agent, but she would not be permitted to pull the entire SVR group and replace it with spies from her Institute.

Pavel Zatsyrko wasn't alone in his opinion of Anna and her agency. Already more than a few men higher up in Russia's intelligence services were griping about Anna Chutesov's all-female group. Typical. The same fools didn't open their big mouths to complain when the men were in control and running Russia into the ground for more than seventy years.

The same old story. Men circling the wagons, protecting themselves and their delicate egos.

Thinking bitter thoughts of the opposite sex, she clicked a slender finger on her mouse. The images went by lazily, one after another.

Petrovina had grouped the photographs by category. The pictures proceeded from the Vaporizer grounds, to the unit itself, then on to some of the personnel.

Anna recognized Mike Sears from the television. Her fledgling agency still relied on the SVR for much of its information. They had little data on the American scientist.

There were a few other people. Technicians and officials from the Mayanan government. As she clicked through them, one photograph caught her eye.

It was of a man somewhere in his early fifties. Dressed as a janitor, he stood near the open Vaporizer door.

The man was talking to Dr. Sears. He held a push broom listlessly. He didn't seem pleased.

The man didn't look Mayanan. While many in the South American country had soft, white British features, a disproportionate number of these were still among the upper classes. The social pecking order almost required that a janitor in Mayana be of local peasant stock.

She enlarged the picture.

The man seemed too refined to be a janitor. For one thing his hands looked too clean. The same for his clothes. The knees of his coveralls weren't worn or baggy in the least. And he held his broom in a way that made it look like an offense that he was even asked to carry it.

Odd that he would wear such an expression while talking to the head of the Vaporizer project....

Turning on her printer, Anna made physical copies of all the photos of the Vaporizer and the grounds around it. She slipped the two stacks of pictures into envelopes and addressed them to the proper government departments. The photos of the personnel she put in another envelope.

When she was finished, she pressed her intercom.

"Yes, Director Chutesov," a female voice replied.

"I have some photographs that I want the SVR to go through for us. Tell them it is top priority."

"Right away, Director Chutesov."

Anna turned her attention back to her computer. She pulled up the picture of the janitor once more.

Something didn't seem right.

Blue eyes suspicious, she reached for her mouse. After a few clicks the printer next to her chair whirred to life once more. When it was done, Anna took the color photograph in slender fingers.

For a long moment she studied the picture of the Mayanan janitor. There was definitely something not right about the man. She would have to tell Agent Dvah to check on him once she was finished with her assignment.

Anna finally set the photo to one side of her desk. Putting the janitor from her mind, the head of Russia's secret Institute returned to work.

12

Toshimi Yakamoto worked late into the evening. It was well after ten o'clock by the time he shut off the lights in his little corner office and headed for the door.

Yakamoto always worked late. His diligence had been applauded on several occasions. With the excitement of this morning, he had no intention of arousing suspicions by breaking with eleven months' worth of tradition.

He shut his office door, locked the dead bolt with his key and stepped out into the warm South American evening.

From the far-off hills came distant jungle sounds.

To accommodate the Vaporizer site, many acres of trees had been chopped back. The creatures that thrived in darkness growled and screeched at a safe distance.

When he first came to Mayana, Yakamoto had been bothered by the animal noises. But it was a fear he had been able to put aside once he had been given a tour of the site.

A great fence stretched all around the vast hilltop area. There were only two routes in. The main road, used by most of the employees and visitors, and the secondary road, which was used for hauling trash up from the harbor.

The gates were staffed by security during the day and locked down tight at night. Nothing could get past that fence without authorization. Including whatever jungle dangers might be lurking in the darkness.

Feeling safe from animal dangers, Yakamoto headed across the well-tended grounds of the visitors' center.

The high fence that surrounded the immediate Vaporizer area was similar to the one that enclosed the entire site. The gate was still open. Yakamoto stepped inside, past the box of special safety boots, to the outer door of the device.

It was secure. Nodding his satisfaction, he headed back out through the gate, locking it carefully behind him.

Routine was very important for him to maintain. They had stressed that back in his training in Japan.

"You must work hard for them," he had been told in that final briefing many months before.

It was in the familiar cold and gleaming conference room back in Osaka. The man who had summoned him there was the same man Yakamoto had called in desperation that very morning. His employer had a deep voice and a bulging neck that made him look like a Japanese bullfrog.

"They must never suspect you are anything other than a loyal employee," his true employer had insisted. "You will remain safe as long as you are a hard worker. Obey the security rules we have taught you. It is likely that they do not know the truth behind their own research. As well, it is doubtful their source will reveal the truth to them. Too much false pride to admit it is all lies. You will be safe in the guise of an average scientist.'' The bullfrog smiled. ''Until the day you bring ruin down around their ears.''

Toshimi Yakamoto was grateful that day had almost arrived.

He headed away from the main buildings, walking calmly down the same road he had run along in panic that morning.

It would be a relatively simple matter to destroy the device. He had worked out exactly which nozzles would have to be misaligned. Several hundred in each of the four major grids would have to be bent. Generally only one out of alignment automatically drew attention from the safety systems, but Yakamoto could easily get the computer to lie. When the device was switched on, extra power would be shunted through those nozzles. The device would overload, feeding on itself. Once started, there would be no way to stop it. When it was done, a smoking crater would mark the site.

Actually, as he walked down the road, Yakamoto doubted there would even be smoke.

He understood why this espionage could not take place before the device was introduced to the world. He could not have tipped his hand four months ago, before anyone knew of the Vaporizer. The Mayanans would have uncovered the spy in their midst quietly, and all Yakamoto would have accomplished was a short delay. It had to come when the eyes of the world were watching, when everyone would see the great danger posed by this machine.

Soon. Now that he had the help he needed, he could be finished with this affair and on a plane back to Osaka by the end of the week. The thought gave him great relief.

A warm breeze brought a foul scent down from the low mountains that crowded the western slope of the Vaporizer hill. There was a great valley beyond the mountains, off-limits to all but a few select individuals. Twenty-five years before, a little corner of that valley had become famous as the home of the Jamestown cult.

Yakamoto crinkled his nose as he walked.

The odor was particularly strong this evening. When they had started their tests there had not been a smell. The more trash they removed, the worse the odor became.

Yakamoto shook his head. The Mayanans were such fools.

The parking lot was empty, save Yakamoto's little Toyota. Even Mike Sears was gone for the night, off at yet another in the seemingly endless functions hosted by the government of Mayana in the days since the machine had been introduced to the public.

At the moment Sears was at a hotel ballroom in downtown New Briton. Four blocks from there, Dr. Hiro Taki would already be waiting for Yakamoto. Yakamoto had made arrangements to meet with his new secret assistant in a corner booth of a restaurant lounge.

Later that week, Dr. Taki would return with one of the tour groups. When the visitors left, Taki would stay behind to assist Toshimi Yakamoto. Today had been a dry run.

An electronic security record was kept of everyone who visited the site. Those managing each tour group used a pocket organizer to check guests in and out. The handheld PCs were tied in with the site computer system. When Yakamoto had used his office computer to remove Taki's name from the computer, no one had batted an eye. When he showed up at the bus to leave, Deputy Prime Minister Jiminez assumed he had missed logging Dr. Taki in at the airport. He recorded his name into his organizer and let Taki on the bus.

It was that simple. Simpler on Friday, when Taki would return with the entire Japanese delegation to the Globe Summit. Then he would be an Asian face in the crowd. No one would miss him when the group left without him. As simple as that. Oh, he might get a little cramped hiding in the well of Toshimi Yakamoto's desk all day, but that was just part of the price of doing business.

Somehow just knowing that he finally had an accomplice in Mayana was enough to bolster Toshimi Yakamoto's spirits. Better was the fact that when they were done, Yakamoto would at long last be allowed to return to Japan.

Yakamoto walked briskly, as if by quickening his stride he could somehow hurry along the future. His shoes scrunched gravel underfoot as he headed for his car.

As he was reaching for his keys, he noted a soft metallic squeak from somewhere above his head. With a sudden sinking feeling, Yakamoto's eyes searched for the sound.

He found the security camera where it always was, mounted to a light post at the parking lot's edge. As Yakamoto watched with growing dread, the automated camera rolled to one side. Again came the soft squeak.

The daytime noises always drowned it out. The squeak was only audible in the quiet of late night.

Yakamoto had forgotten about the camera. After eleven months working at the Vaporizer site, he was so used to it that he had blotted it from his mind. But it was there. Just as it had been there twelve hours before while he was cowering in the back seat of his car with his cell phone.

Alone in the midnight parking lot, his hands began to shake. His keys rattled in his pocket.

He tried to be rational.

Only a camera. Even if it had seen him it did not hear him. He could have been calling anyone from his car. His mother, his sister, his wife. The camera didn't know.

The keys came out, jangling in frightened fingers.

As he tried to steady the key into the door lock, he wondered briefly where the camera images went. There was a security building at the site, but now that he thought of it, he couldn't remember ever seeing a surveillance room there. Strange for there to be so many cameras on the grounds yet no place there to view the images. He would have to mention this to his new confidant, Hiro Taki, the man who had unknowingly become Toshimi Yakamoto's best friend simply by saving the poor frightened scientist from being alone.

The key slipped into the lock.

Yakamoto had just begun to turn it when his shocked ears detected a new sound.

A footfall. Very close by. Almost simultaneous with the sound, looming shadows fell across the car.

When the strong hands grabbed him from behind, Yakamoto could not even find breath to gasp. He was thrown roughly against the side of his car.

There were three men. Two were large brutes. The third was a slight man with a pale face and sagging eyes.

Yakamoto knew the last man. He worked maintenance at the site. He seemed to always be underfoot. Yakamoto had even gone to Mike Sears about the nuisance janitor who seemed to do nothing but get in everyone's way. When he did, Sears had gotten a funny look on his face. The head of the Vaporizer project had brushed aside Yakamoto's complaints.

Now here he was being assaulted by the strange janitor and two men Yakamoto didn't know.

"What is meaning of this?" Yakamoto demanded, forcing the fear from his voice. "What you think you doing?"

He tried to puff out his chest. After all, he was authorized to be here. His heart pounded madly.

The janitor's face remained flat. There was no hint of emotion in those dark-rimmed eyes. "We have been sent to take out trash,'' he replied in heavily accented English.

It was the first time he had ever heard the man speak. When he heard the janitor's voice, an icy fear gripped Toshimi Yakamoto's belly. He knew that accent.

''You are not Mayanan,'' Yakamoto said, his voice weak.

The janitor didn't answer him. He turned his sagging eyes to the big men who stood behind him.

''Bring him,'' he ordered with crisp authority.

Turning on his heel, the janitor marched off. The two men grabbed hold of Yakamoto. They dwarfed the little man as they dragged him back up the road to the hurricane fence.

Yakamoto's mind raced. Pleading eyes darted up at the two who were carting him along.

''What are you doing with me?'' he begged.

In some lucid part of his brain he suddenly realized that there was something familiar about them. He seemed to recall seeing them the day the Vaporizer had been revealed to the press. They had witnessed the test along with the group of Mayanan government officials.

Sweet relief sang in his ears. When he had heard the janitor speak he had feared the worst. But knowing these men were from the government changed everything.

The janitor was just that. A janitor. In his panic Yakamoto had misheard the man's accent.

He might be arrested. But there was nothing he could be charged with. He had not done anything yet.

Probably deportation. He would be sent back to Japan. A failure, yes. Probably fired from his job. But he would be alive. And at the moment he realized that there were things far worse than personal disgrace.

Feeling the tension of months of subterfuge drain from his narrow shoulders, Toshimi Yakamoto offered no resistance as the trio led him back up the road to the small complex of buildings.

He assumed they were going to the security room to call the police. Ahead, he saw the closed gate in the chain-link fence that led to the Vaporizer.

No, not closed. Open now. Which was very strange, since Yakamoto was certain he had locked up everything tight before leaving a few minutes earlier. He must have left them open, since the gates could only be opened by special access codes.

The security building was a simple concrete salt box at the edge of the main road. The fear returned full-blown when the group bypassed the building and headed for the open gate to the Vaporizer.

"No," Yakamoto whined in disbelief as they propelled him up along the alley formed by the high hurricane fence.

"No!" he cried louder when they forced him toward the sprawling black deck of the Vaporizer.

"No!" he screamed when they shoved him through.

The frictionless black deck was slicker than ice. Without the special boots over his shoes, Yakamoto's feet went out from under him. He landed roughly on his back. Forward momentum skimmed him across the surface of the deck. He only realized that the inner fence directly around the pit had been rolled back when he slipped out into open air. The scientist felt a horrible instant of weightlessness.

Then he fell.

The pit walls tapered halfway down. Yakamoto hit the wall hard. Something snapped in his right leg. Daggers of pain shot from his shin as he rolled to the floor of the pit.

He fell onto something soft. In the darkness he couldn't see what it was.

All around was black. When he looked up he saw stars.

"Let me out, please!" he screamed.

His reply was a gentle hum of electricity from the walls. As the sound grew, lights winked on all around him. Tiny dots of yellow arranged in perfect little lines stretching around the four walls of the deep pit.

The nozzle lights illuminated the floor of the pit. He saw what it was he had landed on.

Dr. Hiro Taki was cold in death. The scientist's mouth yawned wide from his last moment of shock and pain.

When Toshimi Yakamoto saw the dead man's belly, his own mouth dropped in shock.

Dr. Taki's stomach wasn't there. There was a wide hole from sternum to pelvis. A perfect circle had been carved through from front to back. Whatever had hollowed him out had somehow cauterized the wound. No blood or organs spilled into the vacant, ghastly circle.

The hum grew in intensity.

"Stop, please!"

Yakamoto was begging, crying.

He hopped on his uninjured leg, scratching at the walls. There was nothing to hold on to. There were no handholds. The nozzles were rounded stubs. In his clawing desperation he tore off a fingernail. He screamed in fresh pain.

By now the air around him was humming like a furious wasp. In all the tests he had never before heard the sound. Somewhere in his terrified brain he realized that sound could not escape the Vaporizer pit once the machine was switched on. He didn't care. He cried and screamed.

The sound was sucked to silence from his parted lips.

And then was a sudden stillness.

Yakamoto held his breath.

And all around nozzle tips flashed to brilliant white.

Stars in a midnight sky, impossibly close. Burning, flaring. The light exploded from every point, all around—dizzying, blinding. And he was suddenly part of the light, and the light was accepting him into it.

Toshimi Yakamoto felt a strange whooshing vibration as his molecules rattled apart. As the world compressed and stretched into a single living stream, the black wall suddenly flew up to meet him. A single glowing nozzle tip burst in warm light all around him.

And then he was in the light and gone.

The black walls of eternity closed in around To-shimi Yakamoto. There was a weird out-of-body experience as he traveled through an endless black tunnel. It seemed to take forever, but he knew that it was only the wink of an eye.

The tunnel opened, the whooshing stopped and Toshimi Yakamoto found himself looking at other stars.

These stars weren't regimented like the false stars of the Vaporizer. These were the real thing, scattered randomly throughout the twinkling night sky.

The warm breeze touched the swaying tops of tropical trees. Though dry, it felt wet on his skin.

When he looked, he saw why.

What should have been skin was now a damp mass of reddish blue, a human husk stripped and turned inside out. Fused bones of rib and spine curled in horrid shapes from pulsing, exposed organs.

There was no horror. In fact, Toshimi Yakamoto didn't mind at all.

The brain had gone the way of the body, twisted in shapes that no longer comprehended pain. When the end came, it came without understanding. The final breath wheezed out, and the quivering mass simply died.

And on the growing mountain of garbage, the rats came tentatively out of hiding. To feast on the inhuman jumble of flesh and organs that in life had been one of the brightest minds of Japan's Nishitsu Corporation.

13

The Caribbean sun rose yellow and beautiful in a cloudless dawn. Petrovina Bulganin watched it sneak over the horizon as if it were a skulking enemy.

This mission was proving more of a nuisance than she had thought it would be. It wasn't just the side trip to the Vaporizer where she was doing the work of the SVR. It was the company she was being forced to keep.

The men on the Russian fishing trawler were blockish, simpleminded things. They lumbered around the deck doing their best to ignore the woman in their midst. As she watched them, she wondered if KGB idiocy was contagious.

Suspicions that extended to the center of the solar system were not typical for Petrovina Bulganin of the Institute, Petrovina Bulganin, formerly of the SVR. That sort of mindless distrust for everyone and everything was an old KGB trait. It was definitely her companions who were making Petrovina suspicious of the sunrise.

They looked ridiculous. Though at sea, they each wore the badly tailored black business suits of the former KGB. And not one of the fools realized how silly he looked.

Although it could have been worse, she decided. For a moment she pictured them in matching black swimming trunks, black socks and dress shoes, their shoulder holsters and guns leaving sunburn lines in their pale flesh.

This was the fault of Russia's current president. The man was former KGB and so trusted almost no one but former KGB. His entourage for the coming Globe Summit consisted almost entirely of Soviet-era KGB dinosaurs drafted from the ranks of the modern SVR. And so Petrovina was forced to work with them or no one.

Petrovina stood on the deck of the trawler. In the distance was floating Garbage City. The foreign scows and other sea traffic had been ordered from the area where the two boats had gone down. There wasn't strict enforcement. Petrovina's trawler had sailed in unmolested.

The men around her were fastening metal clips and checking for holes in her old canvas-and-rubber diving suit.

There was one metal barrel at the edge of the deck. One chance for defense if they were discovered. Not that they would be. This mission was a simple matter of confirming Director Chutesov's suspicions. If the Institute head was right, others would be called in to clean up the mess.

The man in charge of dressing Petrovina picked up a large steel helmet from the dry deck of the ship. He was a thick-necked ex-Party member named Vlad

Korkusku. His eyes were dull, his knuckles were hairy and he had developed an instant dislike for Petrovina the moment he had been told she would be his superior while they were in Mayana. But the command had come directly from SVR head Pavel Zatsyrko.

"Still nothing?" Petrovina asked Korkusku.

Korkusku turned to the bridge where a man in a suit identical to his own was checking the sonar. "Nothing," the man called down.

"Nyet," Vlad told Petrovina.

"I wish to be told the instant anything is detected. Is that clear?"

"Yes, of course," Vlad snarled.

Petrovina allowed Vlad to place the helmet over her head. Others fastened it securely to her suit. A spear gun was hooked to her back.

Her oxygen was fine, but there was a problem with the radio. She smacked the helmet a few times to clear it.

"If radio goes, I will tug line when I am coming up. You tug line if you wish me to return. Understand?"

Korkusku nodded dully. "Of course," he grunted.

The men guided Petrovina to a gap in the rail. Her weighted feet clomped loudly on the buckled wooden deck.

At the deck's edge, Petrovina stepped off into oblivion, dropping like a stone. With a mighty splash, the sea swallowed her up. She sank quickly to the bottom.

The heavy boots touched the sandy soil gently.

Puffs of silt swirled in her wake as she walked along. Shafts of morning sunlight knifed down from the surface, blotted out in spots by floating trash. Nervous schools of fish twitched tails in unison as she walked, flitting off, away from the strange intruder.

She was already sweating in her suit.

Trash was scattered all across the seafloor. A discarded grocery bag floated like a plastic jellyfish before her face. With a slow-motion swipe, she pushed it behind her. It joined other scraps and bits of junk— civilization's castoffs—that danced in lazy sea currents.

When she looked up through the floating garbage, she could just glimpse the underside of her boat.

"Korkusku, come in," she said.

No reply.

"Korkusku, can you hear me?"

Still nothing.

The radio didn't sound as if it were out. There was still an audio hum. A new malfunction. Cursing under her breath, she forged ahead.

At her feet, crabs skittered around broken bottles. A pitted cluster of coral lost from some other world rose up ahead. Bits of trash had snagged the surface. They waved like ghostly fingers as Petrovina passed by.

Beyond loomed the twisted shape of the American scow.

Above the sea the boat would have been big. Below, it seemed impossibly huge—a building toppled into water.

Petrovina walked around the coral and into the long shadow cast by the scow.

As she walked, she felt a tug from behind.

In her suit and helmet, it was awkward to turn around. The metal helmet was the shape of an inverted fishbowl. Three tiny windows, one at the front and one on either side, allowed a limited view of the area around her.

She found that her oxygen line had snagged on coral. Petrovina took the line in her gloved hand and gave it a flick. The line rolled in slow-motion, snaking off the coral and settling to the seafloor.

Loose once more, she headed slowly for the ship.

Some garbage had washed away, but most remained around the wreckage. She was soon wading through ankle-deep trash and climbing on her knees up to the scow. Fish flitted around her, swimming in and out the side of the sunken ship.

The scow had split in two big sections. The rear had broken from the bridge, jamming into the soft sand at the seafloor. The bridge section had nosed down. She saw what she was after at the rear of the angled bridge.

Taking her oxygen line in hand, Petrovina climbed slowly up to the side of the scow. She ran a glove over the metal.

It was twisted back from something that could only have been an impact explosion.

"*Sukin syn,*" she swore beneath her helmet.

As she spoke, Petrovina lost her footing. Some of the garbage on which she was awkwardly kneeling gave way. As her boots slipped, she grabbed around, hugging the broken metal for support. Her glove touched something soft.

The object fell loose, swinging down from the interior of the ship and slapping soundlessly against the hull.

She found herself face-to-upside-down-face with a bloated white corpse.

Petrovina gasped, falling back.

The body of Captain Frederick Lenn swung gently in the fissure that had split his beloved ship. Crabs and fish had chewed his face. His bloated tongue mocked Petrovina.

She held one hand to her belly. Her heart raced. Her breath steamed the glass of her helmet.

Averting her eyes from the body, she quickly climbed back down the hill of garbage.

She had seen all she needed to see. Petrovina could head back to her boat, report to Director Chutesov, leave this place and let the Russian navy clean up the mess. Her work in Mayana was finished. She should have felt relief.

So why could she not catch her breath?

She tried to will herself calm. It did no good.

At first she couldn't understand it. She had seen many dead bodies as part of her Institute training. None in the line of duty. They had all been in a Moscow morgue. Still, most had been in far worse shape than Captain Lenn.

She paused, taking in a deep, calming breath.

She could not. And then it hit her. The problem came not from her, but from above.

Her oxygen line emitted a feeble hiss. Then nothing.

Korkusku! The SVR idiot had cut off her oxygen supply.

It was too far back to her boat. She would never make it. Petrovina started walking. Every step brought the fire of futility to her straining lungs. She could feel the panic swelling inside her. Nothing she could do to stop it.

Every step was agony. Her feet were deadweights.

As she waded through trash, she looked up for a sign of her boat. She could see nothing through the floating debris and the thickening fog within her helmet.

No. That wasn't true. Through the fear and fog she thought she saw something.

No, not something. *Someone.*

He appeared from the haze before her. Swimming as confidently as a shark through the depths of the Caribbean.

Petrovina thought the man might be her savior. If he could share oxygen with her, she could get back to the surface. But with growing despair she saw that he had no diving gear. The man wore only a T-shirt and slacks.

Still, he was an amazingly fast swimmer. At the speed he was traveling, he could help. Maybe he could swim back to her boat. Get help. Uncrimp her line. Do *something.*

As the last gulps of breath struggled from her sweat-drenched lips, Petrovina Bulganin feebly signaled the stranger who had become her last hope to live.

REMO BARELY NOTED the woman in the diving suit. His legs did the work as he swam, propelling him forward with the speed and grace of a porpoise. He knifed toward the twisted hulk that had been the American scow.

He had already seen the Mexican ship. The hull of that scow had been blasted open by an impact explosion.

When he swam past the woman, she grabbed for him.

Remo dodged her gloved hands.

She waved her arms desperately.

He waved hello back.

The woman had stirred up trash and silt. It swirled in the stirring currents beside the American scow.

No matter. He could clearly see the hole.

The metal had buckled at the point of impact, curling back in twisted shards. On the second half he could see a mirror image of the torpedo hole that had cracked the scow in two before it settled at an angle on the seafloor.

Face stern, Remo kicked away from the scow.

The woman in the diving suit was now walking away through an undersea blizzard of trash. She seemed to be having a rough go of it. Every step was a great labor.

Remo swam up to her.

When she saw Remo appear before her, she waved

again, this time with far less energy than before. Assuming she was just being friendly, he waved back once more.

Scowling, she swatted his hand and pointed to her oxygen hose. Her panting was steaming up the inside of her helmet.

Remo trained his ears on the hose. He heard nothing but a few pained squeaks. The light of understanding dawned.

O. He formed the letter with thumb and forefinger.

I. He pointed to himself.

See. He pointed to his eyes.

You. He pointed to the woman.

Can't. He shook his head.

Breathe. He clutched his hands to his throat.

Remo smiled, triumphant at his successful pantomime.

The woman tried to shoot him with her spear gun.

Remo dodged the spear. Frowning, he began to work out in his head how to say "That wasn't very nice" in undersea charades when the woman's eyes suddenly grew wide.

Remo had felt the pressure of something striking the surface of the water far above their heads. Whatever it was, it was sinking slowly. He followed the woman's line of sight up toward the sun.

It was some sort of steel drum. The barrel was heading for the bottom.

Remo assumed it was more trash. The area around the scows was full of it. But if it was just an ordinary metal barrel, why was the asphyxiating woman in the diving suit now running in panicked slow-motion back in the direction of the submerged American scow? He decided to ask her.

Grabbing her breathing hose, he reeled her in like a fleeing fish.

She was running forward. Then she was running in place. Before she even realized she was going backward, she was face-to-face with Remo once more.

The air in her suit was nearly gone. She panted pitiful gulps. Her eyes bulged wide behind her fogging mask.

With a questioning expression, Remo pointed behind them and up. The barrel was fifty yards back and much nearer the bottom.

She yanked on the hose in his hand, desperate for him to let go. In a hysterical voice she yelled something in a language Remo recognized but didn't understand.

When she saw the look of dark confusion pass across his face, she seemed to realize suddenly that this man who could stay underwater without seemingly needing oxygen might actually be able to hear her.

She screamed again, louder this time and in English.

The echo of words in the helmet was like a ringing bell against Remo's hypersensitive eardrums.

"Depth charge!" Petrovina Bulganin gasped.

And as she yelled, the explosion came. Fiery hot,

it rocked the seafloor and hurled metal missiles straight toward them.

Too late, Petrovina Bulganin thought. *We are dead.*

I wonder if the hotel restaurant serves that brown rice I like? Remo Williams mused.

14

The explosion threw them backward toward the ruptured hull of the American scow.

Remo surfed the bubble of water, riding it back as it expanded from the heart of the blast. The jagged metal peaks in the side of the sunken boat caused by the torpedo rupture flew toward them.

Kicking hard once, Remo rode up over the metal ridge. With a gentle nudge, he kept Petrovina from being impaled on a spear of metal. Her limp body was carried up and over with him. Grabbing her by the diving suit, he tugged her to safety behind the exposed inner hull of the scow.

Tiny metal fragments from the depth charge barrel pinged the side of the sunken scow.

An undersea cloud of trash and churned-up silt spread out from the center of the blast. Veils of darkness stretched like clouds of doom across the seafloor, muddying the water and blotting out the streams of sunlight.

From what Remo could tell before the sea went dark, the boat that had dropped the depth charge was the same one Petrovina Bulganin had come from. The woman's useless oxygen hose had stretched along the seafloor and up to the side of the bobbing boat.

He glanced over at her.

Petrovina's boots were clamped to the scow's hold, keeping her upright. But her head was bowed. Her arms floated ghoul-like in the dirty water. She had lapsed into unconsciousness. Asleep, she would last a few seconds longer than if she were flailing awake, but she didn't have much time left. Her heartbeat was already growing thready.

Even worse for Petrovina, a piece of flying shrapnel had cracked her mask. Her helmet was taking in water.

Remo frowned in annoyance. Why did everything bad always happen to him?

Wishing he could find a loophole in his conscience that would allow him to just swim off, he glanced back up.

The sea was still dark, but not entirely. At least not to eyes trained in Sinanju. Where the silt thinned he could just glimpse the outline of a boat's hull. After launching the depth charge, Petrovina's trawler had puttered closer.

Remo zeroed in on the boat through the sea of floating trash. He grabbed a fistful of diving suit in one hand. The dying flutter of Petrovina's struggling heart carried like sonic waves to his hypersensitive ears.

Touching his toes to the scow's rusty hull, Remo flexed his calf muscles. He took off like a fired torpedo, launching straight up at the bobbing boat. The unconscious Russian agent trailed in his wake. A limp, living rag doll in the last gasping moments before death.

THE MEN ON THE TRAWLER had ridden out the explosion gripping chains and rails. The sea had churned, vomiting an enormous bubble of white that rocked the trawler and nearly capsized her. After the waves subsided and the boat began to chug into the spot where Petrovina Bulganin had walked in her diving suit, the former KGB men scrambled over to the edge of the soaking wet deck.

Their matching black suits looked as if they'd been bought off the rack at Woolworth's back in 1977. Three fat ties dangled out over open sea.

Eager eyes searched the field of risen trash and floating fish for human body parts. They were surprised when the part that popped up right next to the boat was not a woman's arm or leg, which was really what they were looking for. It was a man's head. The head was talking to them.

"*Do svidaniya,*" Remo Williams said.

There were three shocked intakes of air. Three meaty hands grabbed simultaneously for shoulder holsters.

Deciding just this once to opt out of the traditional Russian 9 mm handshake, Remo reached up and snagged three fat dangling ties. He yanked, and the men and their guns were dumped overboard.

"I should have known there were Russians in town," Remo griped as the men fell. "A million tons of rotting garbage can't cover the stench of boiled beets and vodka."

As the Russian agents splashed in panic amid the garbage, Remo lifted Petrovina Bulganin from below the surface and tossed her onto the boat. She slapped to the deck with a watery splat.

Another moment and Remo was over the side. He padded barefoot across the deck. His white T-shirt and baggy black chinos clung tight to his body as he bent over Petrovina.

He pulled off her helmet. A shower of seawater poured out, splattering the already soaked deck.

Reaching around, Remo massaged her lower spine. With the other hand he worked the heart and lungs.

Petrovina's pale face reddened. All at once her eyes shot open. Gasping desperately for air, she turned her head, coughing up water. Bleary-eyed, she twisted toward her savior, still gagging on seawater.

"Who are you?" Petrovina demanded as she pushed herself up to a sitting position.

"My name is Mr. Thank-You-For-Saving-My-Life," Remo said. "But you can call me I-Would-Have-Drowned-If-It-Wasn't-For-You."

She hardly heard. Her attention was drawn to the side of the boat where the three former KGB men were pawing through floating trash trying to swim back to their vessel.

A light switched on in her eyes.

"Korkusku," she hissed.

"God bless you," Remo said.

Petrovina scarcely noticed him. Scrambling to her feet, she pushed past Remo. Diving boots clomping the deck, she stormed around the cabin to the front of the boat.

She found the head of her SVR detachment sitting calmly in a deck chair.

Vlad Korkusku seemed uninterested in the action that had taken place on the other end of the boat. A pair of headphones was attached to a twenty-year-old Sony Walkman, and the volume turned up so loud that all ears could hear the blaring, scratchy 1950s Moscow Chamber Orchestra version of the Soviet national anthem. He had a copy of the latest *People* magazine in his hands and was flipping from page to page. Announcing every picture as decadent, he christened each with a glob of fresh spit.

The left rear leg of the big man's deck chair sat squarely on Petrovina's oxygen hose, which still hung useless over the side of the boat.

Petrovina marched up to Korkusku and slapped him so hard across the face that his headphones flew off.

"You tried to kill me!" she yelled.

At first he seemed shocked to see Petrovina Bulganin alive. Almost as surprised to find that she was not alone. He quickly got his bearings, scrambling to his feet.

"What do you mean?" he asked. "Did something go wrong?"

"You deliberately crimped air hose," she snapped.

"Oh," Vlad Korkusku said with hollow innocence. "Is crimp in hose?" He looked straight down at the chair leg.

Beside Petrovina, Remo rolled his eyes. "Couldn't you *pretend* to look around a little first?" he groused.

"Maybe a little look of surprise when you find it? Don't look down at the exact freaking spot where you stuck your chair leg. Cheez, you'd think after seventy years of communism you Russians would actually be *good* at lying."

Korkusku took a step back. "He is American," he hissed.

Petrovina ignored the words of both men. She shoved Korkusku hard in his meaty chest. She was ludicrously small compared to the big man. Korkusku barely budged.

"Is true you try to suffocate me?" she demanded in English.

The SVR man pulled his eyes off the American. His back stiffened. "No, no," he insisted with great bluster. "Was terrible, completely unscheduled accident."

"What about depth charge?"

"Accident," Vlad Korkusku repeated, this time very quickly and very firmly. "We thought we saw phantom killer submarine on sonar, but was actually school of minnow fish." He pointed to Remo. "Do you wish me to kill American spy?"

This time when Petrovina shoved him, her fury was so great that Korkusku stumbled back against his chair.

"Yes, he is American," she snapped, shoving Korkusku again. "But that does not automatically make him spy."

Remo had stripped off his T-shirt and was wringing water out onto the deck. "Actually—" he began.

"And you will not kill him," she continued, shoving Korkusku one last time. "Because if not for him, I would be dead right now. *Idiot!*"

This time when she pushed him, Vlad Korkusku was not taken by surprise by her wiry strength.

Korkusku stood his ground. His flabby face steeled.

"Ridiculous child," he said, sneering contemptuously. "You are the idiot, little girl. Out here playing at game of men."

She heard an angry grunt behind her. When she wheeled around she saw that the three men Remo had thrown into the water had found their way back aboard. Water ran off their drenched polyester suits. Their guns were drawn. Water dribbled out of the barrel of one.

Petrovina spun back to Korkusku. Her wet hair slapped around her neck like angry tentacles.

"Have you gone completely mad?" she barked.

At this Korkusku laughed bitterly. "I mad? Little girl, I have seen the world go insane around me until all that is left is madness." He spit at her feet. "While you were still playing with dolls at your mother's feet, I watched a great nation collapse into anarchy. And now I am this. A baby-sitter to a slip of a girl. This is—as they say—last straw. I will endure no more." He addressed the three men. "Shoot them. Throw their bodies over side."

The three soaking wet men surrounded Remo and Petrovina.

She could see that there would be no reasoning with them. Obviously she had been assigned a group of relics who longed for the glory days of the Cold

War with the West. There was only one option open to her, and it was not one that filled her with much hope. She spun to the American.

"Do something," Petrovina insisted.

Remo was twisting the last drops of water out of his soggy T-shirt. He hadn't been paying close attention.

"Huh?" he said, glancing up. "Oh, yeah."

Remo flicked his T-shirt. The end snapped the back of a Russian gunman's hand. The hand skipped, and the Russian fired into the shoulder of his nearest comrade.

As the bleeding man fell in agony to the deck, the other two disappeared. Vlad Korkusku and Petrovina Bulganin weren't quite sure what happened to them until they saw two faraway splashes in the Caribbean.

Korkusku turned to Remo, face growing pale.

"I'm in a lazy American mood, so two options," Remo said, pulling his shirt back on. "In the first you put *yourself* in the water and you get to keep your arms. Guess the second."

Blinking shock, Korkusku headed for the rail.

"And take him," Remo said, jabbing a thumb toward the bleeding man who was groaning in agony on the deck. "I hear enough Russian whining at the Olympics."

Korkusku took the man by the ankles. He dragged him over the edge of the deck where they made a single splash.

"You're welcome," Remo said once the men were all playing safely in the surf.

''What?'' Petrovina snapped.

''What you said to Bruno the Bear just now. That if it wasn't for me you'd be dead right now. You're welcome.''

Petrovina's full lips thinned. ''Enough nonsense,'' she said. ''What were you doing down there?''

Realizing he had gotten as close as he was going to get to a Russian thank-you when she opted not to shoot him, Remo shook his head tiredly.

''Same thing you were,'' he sighed. ''Looking for subs in all the wrong places.''

''You know about submarine?'' she asked.

''Know about it. Here to stop it. Unlike your pals there, who seem more keen on stopping you.''

He aimed a chin at the water where Vlad Korkusku and his three companions were splashing amid the muck.

''I have met their kind before,'' she said. ''KGB dinosaurs. They do not understand that world has passed them by.'' Petrovina considered for a moment. ''We will work together on this, you and I,'' she announced. ''I cannot do this alone, and it is obvious that you are not as stupid or untrustworthy as the fools who were sent to help me.''

''Stop it, I'm blushing,'' Remo said.

''You will help me stop submarine,'' she said, adding ominously, ''and perhaps help to prevent new eruption of cold-war tensions that could end civilization as we know it.''

''Hey, that's swell,'' Remo said, distracted. He pointed to a distant fishing boat bobbing amid the scows beyond the Mayanan cordon. ''Before we do that, can we stop by my boat? I left my best world-saving shoes over there.''

15

Executive President Blythe Curry-Hume had a name fit for a British lord and the down-to-earth charm of a Mayanan peasant. With appeal that cut across class and political divides, the leader of the Mayana Free People's Party had carried more than sixty percent of the popular vote in the country's last presidential election.

He had slipped onto the Mayanan political stage more than fifteen years earlier, after Mayana had applied for Commonwealth status. His name was made as a voice against Communist-era reforms such as state-controlled industry and price controls. Serendipity put him on the right side of global politics just as the Russian Communist machine and its influence in South America were collapsing.

Curry-Hume was a populist vote grubber. There was no village meeting too small for him to attend, no metropolitan development committee he would refuse to join. As his influence grew, he found himself on university boards, state advisory committees and on dozens of community groups.

In a country the size of Mayana, it was relatively easy to become a household name.

By the time he was finished establishing himself as a man of the people, his fellow Mayanans had practically begged him to run for executive president. No one was surprised at his landslide victory. Least of all, President Curry-Hume.

That was because everything—from his first handshake to his televised victory speech—was part of a meticulously laid-out plan.

If someone were to suggest the lengths to which this professed nonpolitician had gone to attain elected office, they would have been scorned by a disbelieving public. Such was the people's faith in their president. It was a faith constructed on that most flimsy of foundations: personality.

Curry-Hume had charisma by the bushel. When he spoke, it was as if he were speaking directly to every single person in his audience. According to a New Briton newspaper that had supported his candidacy, he could "charm the moon from the sky."

When it was announced that Mayana would host the Globe Summit, the people gave credit to their first-term executive president for drawing attention to their tiny country.

That week, when the people of Mayana learned of the Vaporizer at the same time as the rest of the world, they heaped praise at the feet of their executive president for managing to keep so great a thing secret. When they were told how lucrative the project would be, not just in terms of money to the government treasury but also job creation, the poor of Mayana stood and cheered.

But there was one man in Mayana who wasn't

applauding. One man who didn't buy into the concept of citizen politician. One man who knew what a crock it all was.

Finance Minister Carlos Whitehall was fussing at his jacket cuffs as he entered the office suite of Executive President Blythe Curry-Hume.

Phones were ringing off the hook. The entire building was abuzz with excitement. And the man who was truly responsible was getting no credit whatsoever.

The Vaporizer Project had been the brainchild of Finance Minister Whitehall, who had held the same post in the previous administration. The project was initiated under Whitehall, before Executive President Curry-Hume's election. But were the people told the truth? No, of course not.

Oh, if the project had been a failure, Finance Minister Whitehall would have gotten all the blame. And unlike a slippery politician, he wouldn't have been able to wiggle out of it. He was—to his intense irritation—not a charismatic man.

Whitehall wended his way through the bustle of people, stopping before the desk of the executive president's secretary. "Is he in?" he droned unhappily.

The woman glanced up. She had a phone in one hand and was digging through her desk drawer with the other.

"Oh, good morning, Minister," the harried woman said. "He knows about your appointment, but he's in conference now. Would you mind waiting?"

It was insulting to even suggest such a thing. Carlos Whitehall was a cabinet minister after all. On the other hand, he didn't feel like wading back through two floors of crowded hallways to his own offices. Lips twisting to show his annoyance, he took a seat in the waiting area.

He was dismayed to find that he was seated directly across from the official government photographic portrait of Blythe Curry-Hume. He had to put up with that photo everywhere he went in the building. There was even one hanging in his own office.

As usual, the man so beloved by his fellow countrymen failed to impress Finance Minister Whitehall.

Certainly the executive president's appearance alone wasn't exceptional. In a country where combined Spanish and English features were common, Curry-Hume seemed to be a bland mix of both. His nose seemed a bit two narrow, and his eyes were almost a too-perfect almond shape. His features were white, though his skin was dark. It was as if his face had been voted on and selected for its across-the-board appeal.

Sitting in his little corner of the presidential waiting room, Carlos Whitehall realized that this probably went to the very heart of what constituted a successful politician.

"Mr. Curry-Hume will see you now, Minister."

Whitehall glanced over. A helpful young presidential assistant was smiling at him. Whitehall harrumphed displeasure at the young man. He allowed the aide to lead him back over past the secretary's desk to the executive president's door.

Two men were just exiting. Whitehall recognized Blythe Curry-Hume's brutish bodyguards. The men were new to the government payroll. The executive president had brought them in from his private life. The men swaggered off through the crowded office suite and out into the hall.

The young aide caught the door just as it was closing, holding it open for the finance minister. Whitehall stepped past him without so much as a nod of thanks.

The door closed with a soft click behind him.

In person, Executive President Blythe Curry-Hume was as bland as his official portrait.

Curry-Hume sat behind his broad desk. The back of his gleaming leather chair touched the edge of the mahogany. Brown eyes stared out the window and into the lush hills above New Briton.

Curry-Hume was the one who had insisted the Vaporizer be built in those hills. The original plan had put it closer to the harbor for convenience. Often in meetings his eyes would slip to the window. Cabinet officers would find him staring wistfully at the miles of hills and jungle overgrowth that separated him from the device. He seemed to take strange comfort in the Vaporizer that went beyond what the device would mean for his country.

Whitehall waited a few seconds before clearing his throat.

"Sit down, Carlos," Curry-Hume said. The president did not turn around. He continued to stare.

Finance Minister Whitehall took a seat in front of the president's desk.

"And what is so urgent that the man who has saved Mayana needs to see me?" Curry-Hume asked.

It was an admission only made in private. The world would never know where credit was truly due.

"We might have a slight problem," Carlos Whitehall said. "One of the Vaporizer scientists has disappeared. He did not show up for work this morning. When someone was sent to check, they found his apartment in shambles."

"The Japanese," Executive President Curry-Hume said.

Whitehall raised a surprised eyebrow. "You heard?"

"News travels fast in a country this small," Curry-Hume said as he stared out the window. "I have spoken to their ambassador this morning. Apparently a member of their diplomatic mission never returned to their embassy last night. When the authorities were called, they already knew about your missing scientist. From you?"

Carlos Whitehall's face had paled. "What?" he asked. He shook his head. "No, no. The men who checked his apartment called the police. Mr. President, these men must be found. My God, this could be a disaster."

Curry-Hume finally pulled his eyes from the window.

"I know what you're thinking, Carlos," he said, spinning at his desk to face his visitor. "But I do not believe there's anything to be concerned about."

Whitehall shook his head. "I don't think you understand the ramifications of this,'' he insisted worriedly. ''We hired Yakamoto away from one of Japan's biggest corporations. He signed a nondisclosure agreement like the others, but that is just words on paper if he never stopped working for Nishitsu. If he and this other man were working together, our technology could already be in their hands.''

Curry-Hume offered a paternal smile that crimped the tight skin near his eyes. ''Please, Carlos,'' he said in soothing tones. ''Apparently I'm not a doomsayer like you. But even if it's as you say and they have stolen the ability to create their own Vaporizer, it would take them years to build one. And until that time, the market is ours. Look out at the harbor. We are turning scows away. The Caribbean continues to fill with ships waiting to dock. So what if someone builds another Vaporizer somewhere else? Will it bother me? Yes. But it's probably inevitable. And it is a long way away before they can hope to compete with us. We have everything in place to build more devices—faster than anyone else could, since we have learned from the mistakes of the first. And we have the *first* Vaporizer, Carlos. The only one in the world. It will serve its purpose.''

Whitehall absorbed the executive president's words. He made sense. And though the finance minister was loath to admit it, Whitehall had already considered it inevitable that the technology would one day fall into the hands of others. However, he had always hoped that day would be far away.

He grunted unhappily. "I would still like to know where Yakamoto has disappeared to," he said.

Curry-Hume's smile flickered just a little. "I am certain he will turn up somewhere. For now, the authorities will investigate. Put it from your mind. There is nothing we can do to help by worrying. And we have other business to attend to." He folded his hands in prayer on the desktop. "What about those scows that sank?"

Carlos Whitehall was reluctant to leave the subject of Toshimi Yakamoto, but he knew the executive president was right. With a deep breath he refocused his thoughts.

"There is no proof yet that they were torpedoed," he said. "Boat traffic has been restricted in the area, pending an investigation. We haven't been able to search yet, since our security is stretched thin already preparing for the Globe Summit. But honestly, sir, I doubt we'll find anything to support the American captain's claim. More than likely there was an accident. Perhaps an engine explosion on one that ignited flammable materials that engulfed both ships. The scows are very close to one another out there. It could be that they simply collided and both went down."

The executive president nodded. "Very good," he said. "Well, we seem to have only a few minor problems. Excellent. The Globe Summit delegations are all arriving. New Briton's hotels are bursting at the seams. Nearly all of the leaders of the world will be here by week's end."

Whitehall sensed by his tone it was time to leave. The finance minister got to his feet.

"Thank you for your time, Mr. President," he said.

"Oh, Carlos," the executive president said, "before you go, there is one other thing."

Reaching in a drawer, he passed a large piece of shiny computer paper across his desk. When Whitehall leaned forward, he saw that it was a photograph of two men. One was an elderly Asian, the other, a young Caucasian.

"Do you know these men?" Curry-Hume asked.

Whitehall shook his head. "No. Are they with one of the delegations?"

The executive president nodded. "U.S. State Department scientists," he explained. "They were on one of the tour groups of the site yesterday. There were many men who have come and gone this week, but that one—" he tapped the old Asian "—is the only person in all the groups to speak with your Dr. Yakamoto. They were seen by security cameras."

The finance minister's face grew worried once more. "Another Japanese?" he said. "Mr. President, I strongly recommend that the authorities vigorously investigate the Yakamoto disappearance. Even if we accept the notion that others will one day steal the technology, we can't—"

"Not Japanese," Curry-Hume interrupted. With his fingertips, he spun the picture around so that the two men were facing him. "I would say Korean. Yes, definitely Korean." He twirled the photograph back around.

Carlos Whitehall squinted harder at the older man in the photo. "I do not wish to seem racist, but I don't know how to tell the difference," he admitted.

The executive president smiled. The already taut flesh tightened back near his ears.

"It's the eyes, Carlos," Curry-Hume said. "One can always tell a man by the eyes. As I said, these men are scientists. That is what their identification says they are. The strange thing is, thanks to the Vaporizer we have detailed records now of all the leading refuse experts in the world, and these two men are not to be found in any of our files. You've immersed yourself in this work these past few years. Tell me, Carlos, are you certain you don't know them? Read about them, perhaps? In published papers? Books? Articles? Their names are Doctors Henell and Chiun."

"I don't know them."

Curry-Hume nodded. "Very well," he said, offering his hand. "Thank you for stopping by."

They shook hands and Carlos Whitehall headed for the door. When he opened it, the noise of frantic activity from outside spilled into the room.

"Oh, and don't waste time worrying about Yakamoto, Carlos," Executive President Curry-Hume called as the finance minister stepped from the room. "You have enough to coordinate without wasting time on dead ends."

Curry-Hume continued to smile his tight smile as the finance minister closed the office.

16

Remo had collected his shoes and threw a handful of money at the captain of his rented boat. Leaving the skipper to pilot his way back alone, he rejoined Petrovina on the Russian agent's trawler.

Even more scows had joined the garbage armada since Remo left shore. With Petrovina at the helm, the beat-up little boat had a tough time winding its way through the Caribbean maze of garbage scows on the long way to land. The sun was riding low in the sky by the time they puttered up to a private pier along the Mayanan fishing coast.

Houses that looked picturesque on puzzle boxes but were just squalid in real life slumped up the lush hills. Even away from the harbor, the air was ripe. Overloaded barges waited their turn in a line that stretched up the shore.

Remo had walked the five miles from town. They took Petrovina's car back to the center of New Briton.

The two of them were staying in the same hotel, Petrovina four floors down from Remo. The hotel was on the trash route from the bay. All day long massively loaded trucks rolled by, shaking the walls and littering the streets with trailing bits of trash.

Petrovina had to wait for two flatbeds to pass by before she could turn into the hotel parking lot.

The car's air-conditioning had filtered out some of the smell. As they stepped into the humid dusk, the odor assaulted them anew. On their way into the hotel from the parking lot they made arrangements to meet after dinner.

''I will come to your room,'' Petrovina said.

While she went to the desk to check her messages, Remo headed for the elevator.

He was pressing the button for the eighth floor when a small group of men hustled onto the car.

Most of the men looked like they had pieced their outfits together from the Goodwill bin. Two wore suits with sandals. But at the center of the crowd was a roly-poly little man, well dressed except for a straw Panama hat that didn't quite coordinate with the rest of his outfit.

When Remo glanced at the man's face, he realized with a smile why he was wearing the mismatched hat.

NIKOLAI GARBEGTROV was frowning as the elevator doors closed. When he saw his reflection in the silver doors, he took quick inventory, as he always did these days. He tugged gently on the brim of his hat, making certain the offending pro-American tattoo that had mysteriously appeared on his head was completely covered. Satisfied that none of the disfigurement was showing, he let loose a soft grunt.

The former Soviet leader glanced around the car.

Garbegtrov noted the thin man who was not part of his entourage standing in the back of the elevator. The man seemed to be smiling at some private joke. In his T-shirt and chinos he didn't look like a visiting diplomat. Probably a member of the Green Earth rank and file. The ex-head of the Soviet empire stuck out a pudgy hand.

"Hello, fellow citizen of world," he announced. "I am Nikolai Garbegtrov, concerned passenger of spaceship Earth."

Remo looked at Garbegtrov, then looked at Garbegtrov's hand. He looked back at Garbegtrov.

"Sorry, I don't shake hands with Russians. Got tired of having to take inventory of my fingers afterward."

Confused, Garbegtrov withdrew his hand. "Do you not know who I am?" he asked.

"Know. Don't care," Remo said as he watched the floor numbers blink by.

His sagging frown growing deeper, Garbegtrov retreated to the center of his entourage.

When the doors opened on the eighth floor a moment later, Remo slipped through the crowd. On his way out, he looked square at Garbegtrov's forehead.

"Nice tattoo," Remo said with an approving nod. "I think America's pretty neat, too."

Garbegtrov let loose a horrified gasp. Thinking his hat had fallen off, he clamped his hands to his head. Fat fingers rammed the brim of the Panama hat, knocking it clear off his head.

Shrieking, he plastered an arm up around his bald

head as he frantically tried to catch the hat on the way to the floor. Men scattered as Garbegtrov swatted the hat around a half-dozen times before finally catching it one-handed near his toes. With his bald dome pressed to the corner so no one could see, he quickly tugged the hat back on.

The doors were closing as he straightened.

Panting, the former Russian leader watched the thin young man's retreating back. When the doors closed, Garbegtrov's eyes were narrowed to daggers of suspicion.

REMO HEARD the doors ping shut behind him. He was still smiling as he rounded the far corner of the hall.

When Remo had left earlier that day, Chiun opted to stay at the hotel. After their trip to the Vaporizer, the old Korean had complained about the damage prolonged exposure to the Mayanan air might do to the delicate fabric of his kimono. But Remo saw the look on his teacher's face. He had seen the same expression many times over the past few months. Chiun wanted to be alone to meditate. The old Korean was introspective ever since Remo's ascendency to Reigning Masterhood. It was as if he were trying to come to terms with some great inner dilemma.

Chiun's private problems weren't on Remo's mind as he headed up the hall. Thanks to his chance meeting with the ex-Soviet premier, Remo's spirits were light when he got to his room. He was whistling as he pushed the door open. His face fell the instant he stepped over the threshold.

"Aw, c'mon, we're not starting this again," Remo groused, swinging the door shut behind him.

Chiun sat cross-legged on the floor, face turned to the balcony and the setting sun. Behind him on the carpet two men in suits lay facedown on the carpet. Red stains spread from beneath their chests, darkening the beige rug.

"It was like that when I got here," the old Korean said without turning.

"Cut the baloney. Room service doesn't leave mints on the pillow and goddamn dead bodies on the rug. Chiun, I've got company coming."

"I tried to move them," the old man insisted. "I thought, 'I cannot leave a mess for Sinanju's newest young Reigning Master, even though it is a mess that I did not make, or if I did, was justified in making.' But feeble as I am, I could not lift them. I strained and strained and finally, with great reluctance, surrendered to the inevitable fact of age. I throw myself on your infinite mercy."

Hands on his hips, Remo was scowling at the mess on the carpet. "'Reserve mercy for those with coin to pay; punish the rest,'" he quoted. "The Great Wang."

After quoting the greatest of all Sinanju Masters, he noted a very slight satisfied smile on his teacher's lips.

Remo's shoulders slumped. "Heaven help me, I'm back in the body-dumping business," he muttered.

He flipped over the nearest dead man, searching for identification. There wasn't any. Nor was there any on the second corpse. Both men wore shoulder holsters but had no guns. Remo found their weapons sitting in a planter across the room. There were daisies sticking out of the barrels.

He was relieved. No ID meant they had something to hide, which meant they didn't work for the hotel, which meant his teacher hadn't killed the manager and head bellboy.

"Chiun, any idea what these guys wanted?" he said as he shook the daisies onto a table. He returned the corpses' guns to their holsters.

"They wished to intrude on a delicate flower in second bloom. They wanted to destroy the peace of a kindly old man whose only desire was to steal a moment of tranquillity in order to meditate on his place in the world. They desired to insult the memory of what I was by thinking they could threaten the Master in Retirement with mere firearms."

"So I take it they didn't have a chance to say much of anything before you kacked them?" Remo said dryly.

"When whites speak, who listens?" Chiun replied.

Remo fixed him with a level eye. "I'll be back. Try not to kill anyone in the next twenty seconds."

He ducked out into the hallway.

Two suites down, Remo spied a pile of luggage through a partially open door. Someone was checking in, presumably a Globe Summit mucky-muck, given the elegance of the suitcases. He heard a shower running but saw no one around.

Ducking into the room, Remo selected two trunks that seemed to be around the right size. He cracked the locks and dumped the contents onto the floor. An empty trunk on each shoulder, he headed back to his room.

Chiun was still at the glass doors. The sun was setting over the garbage-mounded scows in the Caribbean.

Muttering Korean curses, Remo placed the trunks next to the bodies. He went into the bedroom and stripped the sheets and blankets. Wrapping the bodies, he stuck one in each trunk. They didn't fit at first. A few strategic crunches and they folded up nicely. All that was left were the two bloodstains. Remo went to work tearing up the carpet.

"And who is your company?" Chiun asked as he worked.

"Huh?" Remo said absently. "Oh, just some spy or something I met. Chiun, the least you could do is put down a drop cloth or something. Or use the tub. You ever think of killing them in the bathroom? Bathroom cleans up nice."

"If you spent as much time working as you spend figuring out ways to avoid work, you would be finished by now."

"I'll finish you," Remo grunted.

He had a big square of carpet up. Tearing it in long strips, he tucked it in the trunks around the bodies. As he was snapping the lids shut, he felt a familiar rumble.

Realizing he might have just gotten lucky for one of the first times in his life, he stacked the trunks on top of one another and made a mad dash for the door. He ran down the far end of the hall where a common balcony overlooked the street. Eight stories below, another trailer truck was driving by on its way up to the hills above New Briton. The open back was filled with garbage.

As the truck passed directly below, Remo tossed the trunks over the balcony railing. They plunged the eight stories, landing neatly in the back of the passing truck. It continued up the street.

When he turned, he saw two elderly women sitting at a metal table on the corner of the balcony. He smiled at them.

"Almost missed trash day," he told them.

Brushing imaginary dust from his hands, he headed back inside the hotel.

"This better not be the start of a revival," Remo announced as he came back into the suite. "I did my time already. I'm not about to start hauling dead bodies for you every other day again."

"That is only fair, for you are now Reigning Master," Chiun agreed. "You may limit the disposal of bodies to those days that fall in between every other day."

"That's not what I meant," Remo said.

He was eyeballing the hole in the carpet. He found one of the sheets he hadn't used to wrap a body. He stretched it over the exposed floorboards. He was just finishing up when the room phone jangled to life. Simultaneous with the ringing phone there came a knock at the door.

The phone was cordless. There was apparently a button on it somewhere Remo was supposed to push. He pushed one. The phone stopped ringing. When he put it to his ear, there was no one on the line nor was there a dial tone. He shook the phone and checked again. It didn't help.

Phone in hand, he headed for the door. As he was pulling it open, the phone started ringing again.

A smiling waiter with a serving cart stood in the hallway. "Room service," he announced.

"I didn't order room service," Remo said.

"I did," announced an authoritative voice from the hall.

Petrovina Bulganin breezed into the room.

The phone in his hand still ringing, Remo spun around Petrovina and the waiter, who had pushed the cart in after the Russian agent.

"I thought you were eating in your room," Remo said.

"I decide is perhaps too dangerous," Petrovina replied. "Hello," she said to Chiun.

The old man eyed the young woman with bland contempt.

"*This* is your company?" he said to Remo in Korean. "A Russian female? I thought you were past that phase."

"Can we not pick that particular wound right now?" Remo answered darkly in the same language.

Petrovina didn't understand what they were saying. Nor did she care. She was looking at the ringing telephone, her beautiful face twisting in a frown of irritation.

"Are you going to answer that?"

Remo looked at the still-squawking phone. "Can you get this for me?" he asked the waiter, who was in the process of setting up Petrovina's meal on the cart.

The waiter took the phone and pressed a button. Remo swore it was the same button he had pressed. But this time instead of dead air, he heard the familiar lemony voice of Harold W. Smith.

"Remo? What took so long? Is everything all right?"

"Just a sec, Smitty," Remo said. "We're reenacting the stateroom scene from *A Night at the Opera* here."

He told the waiter to bill the meal to Petrovina's room, threw him a tip and hustled him from the suite.

When he came back into the living room, Petrovina was lifting the sheet on the floor with the toe of her shoe. She was frowning at the bare floorboards.

"I've got to take this in private," Remo said, pushing her cart toward an adjacent room. "You mind?"

She looked through the doorway. "You want me to eat in lavatory?" she asked in bland disbelief.

"Hey, I've been to Moscow," Remo said. "This is five-star ambience."

He rolled her cart in, pushed a protesting Petrovina in after it and stuck a chair up under the knob.

"Okay, Smitty, we can talk now," Remo said.

"What was that commotion?" the CURE director asked.

"Just a Russian agent I picked up. She was sent here to figure out what's going on, too."

Smith's voice grew concerned. "Who is this Russian?" he asked.

Remo frowned. Stepping over, he knocked on the bathroom door. "Hey, dumpling, what's your name again?" he called.

"Let me out!" Petrovina shouted.

"That your first name or last?"

There was a furious hiss and a stream of muttered Russian on the other side of the door. It was followed by the angry sound of silverware clanking on dinner plates.

"She's not talking, Smitty," Remo said. "I think she said Bulganov, Balganan or something like that before."

"I do not like the idea of you bringing an outsider into this," the CURE director admonished.

"Hold that thought, because you're going to like what we found out even less," Remo said gravely. "The captain of that scow was right. The boats were torpedoed."

The Russian agent was instantly forgotten. "Are you certain?" Smith asked tightly.

"Those weren't love taps on the sides of those scows."

"Have you any idea who is responsible?"

"Not yet. But a couple of guys tried to kill Chiun while I was out checking the boats. Could be related."

"Is Master Chiun all right?" Smith asked.

Near the balcony windows, the old Korean clucked indignantly. "Four months," he muttered to the newborn night sky. "I have not been Reigning Master for a mere four months. Does the mad ghost-face think my skills were scattered to the winds with the relinquishing of my title?''

"Chiun's fine, Smitty," Remo said. "Which is more than I can say for the guys who came after him. They had no ID, no nothing. But dollars to doughnuts they're tied in with whatever's going on down here. They probably saw us when we were taking our tour of that doohickey or something."

"You saw the device in action?"

"Yeah. And you can surrender your skepticism, Smitty," Remo said. "It definitely works. By the looks of what Chiun and I saw today, this machine of theirs is really incredible. I can see why everybody's lining up to haul their junk down here. The world gets cleaner and Mayana gets richer. Seems to me like everyone benefits. Actually I don't see why anyone would want to stop it."

"Since the device was unveiled there have been complaints issued from a number of quarters," Smith said. "Some poorer nations are saying that lack of funds will limit their access to the device. A few in the scientific community have suggested that the technology is too important not to share it freely with the entire world. There are also some groups with environmental concerns. Any one of them has a motive to throw a monkey wrench into the works."

"I suppose there's no lack of screwballs out there," Remo conceded. "So I guess this means the President won't be coming down here after all."

"Unfortunately I doubt this will be enough to change his mind," Smith said. "The Mayanans have successfully kept outside investigators from checking

out the scows—I'm assuming so as not to derail the
Globe Summit. They have too much invested in it,
especially now. The President has already made clear
his intention to go. Unless the sinkings become public knowledge—or expand into something that affects
more than a few garbage scows—I doubt he will
change his mind. However, I will bring the matter
up once more. It would help if you found something
concrete on whoever is behind this. Perhaps that will
help sway him to err on the side of caution.''

"If you wish to know who is responsible, Emperor
Smith, look no further than the Russian pretender
who once occupied beloved Czar Ivan's throne,''
Chiun called. "Not only is his name garbage, but he
once ruled the trough of garbage that poor, late, lamented Ivan's Russia has become.''

"Oh, yeah, Smitty. Garbegtrov's down here, too,''
Remo said. "And it doesn't work that way,'' he told
Chiun. "His name doesn't have anything to do with
anything, other than the fact that he got shafted by
his parents.''

"Believe what wrong things you wish,'' Chiun
sniffed.

"I heard the former premier was there,'' Smith
said thinly. There was a note of disapproval in his
tart voice.

"I know what you're thinking, Smitty, and I don't
want another lecture.''

Smith would not be deterred. "It was reckless of
you to do what you did,'' the CURE director said.
"Breaking in to the former premier's house and tat-

tooing that slogan on his head was not something that I would ever have authorized.''

''Wasn't up to you,'' Remo replied. ''Russia stole some techniques from Sinanju. Three Russian leaders knew all about it, starting with Garbegtrov. That made it a Sinanju matter for punishment, not a CURE one. Ol' Garby was just lucky this wasn't the day of Master Nun. Back then a Chinese baker tried to steal just one ingot of gold from an Egyptian tribute caravan as it passed through his village. Nun flayed him alive and made him cook his own skin in his own ovens. Big mess. At least Garbegtrov got to keep all his skin. He got off easy. Besides, that tattoo was some of my finest work. It's still holding up even after a couple of years.''

''You actually saw him?'' Smith said.

Remo's tone grew sheepish. ''We kind of shared an elevator,'' he admitted.

He could almost see the look of intense irritation on the CURE director's face.

''Did he see your face?'' Smith pressed.

''Yes, but that's not a problem,'' Remo sighed. ''He was asleep during the tattooing. And even though he saw me and Chiun years ago when Russia tried to steal our contract and get us to work for them, we gave him the Sinanju amnesia thing. He wouldn't remember me.''

''Perhaps,'' Smith said. ''But you do not exist in a vacuum. You have operated in Russia several times since then. It is possible you are known to some within their security services. Remember Anna Chutesov.''

"I told Remo the same thing, Emperor," Chiun said.

Remo scowled. "Why does everyone keep bringing her up today?" he complained. "Anna doesn't remember me, and neither does Garby. I wiped both their minds clean of me, okay? And besides, the last time Garbegtrov saw me was before my last plastic surgery, so he wouldn't even know me even if he remembered me, which he doesn't."

There was a reluctant hmm on the other end of the line. "Very well," Smith said slowly. "Still, as a simple security matter in future it would be best to limit your contact with world leaders, current or former. Especially so soon after the Sinanju Time of Succession."

"That's gonna be hard to do if I'm still around here at the end of the week," Remo said. "This place is going to be crawling with presidents and dictators and other assorted assholes in another couple of days. And every one of them got a dead-body-o-gram from me a couple months back."

"Which lends even more urgency to your work," Smith said. "At the time I was uncomfortable with the requirements of the Time of Succession. You came in direct contact with too many leaders of the world. I want you finished in Mayana before too many of them are there, so please work as quickly as you can."

"No problem," Remo said. "After meeting some of them, color me unimpressed. In fact, if you could talk the President into staying home, I'm tempted to leave right now and let them all fend for themselves."

"Absolutely not," Smith said firmly. "Now is not the time for political instability in any part of the world. Regardless whether the President was going, I would still want you in Mayana. Given the climate we now live in, I do not want any of the other world leaders in jeopardy."

"Except for the ones we decide need the ax," Remo said. "Which I don't have a problem with, by the by. Okay, Smitty. I'll try to wrap this up fast."

"Please do," the CURE director said. "Also, bear in mind Mayana has an antiquated phone system. The delegates to the Globe Summit are reporting problems with the phone lines. But satellites will work even if landlines are frozen. If you have trouble calling in to report, find a cell phone. It doesn't matter whose. It will be scrambled from this end so there will be no chance of a trace."

"You got it," Remo said. "Talk to you soon."

He tried to hang up the phone but couldn't figure out which button to press. Shrugging, he took it in both hands, snapped it in two and dropped the halves in a bureau drawer.

He heard a rustling of fabric from the bathroom, followed by rapidly retreating footfalls.

The door was thick. He doubted Petrovina could have heard much.

"Seek your answers from the garbage trough," Chiun instructed as Remo crossed over to the bathroom. "I have heard him speak his native tongue. He commands the Russian language as poorly as he commanded the Russian nation. That one has garbage on his tongue, as well as between his ears."

"I don't know, Little Father," Remo said skeptically.

Chiun shook his head, disturbing the soft tufts of yellow-white hair above his ears. "Listen. Do not listen. I was only the Reigning Master long before you were born. Why would I have anything of value to say?"

Remo pulled the chair out from under the doorknob and swung the bathroom door open.

"Coast is clear," he announced.

Petrovina Bulganin was perched on the edge of the toilet, long legs crossed neatly at the knees. A white napkin was draped across her lap. Knife and fork in hand, she was eating her meal from the serving cart.

The Russian agent turned a bland eye on Remo.

"Oh," she said, chewing a mouthful of stringy beef. "Are you finished insulting my country, keeping secrets from your ally and locking me away in this porcelain gulag?"

"Lose the melodrama, Ivan Denisovich. We've been allies for all of twelve hours."

"Which is twelve hours too long," she replied snidely. As she stood, she slipped the napkin from her lap and dropped it on top of her plate. "This was mistake. Korkusku was idiot, but forming alliance with American agent makes me bigger fool. I will proceed on my own."

"Your funeral," Remo said, shrugging as she brushed past him. Kicking off his shoes, he flopped on the couch.

"You want duck tonight, Little Father?"

"Until you wash the smell of garbage water from

your clothes, you will be eating on the balcony,'' Chiun replied.

It was as if Petrovina weren't even there. Amazing. This was what America had for spies? She had heard stories, of course, but the Russian agent could not believe how lax America was. As the men bickered over supper, she hurried from the room and out into the hallway.

She had her cell phone out of her purse and was pressing the speed-dial button for the special number on her way down the hall.

''Agent Dvah for Director Chutesov,'' she stated when the Institute operator answered. ''Tell her is urgent.''

As she waited, she pressed the down button on the elevator. Anna Chutesov was on the line before the elevator doors opened.

''I have most interesting news, Director,'' Petrovina whispered. ''Is about this strange amnesia you said you experienced and possible American involvement.''

So excited was she that when the elevator doors slid open she wasn't paying full attention.

Petrovina didn't see the strong hands that reached out and grabbed her. Didn't see the faces of the men who dragged her onto the elevator or know the contents of the rag that was slapped over her mouth.

There was a brief struggle during which Petrovina dropped her cell phone to the hallway floor. The fight soon drained from her. She slumped unconscious into the arms of her attackers. The elevator doors slid softly shut.

"Hello, Agent Dvah? Hello? *Hello?*" Anna Chutesov's troubled voice called over the phone to the empty hall.

17

The Jeep bounced down the rough path through the dark South American mountainside. Behind the wheel, its sole occupant perspired in the warm Mayanan evening.

The jungle from which the Jeep had emerged was dense. A wild slice of prehistory lost in time in the modern age.

On the radio a classical music station soothed the driver's ears. This was truly a barbaric place. He would have chosen to be almost anywhere on Earth rather than Mayana. But necessity had dropped him here.

The road led down from a ravine that cut through the mountains above the Vaporizer site. There was a valley on the other side that had been closed off to the public for years. The valley was a site of infamy. It was there that the famous Jamestown tragedy had taken place, where hundreds of cult members had met their end.

Many mothers had lost misguided children that day so long ago. Some said their ghosts still haunted the hills. It was superstitious nonsense that had come in handy.

There wasn't an ounce of concern about running into any wayward ghosts on the face of the Jeep's driver as he threaded his way down the treacherous mountain road.

Eventually the rutted path turned to paved road. The government workers who had rolled the asphalt hadn't been allowed to go too far up, lest they stumble on something they shouldn't see. It was best to keep the remote location as hostile to visitors as possible. The rutted old road above made the special work that much more difficult.

The telephone poles that lined the route had been hauled up by peasant workers, men without families who would not be missed if they disappeared.

He picked up speed on the paved road. Soon the lights of blessed civilization appeared. They were just a few halogen floodlights on poles, but to the man in the Jeep they were like the Star of Bethlehem.

He sped toward the lights, slowing to a stop at a set of gates across the road. From the gates, a fence disappeared into the jungle in either direction, making the rest of the mountaintop inaccessible.

Armed guards manned the special rear booth at all time.

The guard booth and road were in a remote spot, away from prying eyes. Since no one who came to the Vaporizer site down below ever saw them, none had ever questioned what exactly they were guarding.

The guards themselves sometimes wondered. But they never mentioned it to anyone. They were paid well for their silence, and so they never said a word about the mysterious gate and the back road that led to nowhere. Nor did they mention the fact that the only two men who never used the road were Dr. Sears, director of the Vaporizer project, and the strange, rude little janitor who rarely seemed to push a broom or mop and never spoke a word to anyone but Dr. Sears.

The gates were opened for the silent janitor. His Jeep was allowed to pass out of the secret compound.

He stopped on the other side to make certain the gates were closed once more. Only once they were secure did he proceed down the road.

The hill grew steep for the next mile before leveling off. The jungle trees broke apart, revealing the acres that had been cleared for the Vaporizer. Lights from the sprawling complex cast a warm yellow glow to the dark night.

The janitor drove his Jeep around behind the main offices. There was a small one-story building near the rear fence. It was said to be for the custodial staff, although only one custodian was ever allowed to enter it.

When he drew to a stop in his personal parking space, the janitor's headlights sliced across a lone figure sitting on the steps.

The waiting man winced at the light.

The American scientist, Mike Sears, the public face of the Vaporizer project, wore a worried expression. He got quickly to his feet, hurrying over to the Jeep.

"I wasn't sure what to do," Sears said. "It was in the last shipment. They dumped it without knowing it was even there. I only saw it because I was in the booth up above.''

Sears had placed a call to the janitor two hours before. Two hours of waiting anxiously for the man to return from above.

''Where is it?'' the janitor asked in an accent that was neither Mayanan nor American.

Sears was clearly panicked. He was as white as a sheet.

''Here, I'll show you,'' he said.

He led the way to the Vaporizer. Both men put on a pair of special boots before going onto the deck.

Sears had put the lights on bright, illuminating the pit. There was a pile of garbage far down inside. Sitting on top was a big piece of broken luggage. Half-spilled from the trunk, a twisted body lay wrapped in a white sheet.

The man who was posing as a janitor pursed his full lips. ''Come with me,'' he commanded.

They hurried out the gate. Mike Sears helped roll the special scaffolding back in. The two men kicked out the locks, and the scaffolding unfolded into the pit.

Sears waited nervously on the edge of the Vaporizer while the other man climbed inside.

Inside the Vaporizer, the bogus janitor scurried over heaps of rotting garbage to the body. Taking the dead man's chin in his hand, he tipped the head, examining carefully. As he was doing so, something else caught his eye. He climbed over the edge of the trash pile, vanishing completely from sight. He reappeared a moment later. Climbing back across the awkward pile, he scampered back up the scaffolding.

"Is it who I think it is?" Sears asked.

The other man was wiping his hands on a handkerchief. He was clearly more irritated than repulsed.

"Is one of President's bodyguards," he replied.

Sears felt his stomach grow weak. "I thought so," he said. "He looked like one of the men who came with him to the unveiling."

"It is not only body," the other man said, stuffing his hanky in his pocket. "There is second one on far side. Also presidential bodyguard."

"My God," Sears said. "I didn't know what to do. I sent everyone home before anyone could see. I just— With up there and all—" He nodded numbly toward the mountains. "I thought it would be… Who do we tell?"

The other man spoke with clear authority. "No one," he insisted. "I will make call to inform those who need to know. In meantime, clean this mess."

"How—?" Sears began. "Oh. *Oh.*"

He stared down into the Vaporizer pit. At the body lying pale and broken with the rest of the trash.

"But shouldn't we…?" Sears began to ask.

But when he turned, the man who Mike Sears alone knew was not actually a janitor was already gone.

18

Remo had showered and changed, tossing his soiled clothes out the window. After an hour of arguing about what they should do for dinner, the two Masters of Sinanju decided to eat in the hotel dining room. Around the corner from their hotel suite, they found a cell phone on the hallway floor behind a potted plant. Remo scooped it up.

"Hello?" he asked.

Nothing but dead air. Shrugging, he snapped the phone shut and slipped it in the pocket of his chinos.

"Problem solved," he told his teacher. "Smitty says I should be able to get through to him on one of these gizmos."

They rode the elevator downstairs. On the way to the lobby it stopped on the fifth floor. When the doors opened, Remo was confronted by a familiar, surprised face.

Vlad Korkusku blinked in shock at the sight of Remo. One of the other SVR agents Remo had sent for a swim was with Korkusku. Both Russian agents took a cautionary step back.

"Is you," Korkusku hissed.

"Is leaving," Remo replied blandly, pressing the lobby button once more.

It was apparent that Korkusku and the other man didn't want to upset Remo. They smiled to prove that they were friends. When Remo got a close-up look at the products of Russian dentistry, he frantically pressed the lobby button. Everyone seemed relieved when the doors began rolling shut.

"I am not your enemy," Korkusku offered, leaning at an angle toward the closing door.

"Tell that to someone who hasn't smelled your breath," Remo replied. "You're taking the next car down."

Exhaling, Korkusku whispered something in Russian to his companion. Though Remo didn't understand the words, he knew the tone of guilt when he heard it.

"Little Father?"

"He says they kidnapped the woman and are holding her captive in a room down the hall," Chiun said, uninterested. He clucked unhappily. "We should have sent downstairs for a menu first. We do not even know the fish of the day."

Remo wasn't listening. His hand had already shot out, catching the doors just before they closed completely.

Korkusku and his companion had apparently heard the old Korean's loud translation of their worried whispering. When the doors rolled back open, the two men were already halfway down the hallway and running like mad.

Remo tore off after them. Frowning his annoyance, Chiun flounced after his pupil.

Korkusku had slid to a stop in front of a door. Frantic fingers fumbled at a key chain. When he found it, his shaking hands couldn't get the key in the lock. Which didn't matter because by this time Remo was on him.

"Knock, knock," Remo said, banging Vlad Korkusku's head into the door. The lock popped and the Russian agent and his companion toppled in onto the carpet.

The curtains in the big suite were drawn tight on the bright lights of the warm New Briton night. Beyond the living room was the open door to a bedroom. Sitting on a chair in the middle of the adjacent room was Petrovina Bulganin. Her hands were tied behind her back. Cords from the drapes bound her ankles to the legs of the chair.

Remo propelled Korkusku and the other man into the bedroom. A television flickered on a stand in the corner. On the screen a fire burned at sea. Orange flames licked the sky while an endless scroll of text moved on a bar from left to right. The CNN logo was plastered in the corner.

Remo ignored the television.

Four other men were inside the room. Three were Russian agents. The fourth and most prominent individual was a portly little teddy-bear-of-a-man who looked shocked at the sudden, tumbling appearance of Vlad Korkusku. His fear grew to anger when Remo and Chiun slipped into the bedroom.

Nikolai Garbegtrov wore a black sweater and

matching trousers with a black beret pulled tight over his tattoo. The outfit made him look like an overweight beatnik.

"*Ublyudok,*" Garbegtrov said to Korkusku, thinking he had been betrayed.

One of the agents in the room pulled a gun, wheeling on the intruders. On his knees on the floor, Korkusku shook his head frantically, trying to warn the man off. Before he could open his mouth, there was a horrible crack of bone.

The SVR gunman was upside down when he crashed into the louvered closet doors. The doors splintered, and the contents of the closet dumped into the room.

Hundreds of hats spilled from suitcases and hatboxes. There were fedoras and homburgs, baseball caps and toques. Hats of all different shapes and sizes, all collected in the recent past. A black bowler rolled out across the floor, tapping into the toes of Petrovina Bulganin's shoes. Hanging in the back of the closet Remo saw a sorry little sombrero.

Near where the agent had been standing, Chiun tucked his hands inside the voluminous sleeves of his kimono.

"*Now* can we go eat?" he asked.

"In a minute," Remo said. "Okay, what the hell do you turnipheads think you're doing?"

Garbegtrov pulled himself up to his full height, jutting out his chins indignantly.

"I do not know who you think you are to be," he sniffed. "But I am former head of Russia and we are questioning this person for possibility of treasonous acts. You may go now, and we will not involve police. But you *will* go now.''

He spoke with such authority. Standing erect in the middle of the posh Mayanan hotel room, the former Soviet premier was the very haughty embodiment of offended dignity.

Remo flicked off Garbegtrov's beret.

''Aahhh!'' screamed the former head of Russia. There was a brief flash of his pro-American tattoo before he managed to stuff his head between the mattress and box spring.

''Let's try this again,'' Remo said, turning to Petrovina. ''What's going on here?''

Petrovina seemed a little dazed. A result of the drugs they'd injected into her after dragging her down in the elevator. Petrovina tried to keep her lolling head straight as she looked up at Remo.

''Oh, is you,'' she said. ''Hello.''

''Yeah, hi,'' Remo said. ''What are they doing with you?''

''It is there. On television.''

Remo glanced at the TV.

The fire still burned. Remo checked the endlessly scrolling bar as it rolled by the bottom.

'''Rescue ambulance falls in as storm drain collapses, further endangering imperiled kittens'?'' he read.

''Not words,'' Petrovina said. ''That is different story. Look at picture.''

Remo looked more closely at the screen. When he got a good look, his face steeled. He marched over to the bedroom window, drawing back the drapes.

Far out at sea, a fire blazed high into the night. The same image as that on the screen. In fact, it looked as if the action were being filmed from the roof of their hotel.

"Sub's back, Little Father," he said darkly, letting the drapes slip from his fingers.

"Yes," Petrovina said. "Two more scows have been sunk in last half hour. Garbegtrov want to know what I know about sinkings. Is my fault. I should have worked alone. Should have known. Korkusku was former member of KGB who worked presidential security. That is how he knows Garbegtrov and why he is in league with Garbegtrov now. After I left you, his men kidnapped me and brought me here. They knew I was in Mayana to investigate trouble at sea. They only learn now that trouble was caused by that one." With a contemptuous nod, she indicated Nikolai Garbegtrov.

All that was visible of Garbegtrov was his ample rump.

"Whatever she says, she is lying!" he yelled from under the mattress. "I never even met this woman before. Now that I think on it, I do not believe this is even my room."

Still bound to the chair, Petrovina was shaking her head. "I knew was mistake to rely on SVR help," she muttered to herself. "The Institute has agents who could have come down to assist me. Good agents who I know and trust. But Russian entourage for Globe Summit was picked by Kremlin, not Institute. Our president was once KGB and so trusts old KGB men. So I get traitors to back me up."

Remo didn't hear the last. At the mention of the Institute, he glanced at Chiun. The old Korean's eyes had narrowed to slits of deep concern.

"The Institute has field agents again?" Remo demanded. "What kind of agents?"

It was the drugs that replied. Petrovina would never have answered such a question under ordinary circumstances.

"Like me," she said simply. "Espionage agents. I was drafted from ranks of SVR. We are all women. No men allowed. It is like big sorority." She giggled.

Remo let loose an exhale of relief. Beside him, Chiun nodded soft satisfaction. His thin beard barely stirred.

"She has not repeated her previous folly," he said.

"Wasn't Anna's fault that time, Little Father," Remo replied. "Still, I'm glad she's not churning out hack versions of you and me again. Sounds like the Institute's gone all feminist."

In her chair, Petrovina blinked. She seemed to be coming around. "Anna," she said. "Director Chutesov. Yes, you know her, don't you?"

Remo shook his head. "Long story with an unhappy ending," he said. "Let's worry about the here and now. What do you know about the scows that you didn't tell me?"

"Is Russia caused problem," she said. "We suspected it but did not know. Now we do. But we did not know Garbegtrov was behind problem. I only learned that now."

Garbegtrov had wrapped a blanket around his head like a turban and crawled over to his nearest spilled hat. He stood up now, a woolen nightcap covering his great shame. A dangling red pom-pom bobbed in front of a flabby face that was pleading understanding.

The premier seemed resigned to the fact that the truth was about to come out. He at least wanted to be certain that it was his version.

"I can explain," he insisted. "Is not actually my fault. Is his. He has gone insane."

"Do not lie," Petrovina accused, chin aimed squarely at former Premier Garbegtrov. "It is *your* doing. From what you have said, it is all your fault."

"What did he do?" Remo demanded, exasperated.

"He stole Russian submarine and now it has gone completely out of control," Petrovina Bulganin replied. Her eyes burned accusation at Nikolai Garbegtrov. "He wished to silence me, thinking I was only one who knew. But then news came on television of cause of first two scows sinking. He now wants information from me to stop submarine."

Remo looked around the room—from Petrovina to Korkusku and his men to Garbegtrov. Vlad Korkusku was on his feet now, a chastened look on his sagging face. Garbegtrov wore a hangdog expression of guilt.

"So we're all on the same side now?" Remo asked.

"I am on no one's side but my own," Chiun proclaimed.

"No surprise there. Everybody else?"

Vlad Korkusku spoke up for his men. "We will work with you," he volunteered.

"I want to stop sub," Garbegtrov pleaded. "It will ruin me if truth gets out."

"Don't tempt me," Remo warned darkly. "A question for the room. Does anyone here know how to find it?"

Heads shook all around.

"Great," Remo groused. "We're limited to water." He pointed at Korkusku. "You're driving."

They started for the door. Behind them Petrovina bounced in her chair near former Premier Garbegtrov. She was tugging at her ropes. With the others leaving, Garbegtrov seemed at a loss for what to do with the Institute agent.

"Are you going to cut me loose?" she demanded.

"You already cut *me* loose, baby," Remo replied. "Or did you forget your post-eavesdropping snit?"

With Chiun and the others, Remo was heading out the door. Petrovina screeched after him.

"I have keys to boat!"

At the door, Remo stopped. His Russian entourage plowed into one another behind him. At Remo's elbow, Chiun's weathered face puckered unhappily. The old Korean could see the look of surrender on his pupil's face.

"Just remove the harpy and take her keys," Chiun spit. "No good has ever come of consorting with Russian women."

Remo sighed. "I'm sure it'd be easier," he admitted. "But I've already dumped my share of bodies for the day."

He trudged resignedly back to Petrovina.

19

Captain Gennady Zhilnikov did not like having civilians aboard his boat. Unfortunately he didn't have much of a choice. His entire crew were technically civilians. Yes, they had all been sailors at one time. But now they were common civilians. Just like Captain Zhilnikov himself.

It seemed somehow fitting. After all, civilian money had bought and paid for his boat.

Not originally. Way back when the world made sense, the construction of the Charlie-class nuclear attack submarine *Novgorod* had been financed by the glorious Union of Soviet Socialist Republics. No, only its theft had been paid for by civilians.

The *Novgorod* was one of the many submarines in the Atlantic fleet that had been retired at the end of the Cold War. Towed to an abandoned Latvian shipyard on the Gulf of Riga, the submarine was added to the lengthy list of vintage craft from the Russian navy slated to be dismantled or scuttled in the Arctic Sea.

The *Novgorod* was docked for months. A sad, silent, rusting symbol of another era.

When the Russian empire began to collapse faster

than anyone had imagined, the republics along her western border quickly claimed independence from Moscow. Along with independence, Latvia claimed ownership of all of the vessels docked within her borders. This included the *Novgorod*.

Russia hemmed and hawed for a time about wanting the ships returned. In time Moscow decided it would be easier to let someone else worry about disposing of the obsolete vessels. Russia turned control of the boats over to Latvia.

After claiming victory over its former master, Latvia suddenly realized that it had no idea what to do with the rusting hulks it now owned. It was years before someone up the chain of command in the newly independent country decided that a detailed inventory should be made. When the task was finally undertaken, no one noticed that one of their decommissioned Russian submarines had gone missing.

It had happened when the eyes of the world were directed at more important matters. An elite group of former Russian navy officers and men had crept onto the base under cover of darkness and made off with the *Novgorod*. Most amazingly, this daring act had taken place by order of none other than former General Secretary Nikolai Garbegtrov himself.

Back when they first stole the sub, Captain Zhilnikov thought that he was part of a covert mission to restore the glory of communism to the tattered remnants of the Russian empire. He and his men assumed that Premier Garbegtrov was assembling a secret fleet that would force the reformers from power and return him to his rightful place as Party leader and iron-fisted ruler. Zhilnikov and the rest would be toasting their success within the walls of the Kremlin by summer.

But summer came and summer went. American fast-food restaurants opened in Moscow, billboards advertising American products sprouted up around the capital and still the new revolution failed to materialize.

The men of the *Novgorod* began to realize they might not have signed on for the mission they had expected. Premier Garbegtrov seemed more interested in hosting American film, television and recording stars aboard the captured submarine than in seizing control of the Russian ship of state.

Captain Zhilnikov learned the truth one fateful evening off the coast of New England. The *Novgorod* had surfaced in the dead of night to take on supplies. They were met by an expensive American yacht.

This had happened frequently since the theft of the submarine, usually near Martha's Vineyard, where many rich Communist apologists lived. Food, repair materials, oil—anything they needed was given them by the Americans. That night the boat that met them belonged to a middle-aged singer whose well-publicized heroin addiction and institutionalization for mental problems assured him gold records, Grammy awards and plaudits from his peers.

Garbegtrov had given the singer a complete tour of the submarine, from stem to stern. The gleeful songsmith nodded approval, stating emphatically that America had never built anything as impressive as the *Novgorod*.

Captain Zhilnikov knew right then and there they were dealing with a complete imbecile. American submarines had always been superior to Russia's. Zhilnikov complained about the man after the singer had climbed out of the conning tower and the crew of the *Novgorod* closed the hatch.

"That man is a fool," the captain snarled.

"Yes," former Premier Garbegtrov agreed. "But he is a rich fool."

Captain Zhilnikov glanced at his men. They were checking instruments, going about their duties as good Communist sailors. The yacht was puttering away from the submarine. While they were busy, the captain pitched his voice low.

"With respect, Comrade Premier," he whispered, "the men are anxious. When will you begin the restoration of the glorious Soviet Union?"

Garbegtrov looked to Captain Zhilnikov, a hint of amusement in his tired eyes. When he saw Zhilnikov's earnestness, the premier burst out laughing.

Garbegtrov rubbed tears from his eyes as he held on to a bulkhead for support. Still laughing, he glanced back to Zhilnikov. The captain's eyes had grown suspicious. His heavy brow was low.

The laughter died in the premier's throat.

"Oh," Garbegtrov said, amazed. "Oh, you are *serious.*"

"Of course, Comrade Premier," Captain Zhilnikov had said. "Is that not our mission?"

Garbegtrov shot a look over at the other sailors on the cramped bridge. They were busy at work. Only the executive officer was looking their way.

"Come with me, Gennady," Garbegtrov whispered.

The former premier led the captain back to the quarters he used whenever he was aboard the *Novgorod*.

"What precisely do you think we are doing here, Gennady?" Garbegtrov asked once the door to the small cabin was closed and locked.

"I thought we were working to restore Lenin's great vision to Mother Russia," the captain replied.

Garbegtrov sat on the steel edge of his bunk.

"And how will we do this with only one submarine?"

"I assumed, Comrade Premier, that we were the first in a new Soviet fleet. We would build strength, and when the time came our forces would seize control."

Garbegtrov's frown deepened. "I will let you in on a secret, Gennady," he said. "A secret I assumed you knew. We are not only the first ship in this mighty fleet you have invented, we are the *only* ship."

Captain Zhilnikov's face clouded.

"I do not understand," he said.

"Gennady," the ex-premier said, "do you know the cost of keeping this one vessel afloat? We can barely afford it as it is."

"Finance is something capitalist Americans fret over."

Garbegtrov nodded. "You are lying to yourself if you believe communism cares nothing for money. If we did not, this ship would never have been decommissioned. She was left to rust because Mother Russia could no longer afford her. Capital has always been as important to Russia as it is to America. Except they knew better how to spend it.''

Captain Zhilnikov didn't like what he was hearing.

''Respectfully, Comrade Premier, the pursuit of money is not the goal of a good Communist.''

Garbegtrov smiled sadly. ''You and your men are being paid well, are you not?''

Zhilnikov frowned. ''Yes,'' he admitted. ''But that is because we are the new chosen ones. The vanguard of the new order.''

''You are. But it is not the order that you think.''

And Garbegtrov went on to tell the captain how he had gone to a meeting not long before the theft of the *Novgorod*. At this meeting he found a group of people who had given him hope for a new future for the global Communist movement.

''Was it in Moscow?'' Zhilnikov asked hopefully.

''California,'' Garbegtrov replied.

He explained to the former Russian navy captain about environmentalism and an organization called Green Earth. How the Green Earthers were more devoted to socialist dogma than any Duma member. Garbegtrov told the captain that the people who had been ferrying supplies out to the Russian sub were wealthy Americans who belonged to the organization.

''They hate their country, these rich, spoiled children of privilege,'' Garbegtrov explained. ''They hate its freedoms and strength. They loathe the military. Anything that weakens American power and prestige in the world gives them joy. When I mentioned Russia's own diminishing military strength, they were crestfallen. There was a time, Gennady, when we would have destroyed their way of life—crushed the very freedoms that allowed them to act like the stupid children they are—and these people were actually *upset* that Russia was no longer a threat to their survival.

"It was when I told them about the situation with our decommissioned warships that they became particularly interested. One got it in his head that it would be a fitting slap in the face of his own country if Green Earth could have its own Soviet submarine. A way to strike fear in the hearts of illegal dumpers, whalers, oil tankers and the like. Before I knew what was happening it was being voted on by the Green Earth board. The project was green-lighted, I was put in charge and—not long after—you and your men stole me my submarine."

Captain Zhilnikov couldn't believe what he was hearing. He was absolutely crushed. His legs were wobbly. He had to sit down in the little chair near the bolted-down desk in the corner of the tiny cabin.

"We will not use the *Novgorod* to take back Mother Russia?" he asked weakly.

Garbegtrov sighed. "Russia is not as strong as she once was," he admitted. "But Moscow will not surrender to one little obsolete submarine that has to beg for its supper."

And that was that. Out of financial necessity, Captain Gennady Zhilnikov had become a tool of environmental zealots.

For several years the *Novgorod* was kept afloat by Green Earth money. During that time, Garbegtrov moved up the ranks of the organization just as he had risen to the top position of the Communist Party. As time went on, the former premier spent less and less time involved in matters of the *Novgorod,* he was too busy staying in plush hotels paid for by Green Earth. Funding and supplying the sub was turned over to a minor American Green Earth member. The ultimate insult.

By now the men on board knew the truth. Though it sickened them, the pay was good and the work was undemanding. In fact, it was almost as if they had been forgotten.

Then one day two weeks before the Globe Summit in Mayana, Captain Zhilnikov learned that this was indeed the case.

His American Green Earth contact had met the sub in international waters off the coast of Florida. With him was one of the ranking members of the Green Earth board.

The board member was a dotcom millionaire who had cashed out before his online birdseed store had collapsed along with the rest of the Internet market. He was twenty-six, had a social conscience and was a lot more concerned with the bottom line than the rest of the organization's membership.

"You gotta be fluffing *kidding* me," he said as he climbed down from the deck of the *Novgorod.* He looked around at the sailors—still dressed in their Soviet-era uniforms. "No fluffing way, dude," he said, shaking his blond-highlighted head.

"Is something wrong?" Captain Zhilnikov asked.

The kid laughed. "Dude, this is *all* wrong. We've been paying to keep this tub afloat for years." He glanced back at the man who had been Zhilnikov's liaison with Green Earth. "Years, right?"

"Yes, sir. Approximately a decade."

"Dudes, that is *way* nuts," the kid said. "I know some of the older guys thought this was a cool idea and all, but this thing is tapped. I think they were high when they okayed this 'cause there's no way they could ever have used it."

"What do you mean?" Zhilnikov asked. He had taken an instant dislike to this callow American.

"It was *stolen,* dude. The Russians would freak if they found that out. Someone up in Green Earth figured that out, so they kept this floating money pit a secret. But they thought it was cool, I guess, so they kept you around. No more, dude. You're history."

"What does this mean, 'I am history'?"

"You, your little barnacle-butt buddies—you're all gone. Take this tub out and sink it in the Atlantic. We'll get you back on our boat."

Captain Zhilnikov was appalled. The *Novgorod* had been home to himself and his crew for years. He would not surrender without a fight.

"Out of the question," the captain said. "I demand to speak with Nikolai Garbegtrov. He is powerful man in your organization now. He will not stand for such outrage."

The kid laughed. "Dude, who do you think signed off on scuttling this tub?"

Captain Gennady Zhilnikov couldn't speak. He

blinked in disbelief. His mouth opened, but no words came out.

He had believed in Garbegtrov when the politician was first selected premier of the old Soviet Union, only to be betrayed.

Again he personally trusted that Garbegtrov had arranged to steal the *Novgorod* to take back Mother Russia. Again betrayal.

And he had surrendered all dignity to work for these demented Americans who loved trees more than children, only to have Garbegtrov—incompetent, decadent, slave-to-the-West Garbegtrov—betray him one last time.

Zhilnikov tried to gather thoughts now filled with images of rage and hate and revenge. Through the haze he heard a voice.

"It's kinda too bad and all," the youthful visitor to the *Novgorod* was commenting. He was glancing around the sub's bridge. "This is pretty cool. *Das Boot* and all. Hey, dude, you got torpedoes and everything on this scow?"

Captain Zhilnikov's face steeled. He personally took his two American guests to the torpedo room. He made sure several of his men were accompanying them. Zhilnikov spoke low orders in Russian. His guests didn't understand Russian.

"Hey, that's pretty cool, dude," the blond-haired American said as he peered in a torpedo tube. "Hey, are those real torpedoes over there? Hey, what are you dudes doing? Hey, put me down! Hey, open this up!"

The last words were shouted from the wrong side of the locked torpedo tube door.

The second man was loaded into another tube. Both men banged and screamed as the *Novgorod* sank below the waves. The tubes were flooded and the banging stopped.

When their bodies popped to the surface a few minutes later, there was very little time for their companions on the boat that had brought them there to panic. A single torpedo strike from the *Novgorod* sank the boat and all hands.

And on that very special day—a day of liberation for the old Soviet captain—Gennady Zhilnikov had finally found a post–Cold War mission for the crew of his small stolen submarine. The utter humiliation and destruction of the man who had put the *Novgorod* and Mother Russia out to sea.

Zhilnikov already knew through the Green Earth newsletter (printed on 100% recycled paper) that Nikolai Garbegtrov intended to act as the organization's ambassador to the Globe Summit. With the eyes of the entire world squarely on Mayana, there would be no better place to seek public revenge.

On occasion the *Novgorod* had returned in secret to Latvia or one of the other breakaway republics for supplies. It was, after all, a nuclear attack submarine and there were some items that just could not be procured from even the wealthiest American fools. On the black market they were able to purchase scavenged parts from ships rusting all along the west coast of the former Soviet Union.

Captain Zhilnikov had made certain that he had a

full complement of torpedoes on board at all times. No matter what Green Earth claimed about peaceful motives, Gennady Zhilnikov had no intention of putting out to sea unarmed.

His torpedoes had come in handy removing the Green Earth boat that had delivered Nikolai Garbegtrov's doomed envoys to the *Novgorod*. And now, two weeks later, they were proving instrumental in Captain Gennady Zhilnikov's scheme to ruin Russia's untrustworthy former premier once and for all.

UNSEEN BY EYES on sea or shore, the dark shape of the Soviet-era submarine *Novgorod* slid silently through the midnight-black waters of the Caribbean Sea.

After sinking the first two garbage scows three days earlier, the old submarine had slipped out to deeper waters between Haiti and Mayana. There it had waited patiently among coral and schools of swimming fish.

Captain Gennady Zhilnikov expected some news. The world was watching Mayana. The two scows had obviously been sunk by torpedoes. A simple investigation would reveal that fact. Even Mayana with its limited resources would be able to figure it out with just a cursory examination of the scows.

The news would create fear and panic, especially with the leaders of the world converging on the small South American country. The world would focus like a laser beam on the treacherous Caribbean and the unknown danger that lurked beneath its surface. And then, *then* Gennady Zhilnikov could surface, pop the hatch and point a finger squarely at the great betrayer, Nikolai Garbegtrov—the man behind it all.

His men listened in on radio signals for hours.

There were no news reports of the torpedo strikes. That the two garbage scows had sunk was mentioned a few times. But it was attributed to a human error. One scow had struck another, resulting in an explosion that consumed both ships. As the hours dragged into days, no corrections were issued. The captain of one of the scows was to blame for both ships sinking.

There was no mention of a submarine. No one knew of the stolen *Novgorod*. No one knew that Nikolai Garbegtrov, the lying, former dog-of-a-Soviet-premier, was to blame.

It was all too much.

"Human error," Captain Zhilnikov growled. "I will give them human error. Take us back," he ordered.

Even when they returned to the coast of Mayana, the Russian captain thought they might be sailing into a clever trap. But there were no submarines or warships lying in wait for them. Just a cluster of fat blips on the sonar screen.

There were many more scows than had been there just three days previous. The green dots of the scows stretched from one side of the sonar display to the next.

Sitting ducks.

Zhilnikov watched the screen through narrowed eyes. The monitor bathed his pale face in a wash of watery green. He looked like a seasick Martian.

"That one," Zhilnikov commanded, pointing randomly at a blip on the screen.

The order was relayed, the torpedo tubes loaded.

"Periscope," Captain Zhilnikov commanded, spinning from the sonar station.

Far above, the periscope rose like the neck of a steel sea monster.

He found the scow. Silhouetted against a backdrop of lights from the hundred ships beyond it.

Captain Zhilnikov paused for a moment.

They had gotten away with their first attacks. He and his men could slip off and the world would not be the wiser.

He thought of Garbegtrov—the bloated betrayer—sprawled on a bed of American dollars. Laughing at Zhilnikov, laughing at the Soviet Union. Laughing at *Russia*.

The old Russian officer's face steeled.

"Fire!" Captain Zhilnikov bellowed.

And the word launched frothy spittle from between the bitter old captain's furiously sputtering lips.

20

Remo and Chiun stood on the damp deck of the speeding Russian trawler. Beside them, Petrovina Bulganin and Vlad Korkusku studied the Caribbean night. The rest of the SVR agents were up on the bridge.

The two Russians on deck were damp from the spray of the waves that broke across the boat's prow. Both Sinanju Masters remained bone-dry.

The first scows were moored a half mile off the coast.

There had been more torpedo strikes since they left the hotel. In a dozen spots fires now toyed with the twinkling stars in the warm sky. The scows were so tightly packed that flames from the explosions had spread to other boats.

Mayana wasn't equipped for such an emergency. Here and there in Garbage City could be seen flashes of red-and-blue lights—official boats sent from shore. Two undermanned fireboats squirted high plumes of water onto two separate blazes.

When the attack began, some scows had tried to flee. The slow-moving craft were easy targets. The remaining scows were hemmed in by miles of floating trash heaps.

The unnatural firelight cast visions of Hell across the calm sea surface. Petrovina Bulganin's beautiful face was bathed in a ghoulish wash of flickering orange.

She had regained her full senses during the ride from the hotel and the trip out on the boat. Her anger toward the men around her worsened as she grew more alert.

"So you try to kill me for Garbegtrov and his idiotic *environmental* movement?" she said, sneering at Vlad Korkusku. "That is why you try to blow me up and suffocate me?"

"No," Korkusku grunted in reply. He was watching the sea. "At first it was because I just do not like you."

Remo raised his hand. "Me, neither."

"Make that three," chimed in Chiun, who knew only too well his pupil's soft spot for beautiful Russian spies.

"And you," Petrovina said to Remo. "You are a menace, with your kicking in of doors like macho American Rambo. You could have gotten me killed."

"Could've, should've, would've," Remo said. "Sue me for saving your life. And for those of you keeping score, that's the third thank-you I didn't get from you."

"Russian women never show proper gratitude," Chiun confided. "You would think being tractor wenches with cement-mixer hips and shovels for faces they would be grateful for any little attention they receive. But their ugliness has made them resentful. Do not talk to Russian women, Remo, unless you wish to be disappointed or need to know 1001 ways to abuse a cabbage.''

Vlad Korkusku—whose mother, sisters, aunts and grandmother were all Russian women—decided to say a word not for Petrovina Bulganin, but for Russian females in general. He spent the next minute dangling by his ankle from the back of the boat with his head underwater and his face an inch away from the propeller. When he was allowed back up for air, Korkusku vehemently agreed that all Russian women were ugly, nasty harpies.

''You see?'' Chiun said. ''Even through his alcoholic delirium this Russian male understands.''

''I don't think he's drunk, Little Father. Just wet.''

Chiun patted Remo's hand. ''You are still young in so many ways,'' he said paternally.

Searchlights were cutting across the water. The others concentrated on the spots of white. Remo and Chiun searched the darkness between the light. They all scanned the surface of the water for any signs of the Russian submarine.

''This is stupid,'' Petrovina said. ''We have no weapons or defenses even if we do find it. What do you plan to do?''

''Don't know,'' Remo said. ''Maybe toss you at it.''

Another five minutes passed before he spotted the sub sliding up from beneath the sea. The dark, curving shape of a periscope was lost in the darkness. A thin froth of white water broke as it barreled through the waves.

"There it is," Remo said tightly.

Chiun had spied it, too. Petrovina and Vlad Korkusku squinted but could see nothing.

"Where?" Petrovina asked doubtfully.

Remo wasn't paying attention to her. "That way," he hollered up to the bridge. "Angle us that way."

The SVR helmsman had twice seen Remo in action. He dared not disobey. Picking up speed, he eased the boat to port. The line of moored scows drew closer.

"I see nothing," Petrovina said. "How do you see it?"

"You got thirty years, I'll show you," Remo said. "Otherwise butt out. Okay, we're good here," he called up to the bridge. "Stay on this course."

Petrovina opened her mouth to express further doubt, but was interrupted by an excited voice.

"We have submarine on sonar!" an SVR agent called down from the bridge.

Remo and Chiun had already moved to a break in the rail. Remo kicked off his loafers and Chiun shed his sandals.

Floodlights were sent searching the sea. They found the periscope gliding along forty yards off the port bow.

The fishing boat had no torpedoes of its own. Korkusku had squandered their one depth charge. Petrovina Bulganin threw up her hands, helpless.

"So you have found it. What now?" she demanded.

"This," said Remo.

His toes were curled over the edge of the boat's deck. Remo tightened his leg muscles. He shot up in the air, slicing at an angle that brought him parallel to the waves. Chiun did the same.

Ten yards out, both men cut sharply downward. Without disturbing a single drop of water, the two Masters of Sinanju disappeared beneath the gentle waves of the Caribbean.

IN THE BELLY of the submarine *Novgorod,* Captain Gennady Zhilnikov watched through his night-vision scope as the two men jumped from the deck of the fishing boat.

For a moment they seemed to soar like birds before they dropped like stones. Together they vanished below the surface.

They certainly couldn't hope to catch the *Novgorod.* Already they would have fallen behind. Even the boat from which they'd jumped was having trouble keeping pace with the submarine.

"What do they think they are doing?" Zhilnikov asked, puzzled.

"Shall we sink her, sir?" his executive officer asked, thinking Zhilnikov was referring to the fishing boat that had obviously seen their periscope.

"What? No. Target another scow. Any one. It does not matter."

The order went down for another torpedo to be loaded. Another random scow was targeted. Zhilnikov was about to give the order to fire when the sea erupted with a noise so terrible it rattled the captain's molars.

The horrible wrenching noise came from somewhere above his head. It was the sound of tearing metal. The noise reverberated down the length of the *Novgorod,* trailing off at her giant propellers.

In all his many years at sea Captain Zhilnikov had never heard such a sound. It was as if Poseidon himself were squeezing the submarine in his mighty hand.

"What did we hit?" Zhilnikov snapped.

Frantic men checked instruments, surrendering to frightened confusion. "Nothing, Captain!"

Zhilnikov looked up. The ceiling had never seemed so low or fragile. The echo of terrible sound was rolling back up along the metal shell.

"What the hell was that?" the Russian captain whispered.

For some reason his normally logical mind summoned up boyhood images of sea monsters that could drag helpless vessels to a watery grave. He banished the childish thought as soon as it occurred to him. He was on a vessel built by the powerful Soviet Union. There were no ships to match his in the area.

Captain Zhilnikov's confidence returned. He knew in his proud Russian heart that no animal or sea serpent was strong or foolish enough to challenge the mighty *Novgorod.*

REMO WASN'T QUITE SURE at first the best way to break a submarine. He figured anything that would get the water from the outside *inside* would do the trick.

He and Chiun had followed the lowering periscope down to the *Novgorod*. The Russian submarine was a huge dark shape gliding only a dozen yards beneath the waves. At about twenty knots it was easy for the two Sinanju Masters to keep pace.

A wall of displaced water pressed hard against them as they made their way down to the conning tower.

Once inside, the tower protected them from the surging water. They found the hatch—like an oversize manhole. Their fingers searched for a flaw, a lip, anything that could be used for a handhold.

They found what they needed at the front where the hatch hadn't been properly set in the frame. It was just the slightest misalignment in the airtight frame.

Remo jammed his fingers into the opening. Steel-hard fingertips jimmied a gap wide enough for his hands.

Remo ripped once, hard.

The reinforced metal screamed in protest as Remo peeled the hatch back like the lid on a can of sardines. Water flooded in through the mangled hatch door.

Both men let the water take them. The water surge drew them down the tower and to the inner hatch.

The dark tower interior was like working in a phone booth with the glass painted black. The inner hatch had the kind of handle Remo was used to. A round wheel sat at the center bulge of the hatch.

When Remo grabbed it and tried to give it a spin, the locked wheel stubbornly refused to budge.

Remo's exertions thus far had done little to exhaust his oxygen supply. His concern was for his teacher, who, at one-hundred-plus years, would be feeling the effects by now.

He glanced at Chiun. The old man had been studying the hatch for hinges or flaws. When he felt the pressure waves of Remo's stare, Chiun looked up. Through the murky water, Remo saw the look of angry annoyance that creased the old Korean's brow. Beyond that there was no sign of strain on his parchment face.

Chiun raised a hand in impatient warning before returning attention to the hatch. Remo joined him.

There were no handholds. There was only one option open to them. It was Chiun who attacked first.

A bony fist struck hard steel. Then another.

Remo joined in. First right, then left, then repeat. One Sinanju Master built up a rhythm that the other would shatter. The vibrations caused invisible cracks deep in the forged steel. The bowed metal shell dented, then buckled.

When the edge lifted, Remo reached in and yanked up the metal. He felt the pop of a breaking lock.

And with a protesting scream, the hatch began to creak up.

CAPTAIN ZHILNIKOV HEARD the rush of seawater from where he stood beside the ladder to the conning tower. A former Russian navy lieutenant had raced with him to the spot from which the first sound of tearing metal had come. A half-dozen sailors formed a nervous line back to the bridge, where the executive officer awaited orders from the captain.

The *Novgorod* was already coming about. They were heading back out to sea. When the steady drumbeat on metal began to sound directly on the other side of the hatch, Zhilnikov felt his blood run cold.

"What is it, sir?" asked the ashen-faced lieutenant.

"Are we full about?" Zhilnikov snapped.

The question was shouted down the line. The *Novgorod* was passing beneath moored and burning scows in the long arc that would take them out into deeper water.

The pounding at the hatch intensified. The vibrations felt as if they would rattle the sub apart.

"Weapons at the ready!" Zhilnikov shouted, not believing he was giving such an order.

Sailors raised pistols to the hatch. One raised an old Kalashnikov rifle.

The hatch began to bow inward.

The pounding abruptly gave way to a few brief moments of unnerving silence. The men watched the hatch with dread.

Then came another horrible sound of tearing metal like the first that had lost the *Novgorod* her outer hatch.

With a pop that hurt Zhilnikov's eardrums, the inner hatch seal broke. Water sprayed down on the shocked, upturned face of Captain Zhilnikov.

Jumping from the flood, Zhilnikov wiped stinging

salt water from his eyes. When he looked back up, the hatch was tearing upward.

"Have we cleared the scows!" Zhilnikov bellowed.

The answer couldn't come quickly enough. Another, final tear of metal and the hatch ripped free. A high-pressure waterfall began surging through the tower. The deck around his ankles flooded with frothing seawater.

Zhilnikov was thrown back by the surge.

"Surface, surface!" Captain Zhilnikov screamed over the roar of the rushing water. Veins in his neck bulged. His eyes were wild as he stumbled in ankle-deep water.

"Weapons ready!" he shouted to the nearby men. "Whatever comes through that hatch, shoot it on sight!"

And through the flood and the fear, Gennady Zhilnikov watched the water for the first slithering tentacle of the unholy beast that had torn his mighty Russian ship to pieces.

PETROVINA BULGANIN'S fishing boat had tracked the fleeing renegade submarine as far as the first line of moored garbage scows. Petrovina was watching on the bridge when the big sonar blob sped beneath the scows and was gone.

She slammed a hand on a console.

"Dammit," she snapped. "Can you follow them in?"

The fishing boat had already been forced to cut speed.

A fire raged on a half-submerged scow directly in front of them. The water was thick with floating trash, the air with acrid smoke. Someone was shouting something unintelligible through a bullhorn from one of the Mayanan fireboats.

"No," Vlad Korkusku replied. "The scows are too tightly packed. And according to the radio, some in the middle are panicking and trying to force their way out. We would be crushed if we tried to maneuver between them."

The fishing boat was coasting into a slow, wide turn. There was nothing Petrovina could do. She left Korkusku and his men on the bridge and went back out on deck.

Orange flames brightened the dark sea. She saw nothing but more spreading garbage and an oil slick that shone like silver in the flickering light. No sign of Remo or Chiun.

Petrovina was certain they were dead. She had no idea what they thought they were doing when they jumped into the sea, but if they thought they could force the *Novgorod* to stop or surface, they were out of their minds.

The American might have demonstrated amazing abilities before, but they were mere tricks compared to stopping a Soviet-era nuclear submarine. And the old man? Well, it was all simply ludicrous.

Her slender fingers gripped the rail. Jaw clenching, she dropped an angry fist against the wood.

It was infuriating! To think she had come so close to the thing she had been sent to stop, only to lose it. It was ridiculous that she'd allowed Remo to force her out here. Ridiculous that Vlad Korkusku and his men had been so easily cowed by the American.

This wasn't Petrovina's fault. Her record in her short professional career had been without a blemish until now. It would have remained so if she had been given Institute personnel to work with. Every woman who worked for the secret agency was a professional. Not like men. They were like Remo—always out to prove their masculinity. Or like Korkusku, always demonstrating his lack of the same. She was beginning to understand the wisdom of Director Chutesov.

Petrovina was growling at the sea when her angry eyes spotted something strange.

She was looking back toward the scows. The fishing boat had turned completely about and was puttering slowly in the direction from which it had come. As her gaze drifted across the waves a dozen yards behind the small boat, the reflection of fire began to rise into the air.

That was impossible, of course. The water was bulging, swelling up from below. That could only happen if...

Her eyes widened.

"Faster!" Petrovina screamed.

The SVR man at the throttle dutifully followed her command even as another agent monitoring the sonar began to shout excitedly.

"It is back! Directly behind us!"

The fishing boat raced ahead, barely avoiding the leviathan that was the surfacing *Novgorod*.

The conning tower was first to appear. It sliced

slowly through the water, like the dorsal fin of a dying shark.

Water poured from the tower, churning the sea a frothy white. Almost as fast the main deck broke the surface.

The fishing boat had sped ahead and came quickly back around. The small craft bounced against the waves rolling off the sub. Excitement gripping her belly, Petrovina held tight the railing of the fishing boat.

"Korkusku! Get down here with weapons!"

They were parallel to the *Novgorod*. The sub was nearly at a full stop.

Vlad Korkusku and his fellow SVR agents ran to join Petrovina on the deck. When she saw the wrenches and hammers they'd plundered from the boat's tool chest, she fixed the men with a gimlet eye.

"The American threw our guns away," Korkusku explained sheepishly. "He said trusting Russians to know how to use guns properly is like trusting Russians to know how to use democracy properly."

Petrovina spun back to the sub.

The *Novgorod* just sat there.

There was a short, tense moment during which all Petrovina could do was stare helplessly.

There it was, as big as life. And what could she do about it? Throw a net over it? Drag it back to shore?

As she pondered impossible options, something suddenly launched from the submarine.

Petrovina gasped.

For a terrible instant she thought the stolen submarine might have been stocked with more than just torpedoes. But as quickly as the thought came, she dismissed it.

A nuclear missile would not be launched from the conning tower of the submarine. Nor, she realized, would it scream in blind terror as it flew into the air.

The flying thing, which Petrovina now realized was a Russian sailor, was quickly joined by a second and a third. The sailors continued to pop from the tower like champagne corks. They made distant little splashes amid the garbage.

When the supply of rocket-charged men stopped shooting skyward, a head popped into view above the tower. When Petrovina saw who it was, her jaw dropped.

Standing on the conning tower of the submarine *Novgorod,* Remo Williams offered a friendly little wave.

"Hey, Natasha," he called. "How okay are Russians with the high-seas concept of finders keepers?"

"Do not let him have another toy," called Chiun's disembodied voice from down below. "He already has an airplane he hardly ever plays with."

21

The breaking dawn over Long Island Sound found Dr. Harold W. Smith hard at work behind his desk.

The first report had come in after midnight. Thanks to the increased media presence in Mayana, it had turned into an all-night news explosion.

A decommissioned Russian nuclear submarine had been stolen and set loose on civilians in the Caribbean. After a terror-filled night, the sub and its crew had somehow been captured. They were being held by Mayanan authorities.

In any other age it was a news story that would have wrested control of the airwaves from anything else. But the news of the twenty-first century played differently.

It was now early morning and the hard overnight news of the Russian submarine was being set aside, overtaken once more by human-interest puff pieces. On the newscast Smith was watching, the submarine story was supplanted by an update on a frivolous story out in California. From what Smith saw, it was some nonsense about a cat in a storm drain. There was apparently a growing sinkhole that had collapsed part of the street and had swallowed up three fire trucks and a police car. Smith didn't like cats and didn't think such a story had a place on any broadcast, especially when there was serious news to be told.

It was another sign of the changing times. A grave danger had presented itself in South America. Already there were many world leaders on the ground in Mayana. Others were on the way. The last update from the White House was that the President of the United States still planned to attend the Globe Summit. There was carnage in the Caribbean, fires still blazing out of control, a renegade Russian submarine responsible for sinking more than a dozen defenseless commercial vessels and killing an undetermined number of innocents, and the news media was opting to sweep it all aside for a story about a wet pussycat.

Leaning across his desk, Smith switched the channel on his old black-and-white television. The knob had cracked a few years back. There was now masking tape wrapped around it to hold it together.

For a few seconds he jumped back and forth between three newscasts. They were all covering the cat story. He finally gave up, snapping off the TV in disgust.

Smith assumed Remo and Chiun had something to do with the capture of the *Novgorod*. He had phoned Remo's hotel room several times during the night. The phone rang and rang with no answer. Eventually he gave up.

It would be easier for Smith to contact Remo than it would be for Remo to call in. The blasted Mayanan phone system was the problem. The national phone company was a Byzantine disaster of an analog system, rotary phones and party lines. Only recently had the government-subsidized phone company purchased its first modern fiber-optic cables. From what Smith had read, those seemed directly connected to the Vaporizer project. For what reason he had no idea, but many miles of the latest high-tech cables had been part of that project's budget. There was no indication that fiber-optic lines had been used anywhere else in the country.

It was like dialing out of the Dark Ages. Ordinarily for a small nation like Mayana, the system would be more than sufficient. But with the Globe Summit beginning later that day and so many international guests in the country, the lines had only gotten increasingly tangled.

Thanks to the CURE mainframes, Smith didn't have a problem clearing a line into the country. But if Remo was trying to call out on a land-based phone line, it could be days before he managed to get hold of Smith.

With a sigh of weary impatience, Smith turned his attention to his computer monitor. He had accessed an old American surveillance satellite during the night. At first the pictures he received had been little more than a black screen. Here and there were glowing fires. For a time he had watched with alarm as the number of fires increased.

With the coming of gray dawn the fires were fading. From above, the hundreds of scows in the Caribbean were lined up as neatly as Kansas wheat fields. In the wide view the rough coast of Mayana and some of the mountains above New Briton were becoming visible. The image extended up beyond the Vaporizer site.

Already a row of trucks could be seen crawling up into the hills from the harbor. They had been loaded overnight. In spite of the previous night's events, the government was doing its best to conduct business as usual.

Smith admired their tenacity. But he still could not shake his nagging doubts about the technology.

Something on the screen caught his attention.

"Odd," Smith mused.

He was squinting through his spotless glasses when there came a soft rap at his door. Frowning, he checked the time display in the corner of his screen. It was still too early for Mrs. Mikulka to be at work.

"Come in, Mark," Smith called. He returned his gaze to his computer as Mark Howard stepped into the office.

"Good morning, Dr. Smith," the assistant CURE director said, a touch of questioning concern in his voice as he noted Smith's attire.

The older man's gray suit jacket was draped over the back of his chair. He was working in his shirtsleeves, his tie still knotted tightly at his protruding Adam's apple. The only time Smith removed his jacket at Folcroft was when he worked late into the night, and then only rarely.

Smith noted his assistant's tone. "It is not time for our morning meeting," he said blandly. As he spoke, he half stood, shrugging his jacket back on. Brushing the sleeves, he sat back down.

"I figured I'd better check in as soon as I got here," Howard said as he came up to the desk. "Dr. Smith, were you here all night?"

Smith nodded. "I was about to leave when the situation in Mayana grew more dire." He glanced up over the tops of his glasses. "You are aware of what happened?"

"I saw it on the news," Mark said. "Dr. Smith, I *told* you I'd stay any time you want me to. There's no need for you to wear yourself out. And neither of us has to stay at Folcroft. We've both got laptops and phones we can hook into the CURE mainframes from home. If there's a problem, I can take care of it, or if it's too big, I can call you."

It was a discussion they had had before. Mark Howard understood better than anyone else in the world the stress Smith had been living with for forty years now. As their time working side by side grew, Howard had developed more and more familial concern for the aging CURE director.

"I know that, Mark," Smith said, straining patience. "But I've been waiting for Remo to report. And even though his call would be rerouted to my briefcase phone, I prefer not to take CURE calls from home. It is important that we minimize potential exposure, even to our loved ones."

Mark Howard sighed. There would be no getting through to his employer. Smith was too set in his ways.

"I understand," the younger man said. He was standing beside Smith's desk. Glancing over, he noted the satellite image on the canted computer monitor. "That the latest picture?" he asked.

"Yes," Smith said. "It appears that the fires are slowly being extinguished. Brazil has sent fireboats to help. In all, fourteen ships were sunk last night."

Howard had stepped next to Smith's chair behind the desk to get a better look at the screen.

"At least the sub that was doing it was caught. Any idea if it was Remo and Chiun?"

"No," Smith replied tightly.

"Well, no matter. The crisis is over."

"Perhaps," Smith said. "I would like to know if there are any other submarines or ships out there we should know about. The captain of the vessel might have confederates. And certainly if they could steal one vessel, they could have stolen more. The Russians have promised to take a full inventory of their decommissioned ships, but that could take weeks. And there is no way to know if they are one hundred percent accurate even then. We also don't know why this one submarine was even there. The captain could have just been fomenting chaos. We have seen that behavior before from some of their people who refuse to see that the Cold War is over. It would help if the news reported his motivation."

The older man's frustration was fueled by lack of sleep. He removed his glasses, massaging his tired eyes.

Mark Howard was still studying the satellite image on the computer screen.

"What's that?" he asked.

Howard pointed to a small grayish blot in the valley that was nestled on the other side of the mountains above the Vaporizer site. It was the same spot on the landscape Smith had noticed when Howard had first knocked on his door.

The CURE director replaced his glasses. The incongruous spot looked like a smudge in the otherwise green valley.

"I'm not sure," Smith said. "I doubt if it's a settlement or factory. It's too far away from everything else. By the looks of it, it's virtually inaccessible."

"There," Mark said, pointing. "That's a road, isn't it?" His finger traced a pencil-thin line from the back of the Vaporizer compound. It vanished into the jungle.

Smith nodded. "I noticed that. It appears to be new." He hummed, curious. "When you get to your office, look it up. See if it exists on any maps."

As they squinted at the monitor, both men were suddenly distracted by the ringing telephone.

It was the blue contact phone. The computer image was forgotten. Smith scooped up the telephone.

"Remo," he said.

"Hi, Smitty," came Remo's voice on the other end of the line. "You hear the news?"

"Yes," the CURE director said. "The submarine was captured. By you and Chiun?"

"Who else?" Remo said. "As usual, the world makes a mess and we're the ones who have to clean it up. I'm just wondering if I might have driven him to it."

"Driven who to what?" Smith said, concerned.

Remo seemed surprised. "You didn't hear? Nikolai Garbegtrov is the one who stole the sub. Or bank-rolled it, anyway. That cockamamy environmental group of his wanted it, then didn't want it. I guess while they were making up their minds the captain went a little nuts and decided to make things go boom. He was screaming Garbegtrov's name as they were hauling him off. None of this was on the news?''

''Not all,'' Smith said. ''Only mention of a crew of former Russian navy men.''

''No surprise,'' Remo grunted. ''I used to think that birthmark of his was Dan Rather's smeared lip-stick. Probably a hundred more just like it on his ass.''

''So was Garbegtrov behind the actual attacks?''

''Doesn't look that way. The captain was just pissed off the way Russians always get. He decided to vent down here to humiliate his old comrade. Garbegtrov wasn't lying. He wanted the sub stopped just as much as we did.''

Smith's eyes went flat. His chair made a little squeak as he sat up more straightly.

''You spoke with him *again?*'' he pressed.

''It's no big deal, Smitty. He's not talking. The Russians have bundled him off to their embassy. I'm betting he's signed himself up for a nice Siberian honeymoon. Especially when they get a load of what Bartholomew Cubbins has been covering up with his five hundred hats.''

Smith drummed a hand on his desk. ''I suppose this has worked out for the best. Still, I am not pleased if your—'' he hesitated, searching for the right word "—*creative* visit to Nikolai Garbegtrov is in any way responsible for this."

"Know a joke when you hear one, Smitty?" Remo droned, irritated. "The sub was stolen long before I tattooed Garby. I'm not a coconspirator. Sheesh."

"Very well," Smith said, wrapping up the call. "The President still intends to go to Mayana today. I'm not sure if that has changed privately, given the events of last night. If you feel it's safe, I see no problem. I'll call him and let him know."

"Tell him to pack nose plugs," Remo warned. "I'll see you when I get back, Smitty."

The connection broke with an electronic blip, rather than a click. Smith realized CURE's enforcement arm had been using a cell phone.

During the phone call, Mark Howard had taken a seat before the desk. As Smith hung up the blue contact phone, the young man got to his feet.

"You heard," Smith said.

"Enough," Howard said. "You going to call the President now?"

Smith checked his wristwatch. "Yes," he said. "The President is an early riser. He should be up by now."

"Okay," Howard said. "I'll be in my office if you need me. I'll see you for the meeting at nine."

The young man headed for the door. As Smith was reaching for the special White House line in the bottom desk drawer, he glanced at his computer screen. His eye was drawn once more to the blot in the valley above the Vaporizer site.

"Mark," Smith called.

When the assistant CURE director turned, Smith had one hand on the red phone. He was frowning down at his monitor.

"When you check on this road, see what you can find out about the valley above it," Smith said.

"Yes, sir," Howard said.

As Mark left the room, Smith was picking up the cherry-red receiver. His suspicious gray eyes never left the crisp Mayanan satellite image.

"THANKS, BUDDY."

Remo took the cell phone back from the Mayanan dockworker he had asked to dial and hang up for him. He'd held the man by the scruff of the neck throughout the call with Smith. The dockworker was just grateful to be free. Nodding a "you're welcome," he hurried off.

The wide dock on which Remo stood was ordinarily used for cruise ships. Across the broad concrete slab, the submarine *Novgorod* sat exposed to the world. A crowd of reporters, government officials and gawkers crammed the area.

Away from the crowd stood a wizened figure. Chiun was watching the crowd as the crowd watched the sub.

As he crossed the dock, Remo tried to figure out how to snap the cell phone shut. It should have been easy to do—after all, he had done it back at the hotel—but for some reason this time it wouldn't budge.

"I knew I let that guy go too soon," he griped,

struggling with the phone as he walked up to his teacher. "That's it, Little Father. We can get out of here."

"It is high time," Chiun replied. "The stench of this place has permanently corrupted the fabric of my kimono. I will be sending your Emperor Smith a bill."

"'Our,'" Remo corrected. "You're still on the payroll."

Chiun stroked his thread of a beard. "As an uninvolved adviser, perhaps. Until my exact position post-Reigning Master is determined, I am little more."

"You gonna give half the money back?"

Chiun fixed him with a glare he reserved exclusively for rambling mental defectives and Remo at his most obtuse. He was still glaring when Petrovina Bulganin strolled up.

"The crew has largely confessed to working for Green Earth," the Institute agent said. "It looks as if Mayana wants to get rid of submarine and end this matter quickly. UN inspectors are already in the country for Globe Summit, so they will oversee disarming of weapons. Once hatch is repaired, submarine will be towed to rendezvous with Russian ship that will take it rest of the way home."

"Super," Remo said, uninterested.

He was still struggling with the phone. He didn't want to break it, but it looked as if that was the only way to shut it. But that couldn't be the case, because cell phones weren't tossed out like Band-Aids after one use. At least he didn't think they were.

Petrovina saw him grappling and tipped closer to see what was hidden in his hands. She was surprised when she recognized the phone she'd dropped back at the hotel.

"That's it," Remo said, frustrated. "I'm chucking it." He hauled back, ready to heave the phone into the harbor.

"No!" Petrovina snapped. "That's—"

She stopped abruptly, hands outstretched.

Remo paused. "You want it?" he offered.

Petrovina hesitated. For an instant her hand wavered in place.

"Yes, I do," Chiun interjected. He snatched the phone from Remo's outstretched hand. He clicked it easily shut, and the cell phone vanished up a broad kimono sleeve.

"I meant Petrovina, Little Father. And how did you shut that thing? It was stuck or something."

"I don't want it," Petrovina announced.

"Good, because you cannot have it," Chiun stated.

"What are you going to do with a cell phone?" Remo asked.

"Perhaps I will phone my son who offers free gifts to Russian floozies he only just met while his father to whom he has never given anything nice is standing right there. Do you know his number offhand, Remo, or should I just dial I-N-G-R-A-T-E?"

"Say, I just got a swell idea," Remo said. "You keep it." He turned to Petrovina. "Sorry," he said.

"That is all right," she insisted. She seemed suddenly distracted. "I must talk to Korkusku."

"You want us to wait to give you a lift back to the hotel?" Remo offered.

"No, no," she said. "Not necessary." She smiled a stiff-lipped smile. "The Russian Federation thanks you for your help."

"Yeah, okay," Remo said, raising a suspicious brow. "Give it a sloppy wet one from us."

She nodded crisply to Chiun. He scarcely noticed.

"If you will excuse me," she said. With that she turned and hurried off, back to the crowd of people around the sub.

"She's up to something," Remo said.

Chiun had his new cell phone back out. He was clicking the mouthpiece open and closed.

"Fish swim, Russians scheme," the old man said as he played with the phone. "I would be shocked if she was not plotting against you in some way."

"Well, it's going to have to be long distance," Remo said, nodding firmly. "'Cause we're out of here. Let's go, Little Father."

The two men left the crowds and the submarine and headed off on foot to their hotel.

22

When the knock sounded at his office door, Pavel Zatsyrko, head of Russia's intelligence services, sighed deeply. He checked his watch. Right on time.

The SVR head put down his pen and closed the file on which he had been making notes.

"Come in," he called with barely restrained irritation.

His secretary stuck her head in the room. Olga Chernovaya was an ugly, lumpish thing. The broken capillaries around her nose looked like a map of Moscow, she had prematurely gray hair as stiff as wire and her backside had gotten round from a lifetime's worth of government jobs.

"Your appointment is here," Olga snarled.

"Show her in," Zatsyrko said.

Too late. His appointment was already in. Even as the SVR director spoke, the woman he was scheduled to meet slipped around Olga and into the office.

When the beautiful woman appeared, the reason for Olga's disdain became clear. It had everything to do with envy and nothing to do with the fact that neither her employer nor her employer's guest had told Olga this important visitor's name.

With a look of hate-filled jealousy, Olga backed from the room and shut the door tight.

His visitor made certain they were alone before she turned full attention to Pavel Zatsyrko.

"I assume you dragged me all the way over here as some pathetic attempt to assert your masculinity," Anna Chutesov complained.

"Delighted to see you again, too," Zatsyrko droned.

He ordinarily stood when a woman—particularly a woman as beautiful as Anna Chutesov—entered a room. But for the director of the mysterious Institute, he didn't bother.

There was a time when he had acted more chivalrously toward her. It was a brief time back when he first met Director Chutesov and learned of the secret agency that had existed to offer advice to Russia's leaders since the days of the Soviet empire. The few times they met he had stood to greet her, tried to open doors, tried to be a gentleman. She rebuffed his chivalry with feminist insults. And, worse than rudeness, she began plundering his own agency of its best minds—always female—to work at her Institute.

Zatsyrko had been friends with the current president of Russia back when the two men worked together in the KGB. At first he had gone to his old comrade to complain about this nuisance Chutesov woman and her growing sapphic legion.

The president was less than supportive.

"Give her what she wants," Russia's leader

grunted. "She has proved more useful to me and to Russia than all the agents in the SVR combined."

Thus ended all argument.

And so Pavel Zatsyrko was forced to open the personnel files of Russia's premier intelligence service to a woman who would not allow someone to pull out her chair for her and who treated men as if they were...well, *women*.

"You said you had information on the pictures I forwarded to you," Anna Chutesov said.

"Yes," Pavel Zatsyrko said. "I did."

There was a faint glimmer of satisfaction on his face as he got to his feet.

"Please come with me," the SVR head said.

Zatsyrko did not hold the door for Anna as they left his office.

The upper floors of the SVR headquarters were like a library—people talking in hushed tones, practically tiptoeing from office to office. Zatsyrko led Anna through the quiet upper reaches of Russia's chief intelligence agency and to a dusty back hall and elevator, both of which had to be unlocked with special keys. The elevator carried them deep into the subbasement. The doors opened on a long, dingy corridor illuminated by fluorescent lights, many of which seemed on the verge of burning out.

Pavel Zatsyrko marched smartly down the hallway, past locked doors and steel cages stacked high with crates and cardboard packing boxes. As he walked, the SVR head hummed softly to himself.

He was enjoying wasting Anna's time. She refused to give him the satisfaction of showing her impa-

tience. Mouth screwed tightly shut, Anna followed
Zatsyrko to the far end of the hall. The SVR head
led her into a small room.

There were no windows. Cold concrete was flak-
ing from the walls onto the drab green floor. A single
metal table and two old chairs sat in the middle of
the room.

The back wall was lined with a dozen ancient
metal file cabinets. Zatsyrko went to one of the cabinets. From a drawer he produced a pair of manila
files.

The SVR head tossed the files onto the table.

"Those will not leave this building," he said.
"You may go over my head to the president if you
wish, but tell him that if you take those files from
the SVR building, he will have my resignation before
you reach the curb."

Men never changed. They were always involved
in some long-distance urinating contest to prove their
virility. She ignored Zatsyrko's chest-thumping.

When she sat in a chair, the first thing she noted
about the files were the old KGB codes on the flaps.
Reverse Engineering Directorate had been typed in
large Cyrillic lettering below the codes. There were
smaller project code words on each flap. Anna
scanned the file names.

Zibriruyushchiy Kostyum. Lyovkiy Dukh.

"These are not projects with which I am familiar," she said darkly.

"How interesting," Zatsyrko said. He was sitting
across from her, arms folded. "We have finally

found something that you do not know. I will be sure to mark my calendar.''

As Zatsyrko watched, Anna read through the files thoroughly. She seemed to grow more amazed with every turned page. By the time she was done, the care lines around her blue eyes were crimped tight with concern.

''Is this information complete?'' she demanded.

Pavel Zatsyrko seemed surprised. ''I assumed you would ask me first if it was a joke. If this was the first time I was hearing about all this, that would be my reaction.''

Anna shook her head impatiently. ''The KGB was never known to joke,'' she spat. ''Nor does the SVR have the skill to falsify records with this level of believable detail. Even if you could, you do not dis-like me so much that you would waste your time on such foolishness. Therefore the only conclusion I can draw is that this information is real.''

Like most men, Pavel Zatsyrko found that Anna Chutesov's logic was inarguable.

''That is everything except the personnel overview,'' he grunted. Getting up, he retrieved another file from the cabinet. He slipped it across the table.

Anna flipped open the file.

She expected to find the usual dry details. The KGB collected information on everything from eating habits to shoe size. Wondering if Zatsyrko had given her this file to waste her time, she scanned the first page. It contained information about an old Soviet-era physicist.

When she checked the man's photograph, which

was clipped to the back of the sheet, Anna's mouth tightened. She looked up angrily at Pavel Zatsyrko.

Zatsyrko seemed pleased to have finally gotten a rise out of the Institute director.

"I thought you might find that interesting," he said.

Anna wasn't listening. She had clicked open her leather purse. She pulled out a small stack of photographs.

Thumbing through, she found one that she set next to the old KGB photo.

The man was older now. His jowls sagged, and his dark eyes had puffed into fleshy gray bags. But there was no doubt that it was the same man.

Anna picked up the folder and flung it at Pavel Zatsyrko. Papers flew everywhere.

"Idiot!" she snapped. "You drag me down here just so you can strut around and show me how important you are, not even caring that the world is in danger."

Zatsyrko was surprised by the ferocity in her eyes.

"I did not know he was that important to you," Zatsyrko said. "We were lucky to find these files at all. You only gave us the pictures to search for. No names."

"I did not know his name," Anna retorted. Snatching up the small photograph she had brought with her, she flung it in her purse, snapping the latch viciously.

"What is he to you?" Zatsyrko asked. "He is just one of our old scientists. Probably retired. We do not even know where he is."

"*I* know where he is. And now I must do what I always do. Stop you and idiot men like you from blowing us all up."

She didn't wait for Zatsyrko to see her out. Spinning on her heel, she marched from the room.

She took the elevator back upstairs. When a guard saw her marching through a restricted area without an SVR escort, he approached her. Anna chased him away with a glare.

Hurrying through the halls and out the front doors, she emerged into the Moscow sunlight.

She found her car on the street where she'd parked it.

For a moment after she climbed in behind the wheel, she seemed uncertain what to do.

The Institute had an agent on the ground. They had lost contact, but perhaps that was only temporary. Digging in her purse, she pulled out her cell phone. The photograph—a copy of which she had sent to the SVR for examination—fell out on the seat.

Anna scooped up the photo. When she saw the man's face once more, she shook her head angrily.

"They will kill us all," she hissed.

Holding the photo in one hand, she used the other to press out Petrovina Bulganin's cell phone number.

"YOUR KIMONO is ringing," Remo said.

They were strolling along New Briton's docks. The scenery was truly beautiful. This had been a nicer part of town. Tidy buildings, immaculate pleasure boats, lush vegetation. With the wind at their backs, the smell of rotting garbage was almost bearable.

Chiun's hand disappeared inside a wide sleeve. When it reappeared he was clutching the ringing cellular phone.

"I found that, so it's not anyone we know," Remo pointed out. "Maybe you should just toss it in the water."

"Just because it is someone who does not know *you,* does not mean that it is someone who does not know me," Chiun sniffed as he snapped open the phone.

"Here, at least let me answer it for you."

Chiun pressed a button and the ringing stopped. With a thin smile, he raised the phone to his shell-like ear.

"How did you do that?" Remo asked.

"Because I do not take stubborn pride in being an ignoramus," Chiun replied superiorly. Into the phone he said, "You have reached the ear of the most gracious Master who once reigned but who is regrettably between honorifics at the moment. Speak. But speak quickly, for these devices have been known to cause ailments of the brain."

Remo tried to listen but the old man pressed the phone tight to his ear, preventing eavesdropping. He knew something wasn't right when he saw Chiun's face pale.

"What is it, Little Father?" Remo asked.

Chiun glanced sharply at his pupil, as if surprised that he was standing there. "Nothing," he insisted, waving Remo back with a bony hand. "A nuisance call." He pressed the phone even tighter to his ear. "I have told you people before not to bother me," he warned. "Your cards of plastic are more worthless than paper money, and I do not care to answer questions about which baby-kissing white male you install as your leader. If you call again, you invite my wrath." His tone turned grave. "And believe me when I say you do not want that."

The last words were said as hard threat.

As Remo's confused frown deepened, Chiun pressed the Phone Off and hastily switched off the ringer.

"You sure that was a telemarketer?" he asked.

"Of course," Chiun sniffed. "Thanks to you always loitering around, that is all that ever calls me these days."

"Somehow I doubt you were the most popular kid on the assassin's teen chat line before I showed up," Remo deadpanned. "You know, I think I've changed my mind. If that thing works, maybe I should keep it after all." He held out his hand for the phone.

"It is mine," Chiun insisted. "Find yourself another." The cell phone vanished back inside his robes.

His tone was a bit too sharp, his face straining a little too hard at being untroubled. The old man kept his eyes dead ahead as he walked.

From his demeanor alone Remo knew his teacher was keeping something from him. He shrugged.

"Oh, well. Wouldn't be the first time," he grumbled to himself as he trailed the old Korean to the parking lot.

SITTING IN HER CAR outside the SVR building, Anna Chutesov clicked her phone shut.

Anna had been disturbed by Petrovina Bulganin's earlier phone call. Before being cut off, the agent had mentioned something about having knowledge of Anna's strange amnesia.

The Institute director had not tried raising Petrovina directly after that, fearing that she and her phone had fallen into the hands of an unknown enemy. But things had just gotten too desperate not to try.

Anna had no idea who had answered Petrovina Bulganin's cell phone, but it was clearly no longer in the hands of the Institute's agent. No matter. In fact, that was a potential silver lining in this mess. That could be dealt with once the current crisis was past. Assuming the world survived.

There was only one course of action open to her now.

Anna hadn't realized that she had been clenching her other hand. She smoothed flat the photo that Petrovina Bulganin had taken in Mayana.

Glancing one last time at the Vaporizer janitor who didn't seem very interested in his broom, she dropped the photo and the phone in her purse.

Tossing the car into gear, she peeled out of the parking spot and flew out into the heavy Moscow traffic. In the direction of the airport.

23

The Jamestown tragedy of 1978 had propelled the People's Sanctum cult to the front pages, sent Americans scurrying for maps to find out just where Mayana was and had put cult leader Jack James—at least for a time—at the top of a shortlist of the most infamous figures of his age. It was the public end to a private journey along a twisted valley where death was mocked and evil embraced.

Jack James founded the Holy Assembly of God Church in Columbus, Ohio, in the early 1960s. Messianic from the start, he preached a gospel of salvation where he alone was the only bridge between man and God.

"Survival of the soul," James bellowed to the great unwashed, "comes only from intimate knowledge of *this* church's blessed teachings!"

Jack James was fond of sharing this intimate knowledge with his parishioners. Especially the women.

Jack James always had an eye for the ladies. Jack James also had a mahogany cane with which he punished evil. He found much evil in women. With his "rod of persuasion" he chastised many a wayward sister. In their pain the self-ordained pastor found his greatest pleasure.

"The sisters exude the alluring scent of carnality!" he exclaimed under the hot lights of his rented auditorium. "The brothers have in them the seed of Satan! The power to corrupt is in *all* of you! There is darkness in the world and there is light! Who here can say he longs to live in darkness? The light is bright but it does not burn. Come into the light. Forgo the darkness and come to me!"

He spoke the words not with arrogance but with utter conviction. Jack James was the light. Sadly the lost and pathetic souls of his misguided flock seemed to agree.

Preaching impending Armageddon to his followers, James managed to fill to capacity his Sunday-afternoon revival meetings. As the money and membership ranks grew, so, too, did James's belief in his own power. Jack James began to see himself not as God's voice on Earth, but as God himself.

God could not be contained. James began to plot his expansion beyond the borders of Ohio. The catalyst came to him one fateful August day in early 1966.

James had spotted an attractive young woman in the fourth row of one of his services. When it was over, he directed some of his followers to bring the girl to him.

As his flock was driving home, hearts filled with hope of eternal salvation, Jack James was ushering the young girl into his trailer and thinking positively impure thoughts.

She was stunning, this wicked child of Eve's sin. A college student who had stopped by the revival meeting on a whim, the young girl was bubbling with energy and enthusiasm. Her hair was bleached blond and pulled back in a coarse ponytail, tied with a yellow ribbon. The fresh, full womanhood of her chest threatened to burst buttons on her tight yellow blouse.

James smiled in the trailer, which was parked in the shade of an elm tree near a softly gurgling brook.

"Sit, child," he beckoned, patting the edge of his bed. "There are no chairs." He shrugged apologetically.

"I never heard a sermon like yours before," the girl said. "I was brought up boring Episcopalian. That's what Daddy is. Mom was Jewish. At least she was before they got married. We're not supposed to mention it because of Daddy's job, although I don't think he needs to worry about it like you used to have to. But, oh, maybe I shouldn't have said it to you. I guess I shouldn't worry though, you being a man of God and all."

James's smile faded ever so slightly. "I am not a man *of* God," he said dully.

"Oh, I'm sorry. Did I say something wrong? Maybe I should go." She started to stand.

"No, no," Jack James said. He pressed her shoulder, coaxing her to sit back on the bed. "We're fine."

His sermon had touched her. He could see it in her eyes. He could always tell from their eyes. She sat perched on the bed, a bright-eyed, guileless child who would be more than willing to do anything for the leader of the Holy Assembly of God Church.

Jack James excused himself to the trailer's small bathroom in order to change. When he returned a minute later he was stark naked. He held his hands behind his back.

"Oh, my goodness," the shocked girl said, eyeing the excitement of the preacher who was definitely not boring Episcopalian. "Oh, my God," she gasped when he brought his hands out from behind his back.

"Wicked child takes my name in vain," James said. "Wicked child must be punished."

Jack James held a mahogany cane—his rod of persuasion—high in the air. The girl screamed. She fell off the bed and scrambled for the door. Jack James spun around her, breathing her fear, savoring the pain.

James brought the cane down across her leg. The girl had been twisting the doorknob. With a shriek she let it go, falling to the floor.

"Wicked child tempts the flesh to sin," James sang.

A crack to the side of the head. Light blinding bright in her eyes, she tumbled under the small table in the trailer's kitchenette.

She was crying now. A gash bled from her temple. "Please." She tried to crawl to the door.

"Wicked child pleads for mercy," Jack James announced. He was sweating profusely now. Panting with excitement. "But mercy is God's to give. Today, God says—"

He brought the cane back one more time. Frothy white spittle sprayed from the corner of his mouth.

Swing, crack.

The girl slumped face-first to the floor.

"No," the almighty Jack James concluded.

His excitement spent, he left the dead girl on the floor and went in to take a shower. Later, under cover of darkness, he dumped the body in a shallow grave in some woods and rolled her car into a lake.

The story might have ended there for James had he not learned the identity of the young girl who had suffered the ultimate punishment of the wicked temptress. He saw it in the newspaper a few days after the incident. Front page, with accompanying picture.

It turned out that the young college girl was the only child of an Ohio senator who was part of the old Democratic machine. He had powerful friends on both sides of the law. The body had been found and the father was out for blood.

Jack James was not a fool. The day he saw the newspaper photo of that wicked, smiling temptress was the day he realized it was time to seek out sunnier pastures. Four days after the story broke, the Holy Assembly of God Church was renting a storefront in downtown San Francisco.

The move to California, though abrupt, turned out to be a blessing in disguise. In a state where tradition was yesterday and deeply held religious beliefs were last week, it seemed that everyone was looking to buy into the next fad. Church membership flourished. Over the course of the next eight years, James's church—eventually rechristened the People's Sanctum—enrolled tens of thousands of new members.

The public face of the People's Sanctum was a church concerned with the plight of the poor. Food and clothing drives, free beds to indigents and church-sponsored soup kitchens were all part of the church's intensive antipoverty drive. Because of all his good works, Jack James was even appointed chairman of the San Francisco Housing Authority.

The success of Jack James seemed divinely inspired.

His delusions had only grown more firmly entrenched over time. There were no lucid moments. James was now God on Earth. The one eternal, omniscient Deity, come to lead his sheep to his own version of eternal salvation.

And since he was omnipotent God, it came as a shock when everything he had built collapsed from beneath his feet.

He had dodged the charges for years. In the end it took only one betrayer.

A young woman who had barely survived a personal audience with James came forward. She had scars that were the kind that couldn't be seen and the other kind that could. She showed the latter on the evening news.

"Outrageous," said a church spokesman.

"Unfounded," the same spokesman insisted when another woman told a newspaper an identical story.

Soon more former cult members were coming forward. A trickle became a rising flood.

There were allegations of extortion, encouragement of sexual promiscuity and enforcement of discipline among church disciples through blackmail and beatings. One man who came forward knew where some of the bodies had been buried. Literally.

Fortunately for Jack James, he had been warned ahead of time by an acolyte in the media. There was nothing else he could do but flee.

America was no longer safe. Luckily he had purchased several hundred acres of land in the Mayanan jungle a few years earlier. He had hoped to put it to agricultural use—primarily for growing coca plants. The land became haven to Jack James and the six-hundred-odd People's Sanctum members who fled with him from California.

Life in Mayana proved difficult. There weren't the same creature comforts as back in America.

To discourage disloyalty among his remaining cult members, Jamestown—as the property became known—was cut off from the outside world. To break the spirits of his followers, James worked cult members fourteen or more hours a day. As punishment, food and water were often withheld.

There was no longer any need to hide his peccadilloes behind a socially acceptable mask. James roamed the fields of Jamestown administering beatings to men and women chosen completely at random.

Over the years he had let a few close acolytes in on the extralegal aspects of the church. There were twelve in all. In Mayana these apostles became his own private security force. They would serve his every whim and, when necessary, dispose of the bodies afterward.

Jack James might have ruled for the rest of his natural days in the hell that was Jamestown and died a forgotten old maniac in the jungles of Mayana if not for a lone man. He wasn't even very important in the grand scheme of things. Just a run-of-the-mill California congressman.

In November of 1978, word came of an impending visit by Congressman Lenny Rand. Some of his constituents who had relatives in Jamestown were demanding the congressman do something to get their loved ones home. The congressman had decided to plead the case for Jack James's extradition to authorities in New Briton. But first he wanted to take a fact-finding tour of Jamestown. The congressman would be there in less than a day.

James's paranoia reached critical mass. The visiting congressman was an agent of Satan. He was in league with the demons who had driven James from his comfortable home in California. He was cohort to the Ohio senator whose Bathsheba daughter had tempted the flesh of Jack James so many years ago. His world was coming apart. The forces of evil were aligning to destroy Jack James.

The almighty Jack James refused to let Satan win again.

He had no troops to speak of. Jamestown could not survive an attack by America. His security forces were few in number. The regular cult members were starving, emaciated shells. But God was nothing if not resourceful.

When Congressman Rand arrived in Jamestown, he and his party were greeted by the security forces of Jack James. They were slaughtered to a man. James himself beat the congressman's skull in with the rod of persuasion.

That was step one.

After the massacre, stainless-steel vats of the children's fruit drink Kook-Aid were brought forward.

The wasted members of the Jamestown cult were lined up. James's personal security men stood behind folding tables, ladling out paper cups to passing cult members.

The first few people who drank James's special brew quickly discovered there was more than just flavored sugar water in their cups. Stomachs convulsed. Chests heaved. Faces contorting in final agony, the men and women collapsed to the muddy ground of the compound.

Jack James stood on a platform supervising the operation. He wore an untucked dress shirt buttoned to the collar and a pair of dark aviator's glasses. He watched in satisfaction as the second step of his plan was carried out.

"It's the only way for us," he shouted over the public-address system. "The haters of light draw near. The United States government is rallying its evil might against us in the name of the unholy one! We do this now to rob the wicked of their prize!"

James continued to cheer them on even as they dropped like flies, courtesy of the cyanide he had added as a special ingredient to their fruit punch.

Not everyone wanted to drink. These were dealt

with by the twelve heavily armed members of Jack James's security forces.

It took just over an hour.

Once phase two was complete, phase three was quickly put into action.

There were time constraints now. The dead congressman had already been to New Briton. The government there would eventually send someone to look for him.

The bodies of the men and women who had followed their god to South America had already begun to putrefy in the hot Mayanan sunlight as James and his trusted apostles opened the door to the forbidden barn. Inside was a neatly stacked row of thirteen bodies. All had been prepared earlier that day.

They had been selected for their looks. Each body bore a physical resemblance to one of his security agents. Beaten faces and mangled fingertips would prevent positive identification. All wore a special People's Sanctum tag, identifying them as Jack James's chosen disciples.

"Are you sure this will work?" one of the men asked as he dragged his own double into the sunlight.

Jack James smiled. "Ye of little faith," he said, removing his aviator's glasses.

It was Jack James the authorities would be looking for. One of the corpses was thin, for he had been worked hard over the past few years, but his resemblance to Jack James was still uncanny. He had the same general facial features. The same hair color, same build.

James put his sunglasses on the corpse. His wallet

had already been stuffed in the pocket of the man's trousers. There was no record of Jack James's fingerprints anywhere. He had never been in the military, and he had fled the United States before he had been arrested for his crimes there. The dead man had a similarly clean record. His face was bruised only slightly and his fingers were left intact.

God knew that it would be enough to fool Satan.

James and his followers left the look-alike corpses and escaped into the hills of Mayana. When the authorities arrived, they found exactly what Jack James wanted them to find—a cult leader who had forced his followers to commit suicide, killing himself, as well, rather than go to prison. It was instant front-page news.

The legend of Jamestown flared brightly for a time. But news was an ongoing search for fresh blood. As time went on, Jack James was tossed on history's dusty heap of infamous psychotics.

And while the mass suicide he had engineered became the stuff of twisted legend, the real Jack James hid out in a small village in the dense Mayanan jungle. After a year in exile, he ventured out of the forest into New Briton.

James found a gifted plastic surgeon, a British expatriate who had left England under unpleasant circumstances. The man asked few questions. A few years and several operations later—with the bandages off, the scars long healed and the bruises faded away—Jack James emerged from the jungle as politician Blythe Curry-Hume. A true man of the people.

A patient man, he started small. A handshake here,

a small village meeting there. As the years went on, the drip-drip-drip of personal appearances swelled into a river.

It didn't take a great effort to establish a trust with the disaffected element of the Mayanan population. His years in the wilderness had not diminished his ability to weave his charismatic spell. He became champion of the common folk.

The rest took longer. Over time, Blythe Curry-Hume graduated to bigger cities, larger crowds. And when the time was right, he made the final move from the fringes of Mayanan politics. It was a journey of almost two decades.

The Almighty was slow to anger and righteous in his wrath. As executive president, Blythe Curry-Hume's platform was a simple one. He wanted revenge. Revenge against the world that had banished him. Revenge against those who thought him mad. Revenge against the wicked mortals who had persecuted him. And, fittingly, God's scheme of vengeance was truly great.

James had constructed his instrument of revenge on the old Jamestown site. And the fenced-off valley where his followers had met their end hid a special secret.

Finance Minister Carlos Whitehall still thought the Vaporizer Project was his own idea. He resented Blythe Curry-Hume as an interloper who had stepped into office after the project had already been started. The fool.

Carlos Whitehall was a tool, to be used and discarded. A scapegoat if one became necessary. The same was true for all of Mayana if it came to that. But it would *not* come to that.

They were all unwitting pawns. Every last one of them going about their prearranged parts in a play written in blood by a madman who alone knew the final act. And when revenge came, the world would be rocked to its molten core and the heavens would rain fire.

THERE WASN'T A SIGN of fire in the beautiful clear blue sky as Executive President Blythe Curry-Hume watched the heavens. Along with his entourage, he stood on the tarmac of New Briton International Airport. The sun warmed his upturned face, glinting off his sunglasses.

The plane appeared as a dot, growing larger along with its fighter-jet escort. Curry-Hume watched as it landed and taxied slowly to a stop on the main runway.

Curry-Hume stood more erect as the air stairs were rolled up to the plane.

Soon, very soon.

At his side Finance Minister Carlos Whitehall stood at attention. The fussy older man seemed irritated that there were others from the Mayanan government there to intrude on what was actually his moment in the spotlight. Curry-Hume noted the minister's irritation.

No clue whatsoever that he was a minor player. The fool, manipulated by the king.

"Is everything all right, sir?" Minister Whitehall asked, concerned.

"Couldn't be better," Curry-Hume replied. "Why?"

"Well, sir, your smile. It—" Whitehall shook his head. "Never mind."

Blythe Curry-Hume hadn't even been aware he was smiling. A grin of wicked triumph had stretched across his tan face, drawing tight the face-lifted skin at the back of his jaw. A few eyes had turned his way, brows raised. News cameras clicked and whirred in his direction.

The executive president relaxed his smile.

Patience, patience…

Men in black suits with radio receivers in their ears swarmed around the ramp. When the all-clear was given, a lone figure finally emerged from the plane.

The man waved to the crowds at the airport before climbing down the stairs.

Blythe Curry-Hume was there to meet him. The executive president of Mayana extended his hand.

"Welcome to Mayana, my friend," said Jack James to the President of the United States.

24

A series of afternoon thunderstorms swept down from upstate New York, bringing heavy rain and wind. Thunderclaps rattled windows for two hours as people from Westchester County to the Bronx ran to catch runaway lawn furniture and trash barrels. As quickly as they had come, the fast-moving storms blew out to sea, leaving eerie calm in their wake.

As usual, in the sparse office of Harold Smith the severe weather had gone all but unnoticed. If the one-way glass of his picture window had been shattered by a blown tree branch, Smith would have donned a slicker against the gale-force winds and hunkered back down at his computer, ignoring the driving rain on his back.

The storm was several miles out to sea. Soft thunder still rumbled angrily in the distance. The late-afternoon sun was peeking out from behind the black-streaked clouds high above the whitecapped waters of Long Island Sound.

Smith's secretary had already left for the evening. After remaining at Folcroft the previous night, Smith was exhausted. He intended to leave soon, as well.

But there was something that made him linger.

Something scratching at the back of his mind that would not let him go.

He wasn't sure what it could be. All the loose ends seemed to be tied up. The submarine had been taken care of. The crew was in custody. Smith had phoned the President early that morning, clearing the chief executive for his trip to the Globe Summit. Remo and Chiun would soon be home.

So why did Smith still sit?

As a rule he didn't believe in hunches. Harold Smith preferred to truck in cold, hard fact. But there were rare occasions, going back to his days in the OSS in World War II, where Smith had felt the lure of intuition. Being a man not ordinarily given to hunches or even simple imagination, when Smith had a hunch it usually meant something.

Before shutting down his computer for the night, Smith pulled up the Mayanan file.

The file was still active. The CURE mainframes were still drawing information related to the Mayanan situation and dumping them in the growing file. There were a few newer entries since the last time Smith had checked.

News out of Russia on the background of the *Novgorod*'s captain. The Russian president commenting on the situation on his way from Moscow to the Globe Summit. Still no mention of Nikolai Garbegtrov's involvement.

There was a story on the U.S. President's arrival in New Briton. A picture with the story showed the President shaking hands at the airport with Mayana Executive President Blythe Curry-Hume. Smith noted with a frown that Curry-Hume was wearing sunglasses.

Aside from backwater dictatorships, one rarely saw world leaders wearing sunglasses at important meetings. Men preferred to look one another in the eye at such events. But the sun at the airport did seem bright, at least in the photo. Most of the men with Curry-Hume were squinting.

Probably just an unintentional gaffe by Mayana's new leader. And an understandable one, given the fact that his small country had suddenly drawn international attention.

Smith was going to close out the file, but something about the picture made him linger. He was still staring at the image when a message suddenly popped up on his screen: *Dr. Smith, could you come to my office for a minute?*

Casting one last, puzzled look at the picture of Blythe Curry-Hume and the American President, Smith turned down the brightness on his monitor. The picture darkened. Leaving the computer on, he went down the hall.

Mark Howard generally worked with his door locked. He had unlocked it for Smith and was just sitting back down behind his desk when the CURE director entered.

"What is it, Mark?"

"I found something, Dr. Smith," Howard said excitedly. "Though I'm not sure what it means. Take a look at this."

Howard's desk was a sturdy oak slab too large for

his small office. Smith had to sidestep to get in behind it.

Unlike Smith's hidden desk unit, Howard's monitor and keyboard sat on top of the desk. A recessed stud could be used to lower them below the surface.

Standing next to his assistant's chair, Smith peered at Mark's computer screen.

"I've been going over blowups of those satellite images like you asked me to," the assistant CURE director said, tapping at his keyboard. "Here." A picture popped up on his screen. It was in clear focus with sharp lines, cleaned up by special software. "Here's the road we saw above the Vaporizer. Take a look at what's next to it."

Mark had drawn red circles around two objects on the ground. They might have been mistaken for trees from far off. At close range it was clear what they were.

"Telephone poles?" Smith asked. "That should all be uninhabited jungle. There aren't any settlements in that region."

"I double-checked that, too, just to be sure. There aren't. But those are definitely telephone poles. And right there." He tapped the screen between the poles where a few thin black threads stretched from one to the next. "I think this is where your fiber-optic cables went. But what they're doing with them out in the middle of nowhere is a mystery to me. Look. See where they run off here into the jungle?"

Mark quickly accessed several close-up pictures that he had prepared earlier. In breaks in the dense jungle foliage he showed glimpses of the continuing road—now unpaved and rutted. There were underlined markings on each photo to show the telephone wires running parallel to the road.

"It goes clear up the hill," Howard said.

Smith was intrigued. "It can't be a government installation," he mused. "I pulled all those records at the start of the crisis. If it's a secret, it's not one tied to their defense forces."

"I think it's something else. Lemme show you."

Howard pulled up a wider image of the Mayanan satellite picture in order to give Smith a clearer idea where the road headed. He had traced a path up the mountainside, through a ravine and into the valley beyond. The strange grayish blot at the edge of the valley that had caught the eye of both men earlier that morning reappeared.

"It leads there?" Smith asked.

Mark Howard smiled. "Wait," he said excitedly. "Get a load of this."

Typing swiftly, he pulled up another enlarged picture, this one from the valley. It was a super-close-range photo of a single item that had been isolated on the ground.

When Smith saw the familiar image on the screen, he blinked surprise. Assuming he had made a mistake, he leaned in, peering more closely at the picture.

The image was not quite right, but it was clear enough.

"It's a car," the CURE director said, puzzled.

Howard nodded. "Pretty mangled. I'd say it had to be in an accident, but it doesn't look like it was damaged in a crash. The metal's not crumpled and there's no shattered glass. It just looks sort of rearranged. See that shiny stuff on the hood? I think that's the windshield. Or was.''

Where Mark Howard pointed, a thick, clear, uneven substance looked to have thawed and congealed on the hood. It had the rough, rolling edges of solidified lava.

''It appears to have melted,'' Smith said.

''I thought so, too. We can't see too well from this angle, but it looks like that tire has fused with the fender. And right there. See that?'' He pointed to a small rectangle on the car's roof.

Dragging a magnifying glass icon over the spot, Howard clicked to enlarge it. The image of a license plate appeared in great detail. It looked as if it had been grafted to the roof. Smith could clearly make out the numbers.

''I ran the plate through the New Briton driver registry,'' Howard said. ''The car belonged to a guy named Toshimi Yakamoto. He was a Japanese scientist who worked on the Vaporizer.'' He glanced up at the CURE director. ''Someone reported him missing yesterday morning.''

Smith's frown deepened. ''I suppose he could have driven up that road and gotten lost or injured. If so, we should report this to the proper Mayanan authorities. Still, it doesn't explain what happened to his vehicle.''

''This might help,'' Howard said anxiously.

With great enthusiasm he attacked his keyboard. He expanded from the image of the license plate by rapid degrees. The car briefly filled the monitor once more. The picture quickly enlarged to encompass a wide area around the car. When he was done, Mark sat back in his chair, careful to keep his head from bumping the near wall. There was a flush of giddy triumph on his wide face.

Smith's mouth opened a shocked sliver. A cloud of dark confusion passed across his gray features.

The car sat on a mound of heaped bags and paper. All manner of metal and plastic jutted crazily from everywhere around the pile. Since it was a still image taken from above, Smith could distinctly see the backs and outstretched wings of several seagulls frozen in flight as they swooped over the piles.

Smith tore his eyes off the screen, glancing in confusion at his young assistant.

"Trash," the CURE director said, frowning.

Howard nodded. "*Tons* of it," he said. "It looks like a big blur from above because it's pretty much shapeless. It almost looks like that's where they're dumping everything they're bringing up to the Vaporizer."

"How?" Smith asked. "They aren't using that road. It's far too narrow and remote. And there are no others up into the hills. Besides, they are driving to the device on public roads. They would be missed if they detoured for as long as it would take them to get all the way up there."

"I know," Howard said, pursing his lips in thought. "I've tracked some of the trucks off and on today. They go from the harbor, up to the Vaporizer, dump their stuff in and then go back down." He crossed his arms, frustrated. "Unless they found some way to beam it up there from down below, it's getting vaporized, just like they claim."

Smith raised an eyebrow. "Beam?" he asked.

Howard had learned this about his employer early on. The CURE director knew little about popular culture.

"From a TV show, Dr. Smith," Howard said. "They could transport matter from one spot to another." He was peering at his screen. "I don't know. I thought this might be something, but it must just be an old dump," he concluded. "It's probably stuff they've been dumping there for years. Doesn't have anything to do with the Vaporizer. Still, I'd like to know how that car got all the way out there."

He was still staring at his screen when he heard a soft hiss of air beside him. When he glanced up he saw a flush of color on his employer's normally gray face.

"The scientist you mentioned," Smith pressed urgently. "The one whose car that was. You said he was Japanese. Did you research him—specifically employment history?"

"Some," Howard said. He pulled up the file on Toshimi Yakamoto. "Not much here. Hired a year ago by the government of Mayana. Before that he worked for fifteen years for the Nishitsu Corporation of Japan. I can do more if you'd like."

Smith was shaking his head. There was a look of quiet triumph on his face.

"Of course," he said. "It all makes sense."

Mark Howard looked from Smith to the monitor, then back to Smith once more. "It does?"

The CURE director shooed the younger man from his seat. Mark Howard stood back in the tight corner as Smith sat down before the raised monitor. The older man's hands flew over the keyboard, keys clattering madly.

"I gave you some research material from our old files after you came to work here," Smith explained while he typed. "Out of necessity I condensed much of it." He finished with a flourish. "Here it is. Read this file. It's more complete than what I gave you before. Digest the broad details as quickly as you can. Skim the rest for now. When you are finished, meet me in my office."

He vacated Howard's chair. The younger man was slipping back in the seat as Smith hurried back into the hallway.

The CURE director marched back to his own office. He slipped into his own familiar chair and grabbed up the blue contact phone. From memory, he called Remo's hotel room directly.

There was no answer. He tried the number a few more times before calling the main desk. Remo and Chiun had not returned, nor had they checked out yet.

That was at least a good sign. Remembering that Remo had checked in by cell phone, Smith spun to his computer.

When he turned up the brightness on the monitor, he found the picture of Mayanan Executive President

Blythe Curry-Hume smiling on the tarmac of the New Briton airport.

Feeling a stir of something in the back of his brain, Smith dumped the picture, activating CURE's tracer program.

He quickly traced the line Remo had used to report in. He was concerned to find that the phone was registered to a Russian telephone service.

Smith tried the number several times.

No answer. Knowing Remo, he had most likely tossed the phone in the trash once he was through with it.

Smith was sitting back in his chair and frowning in deep frustration when Mark Howard entered his office. The young man was shaking his head in amazement.

"You read the material?" Smith asked.

"Enough," Howard said. "You sure about this?"

Smith nodded crisply. "It all fits," he said.

Mark seemed to still be digesting everything he had just read. "How did all this end up down there?"

"I have a good idea on that, as well," Smith said, tapping a frustrated hand on his desk. "Fortunately this is not necessarily a major problem. Not for CURE anyway. As long as Remo is down there, I would like to have him confirm my suspicions before he leaves."

He reached once more for the contact phone. Maybe Remo had returned to his hotel by now.

"I can see them choosing that valley," Howard mused. "It's the perfect site. That's the exact spot where Jamestown was. No one's allowed out there."

Smith already knew the location of Jamestown. Yet it took someone else speaking the word aloud for the little nagging doubt that had been playing persistently at the edges of his mind to finally crystallize.

He dropped the blue phone. The color drained from Smith's face. His mouth went as dry as desert sand. His hands were shaking as he reached for his keyboard.

''What's wrong?'' Mark Howard asked, noting with dread the sudden change in his employer's demeanor.

Smith didn't answer. His ears rang as he pulled up the photo that had been taken an hour before on the tarmac of New Briton International Airport. President Blythe Curry-Hume stood shaking the hand of the American President, sunlight glinting off his dark glasses. Smith enlarged the photo for a close-up on the face of the Mayanan executive president.

Delving into the CURE archives, Smith retrieved a picture that had been taken twenty-five years earlier. He set the old photograph next to the new one.

The instant he saw them side by side Smith felt a tightness in his chest. As if a cold hand had reached in to clench the life from his struggling heart.

The skin was darker now, but it seemed unnatural. A salon tan rather than natural pigmentation. The nose was oddly sharp, the hairline plucked back. The hair itself had been dyed jet-black. But the build and the general facial structure remained the same. The men in both pictures were even wearing the same aviator-style sunglasses.

Mark Howard had come around the desk and was peering at the pictures of the two men.

Smith had been guided by instinct. Since Remo had undergone several operations to alter his appearance since coming to CURE, Smith had also become adept at spotting plastic surgery. Mark Howard, on the other hand, had his own sixth sense, an ability to see that which others could not. That the young man saw what Smith had seen was clear.

"My God," the assistant CURE director croaked. "But Jack James is dead. That can't be him."

Smith scarcely heard. His hands were on the leather arms of his chair. Deadweights at the ends of his wrists.

A peal of distant thunder rumbled in across Long Island Sound. The sound registered dully on Smith's ears.

It could not be. Yet there it was.

Jack James, the psychotic. Jack James, the murderer. Jack James, long-dead leader of the People's Sanctum, the man who had killed hundreds of his own followers at Jamestown.

There now, shaking hands with the President.

The President of the United States and dozens—*hundreds*—more world leaders and high-ranking diplomats were in Mayana for the Globe Summit. And their lives, perhaps the fate of the world, were in the hands of an utter madman.

And not one of them knew the truth.

25

Remo had hoped to get a quick flight out of Mayana. Unfortunately the opening-day ceremonies of the Globe Summit tied up all air traffic in and out of New Briton. With dignitaries from around the world swarming the city, the earliest flight he could catch was the following morning.

He tried phoning Smith to speed things up, but Mayana's phone system was worth spit. After hours of trying, he still couldn't get through.

"You know, maybe we could get out of this dump faster if you showed me how to use that cell phone I found," Remo complained to Chiun after his hundredth time pressing the redial button on their hotel room phone. The hotel had given them a new phone with an actual cord that actually plugged into the actual wall, replacing the phone that Remo claimed was already broken in two when they checked in, honestly.

"What phone?" Chiun asked. The old Korean was watching the sun sink out over the Caribbean.

"Ha, ha," Remo said. "Come on, where is it?"

"I lost it."

"Right," Remo droned. He gave up, hanging up

the phone. "Looks like we're stuck here tonight. What say we put our best clothespins on and go out to dinner?"

Still wearing a look of serious contemplation, Chiun nodded agreement. The two of them headed out the door.

The moment they stepped out into the hall, someone tried to shoot Remo in the head.

"What the hell?" he snarled, whirling. A bullet whizzed an inch from his ear, burying deep in the hallway wall.

At the far end of the corridor, two men in dark suits braced themselves in doorways, guns aimed at Remo and Chiun.

They seemed surprised to have missed with the first shot. Both men began squeezing off rounds. Silenced bullets sang left and right around the two Masters of Sinanju.

"I thought we were done," Remo griped, dodging bullets as he turned to his teacher. "Who are *these* guys?"

"They are dressed like the two braying fanatics who intruded on my peace yesterday," Chiun replied.

"I thought those guys didn't say anything."

As hot lead sliced the air around his frail form, Chiun waved an impatient hand. "They might have. I have weighty issues of my own to consider. I do not have time to entertain the wrong thoughts of every door-to-door religious crackpot who intrudes on my peace."

"Religious?" Remo asked, frowning.

Chiun was tapping his foot impatiently. "Are we eating or aren't we?"

"Smith gave us the okay to get out of Stench-burg," Remo mused. "If someone wants to kill us, they're going to have to follow us back home."

He turned to the gunmen who were still trying to shoot them. "Sorry, boys," he called to the increasingly frustrated men, "but we're officially off duty."

As the bullets ran dry, Remo and Chiun headed down the hall in the opposite direction. Leaving the baffled gunmen helplessly reloading, the two Masters of Sinanju ducked into the stairwell and were gone.

AFTER HOURS SPENT at the docks of New Briton, a tired but triumphant Petrovina Bulganin returned to her small hotel room flushed with success.

She had accomplished much more than her mission's original objective. Not only had she proved the *Novgorod* was behind the scow sinkings, she had also captured it. The renegade submarine had been stopped, its crew was in custody and—as a bonus—former Premier Nikolai Garbegtrov had been collected and quietly locked away at the Russian embassy.

In a serious crisis, Petrovina had both proved her own mettle and demonstrated the effectiveness of the Institute to Russia's male-dominated espionage community.

Yes, Remo and Chiun had helped. But no one need ever know the extent of the American agents' involvement. Vlad Korkusku wouldn't talk. Who would believe him if he did? The same with his men.

They would be laughingstocks if they mentioned any of what they had seen. Thrown out of the SVR. No, this was Petrovina Bulganin's victory to savor.

She pulled her suitcase from the closet floor, setting it on her bed. Removing her laptop from a zippered flap, she sat down at the small writing desk.

Since the ground lines were useless and she was now without a cell phone, her computer's satellite hookup was the only way she could check in with the Institute. As she booted up her computer, she thought of her special cell phone. Another exultant smile passed her full lips.

Even an unplanned accident had worked out in her favor. Everything about this assignment was working out perfectly.

When she checked her mail she found several urgent notes from Director Chutesov. Checking the time, she found that the first was already many hours old.

As Petrovina scanned the first note, her smile of triumph slowly faded. By the time she finished the second and third notes—written by Director Chutesov on a flight from Moscow—Petrovina's hands were shaking.

They were still shaking as she stabbed out the number to Remo's room. The internal lines worked. The phone rang and rang without answer. Woodenly she hung up.

Petrovina fumbled in the suitcase pocket where her computer had been hidden away. For a moment she didn't seem to know what to do with the pistol she pulled out. Finally she stuffed it in her belt, zipping her jacket up over it.

When she stepped numbly from the room a moment later, the usually efficient Petrovina Bulganin didn't even notice that she had left her computer on and the door wide-open.

26

Captain Gennady Zhilnikov was lying on the bunk in his New Briton prison cell when he heard the distant clacking of footsteps far up the corridor beyond the iron door.

Zhilnikov tuned out the sound.

People had been coming and going all afternoon. Ever since he and his men were brought here by the local authorities. There had been local and federal police. The Russian ambassador stopped by, voicing disapproval of this whole affair. One of the SVR agents who had been on the boat that helped capture the *Novgorod*—an SVR neanderthal named Vlad Korkusku—came by with the ambassador. He growled and threatened and puffed out his chest in the way only old KGB could do. When he left, Korkusku told Gennady Zhilnikov that he was looking forward to seeing him back in Moscow.

Now, hours later, hands behind his head as he stared up at the springs of the empty bunk above him, Captain Zhilnikov smiled. As prison cells went, this one was not so bad. In fact, it was more spacious than his quarters on the *Novgorod*.

Despite Vlad Korkusku's bluster, things were not

as dire as they could be. Zhilnikov had chosen the right time to go mad. With all eyes focused on Mayana, there was no way the Mayanans would deal harshly with their prisoners. Even a return to Moscow would not necessarily be the end. Ten years ago death would have been certain. Now? Who knew?

He had been told that the Russian government was already working to extradite the crew of the *Novgorod*. If they succeeded, the cell he would end up in would be nowhere near as pleasant as his current accommodations.

Zhilnikov didn't care so much about himself. He was more concerned about the treatment of his men.

Still, the most important thing of all was that revenge had been served. There were cameras waiting when he arrived at shore. He shouted Garbegtrov's name at all of them. Although Zhilnikov hadn't heard anything yet, the former premier was certainly disgraced by now.

The captain of the *Novgorod* was smiling once more when he heard keys jangling outside his door.

The cell door swung open. Two men in suits loomed in the doorway.

"Get up. You're coming with us."

Zhilnikov assumed he was being brought before some sort of magistrate. Climbing out of his bunk—which was more comfortable than his old worn mattress back on the *Novgorod*—he followed the two men out of the cell.

When he saw some of his men already standing in the hall, Zhilnikov frowned. There were more Mayanans in suits in the dank corridor. They were turning keys in locks, releasing the rest of the Russian submarine crew.

"What is meaning of this?" Zhilnikov asked.

"It's judgment day," the Mayanan replied. "And you fellows have bought yourselves a front-row seat."

Puzzled, Zhilnikov looked to his men.

The Mayanans had drawn handguns. They were waving the weapons at the sailors, herding them together and steering them toward an open rear door. The door didn't lead to the main street. Zhilnikov saw an alley wall. The men began shuffling out into the late-afternoon sun.

"I am confused," Gennady Zhilnikov said, hesitantly trailing his men. "Are we going before judge now?"

At this, the Mayanans shared a wicked smile.

"You're going before the *ultimate* judge," one promised. "And woe to you sinners, his wrath shall be great."

With a rough shove between the shoulder blades, the Mayanans propelled Captain Gennady Zhilnikov out the prison door and into the lengthening afternoon shadows.

27

By the time Remo and Chiun finished supper, dusk was sweeping away the last of lingering daylight.

He'd asked for recommendations from the hotel staff. Their restaurant was near the dock where the *Novgorod* had been brought. Remo parked his rented car near a seaside bar that had been built on a pier above the gently lapping waters of a deep inlet. The windows of the bar had been recently boarded up. A closed sign hung on the door.

The inlet was home to a large marina that was virtually abandoned. There were no people to be seen. Unused pleasure boats lined both shores. The houses on the far side were walled and gated. Remo saw for-sale signs on many of them.

It was no wonder. Junk from the scows that had sunk in the Caribbean had washed in to shore. Garbage from around the world clogged the beaches. Chunks of Styrofoam, plastic bottles and other trash floated atop the sparkling water.

"Tough luck for anyone who bought retirement property down here," Remo commented as he and Chiun strolled the sidewalk along the shore. "Although, actually the climate's pretty good. If the land's selling for cheap enough, maybe we should relocate the entire population of Sinanju here. It's a lot warmer, and the shit smell isn't half as bad.''

He glanced at his teacher for the reaction his Sinanju-bashing usually provoked.

Padding along beside him, Chiun wore a concerned frown. Through the afternoon and into early evening, the old man's expression hadn't changed. It had started when he answered the cell phone Remo had found in the hotel hallway.

''I have a dream,'' Remo announced all at once.

''If I give you a dollar, will you promise to keep it to yourself?'' the old man asked blandly.

Remo was undeterred. ''I have a dream,'' he repeated, ''that one day you'll let me in on everything. I have a dream that you won't just make me memorize every Master of Sinanju without telling me their legends, just so you can dish the stories out on a need-to-know basis. I have a dream you'll let me in on what kind of contract you cut with Smith. I have a dream you'll let me know exactly what you're planning for your retirement, so I don't wake up one morning to find you've gone back to Korea forever. But mostly I have a dream that now that I'm Reigning Master of Sinanju, you'll finally let me in on all those tiny little everyday secrets you've insisted on keeping from me for the past thirty years.''

Chiun nodded thoughtfully as Remo spoke, giving weighty consideration to his pupil's words. When Remo was finished, the former Reigning Master of the House of Sinanju raised his wattled neck from his kimono collar. He turned as if to address an equal, not a student. And he did say, in low and serious tones, "Keep dreaming, round eyes."

"Why am I not surprised?" Remo said with a shrug.

"As long as we are on the subject of desires, I would live in an ideal world where I would have trained a pupil who trusted his Master enough to mind his own business."

"In an ideal world Julio Iglesias would have been born sterile. We play the hand we're dealt."

As they closed in on their car, Remo noted something in the air that was more than just the omnipresent odor of garbage. Soft pressure waves were directed at the two men.

"For cripes' sake, not again," he complained.

Up ahead, Remo caught sight of a man in a suit lurking behind a bunch of shrubs. He recognized him as one of the gunmen who had attacked them outside their hotel room. He spied the other man behind some drying fishing nets.

"What did you say those guys you killed yesterday were—religious fanatics?" he asked Chiun. "What did you mean?"

"They mentioned something about suffering the wrath of their deity. In truth I did not listen to all they said. The selling moments were over and my show had begun again. Besides, I would give audience to a Calcutta leper before I would an American who knocks on my door to discuss religion."

"American? What makes you think that?"

"The rudeness? The smell? The big mouths? Stop

me when you hear something you do not already know.''

Remo was only half listening. Through narrowed eyes, he noted that another figure had joined the party.

Up ahead, a man was snooping around Remo's car.

As he lurked, Vlad Korkusku scowled at the world as only ex-KGB agents could. When he spied Remo and Chiun coming toward him, the scowl flashed to dread.

''Hello, American friend who frightens me,'' said Vlad Korkusku, slapping on an insincere smile.

''I'm not your friend. And if you're the one trying to kill us, you're going to get the Chernobyl of wedgies.''

''Kill you? No, no. Am not killing you,'' Vlad Korkusku insisted. ''Hotel worker said I could find you here. I have come with message from Agent Bulganin. She is in needing of your assistance.''

''Soon as I get a thanks for the first twenty times I helped her in the last two days, I'll consider it. Until then, Mother Russia can take a flying leap.''

The SVR agent was standing in his way. Remo picked up the big man with the ease of a grandmother rearranging the wicker furniture. He set Korkusku to one side.

''Is important,'' Korkusku pleaded. ''I was away from embassy for a time. Only just found message she left. She did not give full details for sake of security. Just said that there was great danger and to find you if I could, and to reassemble my squad if I could not. She took only one SVR agent with her to presidential palace. I have to be coming to *Novgorod* to round up rest.''

''Yeah?'' Remo scowled. He turned to his teacher. ''Say, Chiun, maybe they don't care about us at all. Maybe they followed this schmuck.''

''They are not watching him—they are watching us,'' the old Korean pointed out.

Korkusku was confused. ''Who is watching who?''

''The killers who have us surrounded,'' Remo said, peeved. ''Do you mind?''

Startled, Vlad Korkusku reached under his jacket. He found an empty holster. He looked pleadingly at Remo.

''No, I am not telling you where I hid your guns,'' Remo said impatiently. ''If you've got the urge to kill and maim, use a Russian cookbook. Besides, they don't want you. Now beat it. I've had it with cleaning up bodies.''

Korkusku didn't seem to know what to do. With great reluctance—and all the while studying the growing shadows—he left Remo and Chiun to get in their car.

The SVR man got no more than a few feet when there came a sharp pop. His black shoes skidded on pavement. There was a gasp that seemed strangled in his throat.

Korkusku spun back to Remo and Chiun, a look of panicked bafflement on his sagging face. One hand was clutched to his chest. Blood gurgled between his fingers.

''Crap,'' Remo said. ''Never a minute's peace.''

This time when the men opened fire on him, Remo

didn't head in the opposite direction. With an angry frown he headed straight for the gunman in the bushes.

The man took careful aim at Remo and fired. When he missed—and continued missing—he grew more and more panicked. With one bullet left and realizing now that there was no chance of hitting the stranger he had been sent to kill, the man sprang abruptly to his feet.

"Brother, the rapture is upon us!" he cried.

And, placing the barrel of his gun against his own temple, he pulled the trigger.

The man on the dock followed suit. By the time Remo reached them, the gunmen were two twitching corpses.

Remo checked for ID. Like the men in their hotel room, they had none. He returned to his teacher's side.

"You were right, Little Father," Remo said. "That guy wasn't Mayanan. He sounded like he was from the Midwest."

There was a gurgle from the ground. He went over to where Vlad Korkusku was gasping for breath on the pavement.

When Remo saw the condition of the SVR man's wound, he frowned morosely. "Too bad."

"I am going to die?" the Russian pleaded.

"Worse for me. You're gonna make it." He shook his head. "Life. Always it's gotta make more work for Remo."

Scooping the Russian agent off the ground, he dumped him like a sack of Ukrainian beets in the back of his rented car.

28

The President of the United States leaned in close to hear the whispered words of his chief of staff.

As he listened, he tried not to chew the inside of his cheek. His wife had been on him to stop this old habit, which the Washington press corps had dubbed a smirk.

The press held the smirk up as proof positive that this President was an unserious frat boy who had somehow stumbled into his role as national leader. Which was strange, really, because the same press that dubbed this President unserious for a smirk found very serious his immediate predecessor, a man who had devoted so much time and energy to exposing himself to women during his time in office that once—after one exhausting, zipper-free summer vacation on Cape Cod—naval doctors at Bethesda had had to apply sunburn ointment to his very raw, tenderest of presidential areas. But that was then and this was now and this grown-up President who had learned from his mommy as a very little boy how to keep his belt buckled and his pants up at his waist was regularly eviscerated by the Washington press for his unserious smirk.

"I'm not sure who he was," the chief of staff was saying. He kept his voice pitched low. "But he had clearance. He wanted to talk directly to you."

"Let me guess," the President said, exhaling unhappily. "General Smith, right?"

"No," the chief of staff said, a hint of surprise in his voice. "Undersecretary Smith, actually. With the Treasury Department. You know him?"

"Just by reputation," the President replied.

"Oh. Well, I don't know who he is, and neither do any of the Secret Service here. He's in their database as a Treasury employee, but when I had them check out his office they said it was a storage closet."

"He doesn't have a regular office there," the President said, vaguely uncomfortable. "He's more of a floater."

"Oh." The chief of staff seemed to expect a more complete answer, but when he saw one was not forthcoming he forged ahead. "Well, it's just lucky the treasury secretary was with us to confirm this wasn't one of his regular staff. Otherwise they might have dragged you out of here."

"I'm not going anywhere," the President said firmly.

The chief of staff nodded. "I knew that," he said. "I just thought you should know. He sounded so serious. Like it really was life and death. But as long as you seem to know, I suppose everything's okay. Excuse me, sir."

The chief of staff hurried over to confer with the chief executive's press secretary.

As soon as he left the president's side, yet another group of men came up to shake the President's hand. The President politely obliged.

He couldn't begin to guess how many hands he had shaken since arriving in Mayana earlier that afternoon. Hundreds since that first handshake at the airport with Executive President Blythe Curry-Hume. There would be hundreds—perhaps thousands—more before this Globe Summit was over.

As he shook the hands of a delegation from a country that regularly denounced the United States at the UN, he considered his chief of staff's message.

The President wasn't surprised his chief of staff would be concerned. The man who had called had access to his private number and knew all the special codes. And the President himself might actually have been concerned. That was, if he had not been expecting the call.

So far the President had had members of his staff bring warnings to him from General Smith, Special Agent Smith, Field Director Smith and now Undersecretary Smith.

The President had to hand it to Dr. Harold W. Smith. The director of CURE was tenacious.

Smith had expressed reservations about the President's plan to attend the Globe Summit right from the start. His concern had only grown more acute these past few days. With the capture of the Russian submarine, the older man had relaxed some of his concerns. But now, not one day later, he had doubtless found yet another reason for the President to cut short his visit.

The President was not about to leave. Yes, there was potential danger in coming to South America. But the greatest threat had obviously been the rogue submarine off Mayana's coast, and that had been dealt with. According to intelligence, the Russian government was telling the truth. It was not behind the sub attacks. The Globe Summit was as safe—and as dangerous—as everywhere else in the world. The President of the United States couldn't alter his schedule based on undefined risk or he would spend his entire tenure in office hiding in a bombproof cave under the Rockies.

"Mr. President?"

The voice intruded on the President's private thoughts. He had been shaking hands with members of the Chinese delegation. He looked up to find Mayana's executive president standing before him. Some of the other world leaders had begun to gather around him.

"We're nearly ready for the demonstration," Blythe Curry-Hume said. "I'm sure you will find it fascinating."

With a friendly sweep of his arm, Jack James herded the world leaders through a nearby gate.

As he followed the Jamestown cult leader through the gates to the deck of the Vaporizer area, the President of the United States concentrated on controlling the smirk that so bedeviled and delighted members of the fourth estate.

REMO DUMPED Vlad Korkusku at the hospital in downtown New Briton around the corner from the presidential palace. After the injured Russian was wheeled off to surgery, Remo decided to try Smith again.

This time he didn't even bother to ask Chiun for the cell phone he was sure was still stashed up the old man's robes. Chiun was acting too weird and possessive to even try arguing. He went off and scraped up his own phone. He was back in a minute. He was happy when he managed to open it but stood blankly staring at the buttons for a long moment.

"Do you know what you are doing?" Chiun asked.

The two men stood near the glass-enclosed entrance to the emergency room. Outside, streetlights were winking on.

"Of course I do," Remo said. "A phone's a phone." He stared at the cell phone for a few more seconds.

"You have to press those little buttons," Chiun offered.

"I know that," Remo snapped.

He pressed some of the little buttons. Nothing happened.

"Nothing happened," Chiun pointed out.

Remo gave him a withering look. He tried pressing the buttons again, this time in a different combination. Still nothing. Frustrated, Remo collared a passing doctor and asked him for help.

"I think it's broken or the batteries are dead or something," Remo said as the balding man took the phone.

"No, no," the physician said with a helpful smile.

"See this little button here? You've got to hold that down for four seconds before you can make a call. That way it won't accidentally turn on if it's jostling around in your pocket. See? You're ready to make a call now. It's not that complicated really. I've got the same model."

"Thanks," Remo said, taking the cell phone back and feeling a little guilty for the fact that this nice and helpful man actually no longer had a phone like this one, since it was his pocket Remo had swiped the phone from in the first place.

Through some miracle he was able to place the call. He was amazed when Smith answered.

"Remo, thank God," the CURE director blurted, his tart voice straining with barely controlled panic.

When he heard Smith's tone, Remo's brow furrowed.

"What's wrong?"

"My God, he's still alive," Smith spluttered. "No one knows it. I tried to contact the President, but he will not take my calls. I almost issued a warning through some of the other governments there, but who would believe it? It sounds too incredible. But it's true. My God, I was helpless. If word got out, he might be alerted and do something rash."

"Deep breaths, Smitty. He who?"

"*Jack James,*" Smith insisted. "He didn't commit suicide with his cult at Jamestown. He is still alive."

Remo took a second to absorb the CURE director's words. "Is he still in Mayana?" he asked.

Smith blurted the whole story, as quickly and concisely as was humanly possible. When he was finished, Remo didn't bother to say goodbye. He tossed the phone into a trash can and whirled to his teacher.

Chiun had heard everything. His parchment face held a look of deep concern.

"Next time I say I'm bored just hanging around Sinanju, remind me to take up basket weaving," Remo said.

Side by side, the two men raced out the emergency-room door and into the warm South American night.

THE WORLD LEADERS were asked to leave their entourages out in the parking lot. There was only a limited number of protective boots to go around, they were told, and this test would be a nice shared moment for the men who held the environmental fate of the world in all their hands.

The Vaporizer was just as most of them had seen on television. The black deck was surrounded on all sides by a wall made out of the same material that lined the pit. A chain-link fence prevented the men and women from falling in.

"What you witness here today is something the world will talk about long after you have all turned to dust," Executive President Blythe Curry-Hume promised as he ushered the last of the world leaders out onto the deck. "If you will all step to the fence. We will be ready to begin momentarily."

The President of the United States fell in with the prime minister of Britain and the president of Russia.

The first few leaders had reached the fence. A ripple of confusion passed through the group as they looked in the pit. As the men and women glanced at one another—muttering in dozens of languages—another sound rose above them.

The President heard the muted sound of shouting voices.

"What's that?" he asked.

America's chief executive and the others hurried to the fence at the edge of the pit. When they looked down inside the Vaporizer, they were stunned to find not garbage, but human faces staring up at them.

Captain Gennady Zhilnikov and the rest of the crew of the ill-fated *Novgorod* looked pleadingly up at the world leaders.

"What is the meaning of this?" the President demanded. "Is this supposed to be some kind of sick joke?"

He turned to look for Mayanan Executive President Blythe Curry-Hume. Only then did he see that the black door had slid silently shut behind them, sealing them in. In the crowd of confused world leaders he didn't see the face of Mayana's executive president. And then he heard Curry-Hume's voice. It boomed at them over the public-address system.

"'And there was given to him the key of the bottomless pit,'" Curry-Hume recited in a tone suited more to a carnival revival meeting than a summit of world leaders. "'And he opened the bottomless pit and there came up smoke out of the pit like the smoke of a great furnace; and the sun and air were darkened by the smoke of the pit.'"

The President felt his blood run cold. There was

no way out. The door was sealed. He glanced into the pit.

The crew of the *Novgorod* was growing more frantic. Some clawed at the walls. The President now saw why. The lights in the walls had gone from a dull glow to a brilliant white. The deck beneath their feet hummed with energy.

"'For they are spirits of demons working signs,'" Blythe Curry-Hume shouted, "'and they go forth unto the kings of the whole earth to gather them together for the battle on the great day of God almighty.' That day is upon us!"

There was a flash. White and all-consuming. And in a series of pops so fast they seemed to happen simultaneously, the crew of the *Novgorod* vanished from sight.

Even as understanding of what had just happened was sinking in, the world leaders had a fresh shock.

All around the upper deck, little pressurized caps began popping off the walls, one at a time. Beneath the caps winked on the sightless eyes of glowing nozzles.

The realization fell softly over the crowd like a settling shroud. And like the crew of the *Novgorod,* many of the leaders of the world screamed and ran for the walls.

"'And there came forth a loud voice out of the temple from the throne, saying, "It has come to pass!"'" the man who had been Jack James cried out with joy.

And at the edge of the upper deck, a few of the leaders who held their ground—the President of the

United States included—watched with stoic countenance as the little lights continued to twinkle to life in the walls all around.

REMO'S CAR SQUEALED to a stop at the rear gate of the Mayanan presidential mansion. As it rocked on its shocks, he and Chiun were already out the doors and racing to the gate.

Two uniformed guards tried to stop them. Remo put them to sleep and dumped them in the bushes while Chiun kicked open the gate. The old man swirled inside, Remo behind him.

They met no other guards on their way to the building.

"I don't like the looks of this," Remo said. "This place is like a ghost town."

"The Reigning Master of Sinanju Emeritus fears neither ghosts nor living men," Chiun intoned.

Ducking beneath the shadow of a long canopy, the old Korean cracked the shatterproof doors that led into the mansion. Sheets of bulletproof glass imploded, crashing to the floor and scattering like glistening sand.

The sound finally attracted attention. Guards came running up the hall, rifles aimed at the two men who were charging toward them.

"Emeritus?" Remo asked as the men opened fire. He twisted and twirled around volleys of screaming lead.

"It is a title conferred on Masters who, while technically on the edge of the Time of Seclusion, still actively ply their trade," Chiun explained.

The guards were upon them. There were seven of them. Some dropped their rifles in favor of handguns. Others tried hand-to-hand attacks.

"How come I never heard of this before?" Remo asked suspiciously as he slapped a palm into a soldier's forehead. The man's eyes rolled back in his head and he slumped unconscious to the floor.

"If I am now expected to catalog those things which you do not know, I will have to plead with the gods to extend my life by another five hundred years," the old Korean replied. Darting hands slipped past the defenses of two charging, screaming men. Slender fingers pressed two throats and the men collapsed.

They made short work of the remaining guards.

Leaving the men asleep on the floor, the two Masters of Sinanju flew for the stairs.

They found the presidential suite of offices all but deserted. Only one heartbeat issued from a back room. Remo kicked the door open. It screamed off its hinges, cracking to kindling against the far wall.

The Mayanan president's office was empty.

They traced the heartbeat to a locked bathroom. Inside, Petrovina Bulganin was bound and gagged on the floor. The Russian agent had shattered the vanity mirror and was using a fragment to saw through the ropes at her wrists. Her hands and forearms were covered in blood.

On the floor near her was the male SVR agent she had brought along to help. The man had not fared as well as Petrovina. His skull had been fractured in several places. The body was rolled toward the wall.

When the door burst open, Petrovina looked up with fear. Her face quickly collapsed into relief.

Chiun cut the ropes at her ankles and wrists with his long fingernails while Remo removed her gag.

"Jack James!" she exhaled the instant the gag was loose. "He is alive!"

"Not for much longer," Remo replied coldly. "You know where he is? This place is deserted."

"He has gone to the Vaporizer site," Petrovina said, scrambling to her feet. "He was keeping me alive for his pleasure later on. I heard his plans. He will claim to give them a demonstration, but he intends to murder them all."

"Murder who?" Remo asked.

"Every leader in the world who is in Mayana," she answered. "World will be thrown into chaos. Governments will collapse. Panic could destabilize entire continents." There was a look of terrified urgency on her face.

"Every leader in the world, you say?" Remo asked, sitting down on the closed toilet lid.

"Yes," Petrovina replied sharply. *"Hurry."*

She was edging anxiously for the door.

"Don't rush me," said Remo. "I'm thinking."

29

From the window of the Vaporizer control shed, Jack James watched the frightened little men who thought they ruled the world. As the caps popped off the fully functioning upper level of the device and the lights of doom glowed brighter, the men and women tore at the walls. They screamed and climbed over one another in blind panic.

The walls were too smooth. There were no handholds. Thanks to distance and the weird soundproofing quality of the frictionless walls, their yelling wouldn't be heard by their staffs and the press gathered out in the parking lot.

Their cell phones had been confiscated. They'd been told that the devices could interfere with the operation of the Vaporizer. Trusting, wicked fools.

As the little men ran around in fear, James smiled.

The sheep were scattering.

The history of this day would be written in blood on scrolls for wicked mankind. They would call it Judgment Day. The day that he, Jack James—*Almighty* Jack James—punished the evildoers for their sins and washed clean the face of the earth. It was the Flood, the rapture, the expulsion from Paradise.

All the sins of the world were concentrated in the hands of these, the stewards of this modern Sodom.

With a calm that chilled the cold air-conditioned room, Jack James glanced down at the control monitor. The power levels were nearly at maximum. Only a few minutes more.

He was glad he had told them to simplify the Vaporizer commands. At the moment he was the only one there who could operate the device.

In the corner of the room lay Mike Sears.

When he realized what the executive president of Mayana had in store for the crew of the *Novgorod,* the Milquetoast American scientist had grown a backbone. It hadn't been enough to withstand the mighty rod of persuasion.

James's precious cane hung on the edge of a table. He had kept it throughout his years in exile. Through a life of adversity and persecution.

Blood dribbled down from the scientist's forehead. Sears was unconscious. For his disloyalty, James would finish him off when this was over. Just a few minutes more.

James sat down in Sears's well-worn chair to await the end. As he watched, the last of the little lights continued to come to life. Just as the very first light had been brought into existence on that first long-ago day, the day Almighty Jack James created the heavens and the earth.

THE ROAD UP to the Vaporizer was jammed with abandoned cars. Buses were being used to cart reporters and lesser dignitaries to the site. When Remo and Chiun arrived with Petrovina, they found that only VIP limos were being allowed past the yellow sawhorses.

"They took my purse with my diplomatic identification back at presidential palace," Petrovina said, frustrated. "Have you ID?"

Remo was hardly listening as he glanced around. "My dog ate it," he said.

"There is no way we will get in," Petrovina said.

"I hope you are listening to this, Remo," Chiun said. "You who would invite all manner of Russian trailer trucks to drive into your bed should realize that if you make a baby with this one, it will inherit not only its mother's mustache and swollen ankles, it will get that optimism for which all Russians are famous."

Remo was looking down the road. "Not all Russians are bad, Little Father," he said absently. "Anna was okay."

Face tight, Petrovina glanced sharply at Remo.

"That's right," Chiun said. "Drive the knife deeper into your poor old father's dying heart."

A limousine was driving up from New Briton. It had diplomatic plates. One of the attendees of the Globe Summit was arriving late for the Vaporizer test.

When the car drew past them, Remo reached over and popped open a rear door while Chiun opened the driver's door.

Remo found himself looking into the familiar bushy-bearded face of the president of Communist Cuba.

Remo had met the man years before. There was a flash of recognition. When he opened his mouth to scream, his cigar flopped out, scattering burning ash on his drab fatigues.

"Glad we don't need a reintroduction," Remo said. "C'mon, Fuzzy, move it *o muerte*."

Unseen by the roadblocks up ahead, Remo dragged the Cuban leader out of the car, stuffing him in the trunk.

By the time he got in the back seat, Chiun had already persuaded the driver to continue without question. The Cuban behind the wheel was driving with one hand. The other arm hung limp at his side. He gritted his teeth against the pain.

They kept the tinted windows rolled up tight.

Remo, Chiun and Petrovina were waved through the roadblocks and onto the main grounds. At the site they abandoned the limo, racing for the fenced-in Vaporizer.

The two Masters of Sinanju could already feel the thrum of power from the machine. It was the same buildup they'd felt during the test two days previous.

"It's close to going off," Remo warned.

Luckily the rest of the dignitaries and reporters had been herded into the visitors' center. There were only a few guards and security personnel near the main gate. When they saw the small trio racing toward them, the men drew guns.

There was no time to argue. Remo and Chiun swept into their midst, fingers and palms putting to sleep all who came at them. As the men toppled left and right, Remo yelled over his shoulder at Petrovina.

"Get to the control booth! Try to shut it down!"

She nodded, scooping up the pistol of a fallen Secret Service agent. She ran through the open gate and up the narrow, fenced-in corridor that separated the main driveway from the exterior Vaporizer wall.

Remo and Chiun quickly removed the remaining guards. The last man had not yet hit the ground when they were flying through the fence to the Vaporizer wall. Near the bin with the protective boots waited Jack James's disciples.

Only eight of the twelve remained. They had been ordered to hold their ground and not let anyone inside.

"The Lord shall punish the wicked!" one man shouted as the group assembled around Remo and Chiun, weapons drawn.

"Show of hands for whoever has heard enough of that crapola," Remo said. One hand rose. It, as well as the arm that went with it, was no longer attached to its owner.

Remo tossed the arm to the ground, taking out the one-armed gunman with a sweeping toe. He and Chiun flew through the rest. When the last disciple had fallen, the two Masters of Sinanju raced to the sealed Vaporizer door.

They could feel the hum coming through the black wall.

"Stay here, Little Father," Remo said.

The old man shook his head. "We go together."

"Can't risk it. Not both of us in there."

"I expect your superior knowledge of garbage to save me," the wizened Korean sniffed, reaching for the door.

"This isn't a debate," Remo snapped. "I'm Reigning Master. It's my decision. I *need* you out here."

Chiun saw the look of determination on his pupil's face. Jaw tightening, the Reigning Master of Sinanju Emeritus nodded sharp agreement. "Have a care," he warned.

Despite his concern, Chiun felt his heart swell. It was a moment of great import. Significant not just in Sinanju, but throughout the history of mankind. Fathers and sons. The passing of authority from one generation to the next.

Remo didn't seem to realize it. Like all the young, he was too concerned with the present.

Remo's face was grim. Whirling, the latest Reigning Master of Sinanju reached for the door.

THE PRESIDENT of the United States never dreamed he would meet his end like this.

Mayanan Executive President Blythe Curry-Hume had apparently gone insane. The President could see the crazed man's shadowy face peering down from the control booth.

There was nowhere to go. No way to call for help. The President and the other world leaders were effectively standing inside the Vaporizer. The President had seen the device being demonstrated on television. He understood what was about to happen to all of them.

Many of the others couldn't seem to accept the inevitable. Across the deck they kicked and screamed, pummeling one another with fists as they pounded on the door.

As the lights glowed brighter all around, the President stood his ground, determined to meet his end as a man.

In his mind he recited the Lord's Prayer. He didn't know he was speaking the words aloud until he heard the prime minister of Great Britain saying them alongside him.

The two men glanced at each other. The President gave a smile and a sharp nod. As he did so, he heard fresh shouts from over near the sliding door.

The other world leaders were backing fearfully away from the door, babbling in dozens of languages.

As the President watched, hope tripping deep inside his chest, the door began to bow inward. The regimented lines of glowing lights stretched out across the bubbling surface.

With a shriek the door burst off its sliding track. Men scattered. Trailing wires, the door slid across the deck, bouncing off the chain-link fence and skittering away.

A man appeared behind it. With dark, deep-set eyes, he viewed the stumbling, panicked world leadership.

''There's six billion people out here who'll probably want to lynch me for this,'' Remo Williams grumbled.

And with an unhappy scowl, Remo grabbed the collars of two nearby diplomats.

With a sharp tug, the chief of government of the Principality of Liechtenstein and the president of South Africa were dropped to their backsides. The deck was black ice. The two men zipped across the frictionless surface and disappeared through the opening.

And like a shot, Remo launched himself out on the deck.

He had not donned a pair of frictionless boots. Forward momentum carried him on sliding soles.

He snagged the prime minister of Niger and the president of Honduras. Both men were launched back across the deck.

Outside the open doorway, Chiun grabbed these two as he had the first. The old Korean stopped them, stacked them to one side and spun back just in time to accept the next pair.

Inside the Vaporizer, Remo was picking up speed. They flew in his wake—blurs of presidents, prime ministers, princes and kings. He banked off each set, changing direction in a slivered second, flying off to the next.

By the time he reached the President of the United States, prime minister of England and president of Russia, Remo was a barely visible blur.

Each man felt a sharp tug. In the next instant he was flying through the door of the Vaporizer and into the flashing hands of the former Reigning Master of Sinanju.

And in a flash Remo was off to the next set of world leaders, ever mindful of the awesome man-made power that was swelling up all around him.

AT FIRST JACK JAMES didn't see the commotion down on the upper level of the Vaporizer. He had been preoccupied watching the monitor. The device was nearly powered up.

When he glanced down, he blinked in shock. There were fewer men than had been there just a moment before.

Impossible. There was no way out. He had sealed the door himself. They couldn't have broken out. And yet there were definitely fewer world leaders on the deck.

As he watched in amazement, more vanished.

It couldn't be. The device wasn't yet ready.

Blurs across the deck. On the security camera he caught sight of men appearing through the door. The *open* door.

In that moment the impossible registered in his dull mind. Something was throwing the men to safety.

There was still a way. He had hoped to savor his victory, hoped to live to tell the tale. But the fools didn't know. Jack James would go, but he would take them all with him. And Jack James was eternal. Jack James was light. Yes, he would die this day but, after, he would live forever in glory while all the other, lesser beings were thrown into the dark, there to wail and gnash their teeth.

A light flashed green. The Vaporizer was at full power. James reached for the keyboard, tapping a single key. The instant he did so, a voice shouted at his back.

"Step away!"

James wheeled.

Petrovina Bulganin stood in the control booth, her pistol trained on the infamous Jamestown cult leader.

James smiled a twisted grin of triumph.

"Too late!" he cried, laughing maniacally. "You can shoot me if you want, but you are all dead! They told me the machine needs to remain perfectly balanced. With the door missing, it's not. When it goes off, the Vaporizer will consume itself, this hill, these grounds and every last one of us. I've won."

For an instant Petrovina Bulganin weighed her options.

Abruptly she turned the barrel of her gun from James, aiming it at the upright computer nearest the Mayanan president. Petrovina unloaded her clip into the hard drive.

Sparks exploded in the small room. There was a spluttering hiccup in the swelling hum of power.

"No!" James flew to the window. He didn't care that the Russian woman whom he'd carelessly left alive back at his presidential palace turned and ran from the control room. Didn't care about anything but his failed act of vengeance.

He had been too slow. As he watched, the lights in the upper level dimmed. The newer section would shut down first. The lower level still glowed brilliant white.

Not that it mattered. The deck was clear.

He saw something rocketing toward the pit. It had the blurry shape of a man.

For an instant as it struck the fence that surrounded the lower level, James saw a face frozen in time. The dark eyes of the Angel of Death himself stared deep into the cold black soul of Jack James.

The fence bowed out over the pit.

The lights still glowed bright. There was a flash.

And the man with the face of doom promptly disappeared. Vaporized into oblivion.

30

The force needed to hurl the final world leader out to safety created an opposite reaction that had to be channeled somewhere. Remo used it to propel himself back toward the fence that surrounded the deep Vaporizer pit.

Up and out into empty air.

The soles of his loafers hit the chain link, bowing it out over the pit. Brilliant white lights glowed beneath him. The charge of ionized particles filled the air. But the true forces of nature could not be known to mere machines.

Remo was a full Master of Sinanju, his body trained to the perfection that lived unrealized in all men.

Out over empty air, the vast blackness of certain death stretched out beneath him, Remo Williams, Reigning Master of the House of Sinanju, felt the world flood his senses. And to every last atom, all was right and perfect.

The fence was a bow that launched him like an arrow back across the deck.

At a speed even his teacher could not follow, Remo was out through the doors. The shaken world leaders who stood with the old Korean felt little more than a hiss of violent wind as he zoomed through their midst.

Down the path he flew, banking up along the inside of the chain-link fence. He was up the stairs and in the control room even as Jack James was still registering his disappearance from below.

When the cult leader saw Remo appear before him the instant after he had seen Remo disappear from down below, his eyes grew wide. He fell back, shocked.

''You can't be alive,'' James gasped.

''Said one dead man to another,'' Remo replied. ''In your case what say we make it official?''

And he lifted the cult leader off the floor.

Jack James saw the control-room window come toward him very fast. The glass shattered and he was out in empty air. And like a god, Jack James soared on angel's wings.

He flew until he fell.

All at once the lights of the Vaporizer, which had been distant, grew very large all around him.

And Jack James looked into one of the lights, and that light became very bright, and Jack James was flying toward it. And then he was one with the light. A god propelled forward on a stream of pure energy in a tunnel that was warm with the heat of his creation. For an instant Jack James was the god he always knew he was.

Then the mouth yawned open at the far end of the magnificent, light-filled tunnel.

It was not heaven waiting on the far end. For Jack James it was an altogether other place.

And in one terrible instant, a lifetime of all the pain and anguish he had ever inflicted on others was heaped upon him. And in the first moment of his ultimate fall from grace, the wonderful path of light to the kingdom that was never his collapsed behind him, sealing the distinctly ungodly Jack James in misery and torment for all eternity.

FROM THE CONTROL BOOTH, Remo watched the lights of the Vaporizer splutter and die. The pit went dark. The power hummed silent beneath his feet.

Jack James was gone. The Jamestown cult leader had disappeared in the instant just before the lights went dark.

Alone, Remo nodded satisfaction.

"Garbage in, garbage out."

Turning, he headed back out the door.

31

It was all over.

He could tell from the shouts and from the activity out near the Vaporizer. He could see it all through the tiny window in his little cinder-block shed. Security personnel from dozens of countries were swarming in. Tires squealed. Dignitaries were being hustled out to waiting cars.

Yes, it was over. At least for now.

He would find another. There was no doubt that he could. He had skills that the shadow world would pay dearly for. Jack James had been a client. Not a partner, not a visionary, not anything. There were plenty of other clients out there just like James.

The man who was thought to be a janitor, but who had been the real mind behind the Vaporizer, hastily stuffed a few items in a knapsack. A few floppy disks, some schematics. He had already destroyed his hard drives. All of the data he had stolen. He could use it to re-create his work here. Or adapt it in other ways the world would not expect.

This last thought flitted through his racing mind even as his hand brushed across an item on his workbench.

It looked like a soldering gun with a miniature satellite dish attached to the end. He picked it up to put it in its special case when a voice from behind startled him.

"You stupid fool. You stupid, stupid fool."

The woman's voice was flat with cold contempt.

Keeping his back to her, he looked up only with his eyes. He saw her reflection on the screen of his dead monitor. The beautiful woman with the blond hair was framed in the open doorway of the shed. In her hand was some sort of pistol. She had it aimed at his back.

"Did you even care what might happen?" she asked. She spoke in his native language. "I read the data. Shifting atoms like this is dangerous on a small level. An accident where a single atom materializes inside another could cause a nuclear explosion. With what you have been doing here, we are lucky all of South America wasn't blown into orbit. Or worse. You *knew* this, yet you did not care."

His hand still rested on the strange-looking gun on his desk, shielded by his body. Unseen by his guest, he lifted it, a smile brushing his pale features.

"I was paid handsomely for my skills," he admitted. "But I was not paid to care." And he whirled.

He squeezed the trigger once. But only once.

He had fired wide. Anna Chutesov did not.

Anna's bullet caught the janitor square in the chest. With a shocked look on his face, he spun on one heel. He died sprawled across his workbench.

Still scowling, Anna crossed to check the man's pulse. Satisfied that he was dead, she holstered her weapon. When she heard scuffling feet behind her, she glanced up.

"Director Chutesov!" Petrovina Bulganin exclaimed from the door. She noted the janitor's body. "Is that him?"

Anna nodded. "I came just as this confusion began," she said, aiming her chin to the bedlam out in the parking lot. "They were all more interested in spiriting their charges to safety. No one saw me come here."

She began collecting the janitor's things. She would destroy everything the first chance she got.

"Those men are here," Petrovina said. "The ones who know about your amnesia. They both seem to know you."

"Your phone?" Anna asked as she hurriedly worked.

"The old one still has it as far as I know."

"Good." The last thing Anna picked up was the strange gun the janitor had used against her. With careful blue eyes she followed the path the fired weapon had taken.

A hole as big around as a coffee mug was visible in the door frame. There was no splintering of wood. No bullet had been fired. Beyond, in the same path of the fired weapon, a similar hole had been bored through the trunk of a tree.

Anna's eyes narrowed as she studied the strange phenomenon. "I was never here," Anna Chutesov announced.

Tucking the gun into its box and tucking the box up under her arm, Anna hustled past Agent Petrovina Bulganin. And was lost in the growing confusion.

32

They drove a government Jeep up into the hills.

Mike Sears was behind the wheel, a bloody bandage wrapped around his injured head. Remo sat beside him. Chiun and Petrovina sat in the back.

When the guards at the booth saw Sears, they obediently opened the gates to the special road above the Vaporizer.

It was nearly a two-hour drive, from paved road to treacherous dirt path. All along the side of the road, even in dense jungle, ran telephone poles. Black lines of cables stretched up from far below, sometimes hidden by the jungle canopy, sometimes breaking out into stark sunlight.

"What happened to the people who put up the poles?" Remo asked Sears as they drove.

The scientist looked sickly. "I don't know," he admitted. "When they were done, they just sort of vanished. Maybe they work for a utility company in town?" His look of hope faded when he saw Remo's hard expression.

The ravine between the mountains brought them to a vast valley. Sears stopped the Jeep on a plateau above.

A sea of rotting garbage stretched out before them—every scrap of trash that had been processed through the Vaporizer from the first moment it had been switched on.

In the back seat, Petrovina turned to the scientist. "It was all hoax," she accused.

Sears nodded. There was shame on his face. "It would have taken years to fill this valley. We had plenty of room. I always figured it would be found out sooner or later, but by then everyone would be in the habit of sending their trash here and wouldn't stop. I mean, it didn't matter where it ended up as long as someone was willing to take it, right? But I guess that wasn't the plan at all." He still seemed shell-shocked from the events below. "See, the Vaporizer doesn't disintegrate trash, it just sort of moves it."

The telephone poles fanned out in either direction, forming a semicircle around the near end of the valley, connected by cables. At the top of each pole a black box that looked like a miniature outdoor speaker was directed down into the valley.

"The demolecularized trash we sent up from the Vaporizer traveled the cable and was redirected back out through those," Sears explained. As the four of them climbed out of the Jeep, he pointed up at the boxes on the poles.

In the distance some trash had materialized on trees, bending them low. In most places it had obliterated the local flora. The valley floor was a growing mountain of trash. Seagulls flew above while rats played on the piles.

"Your great work," Remo said acidly.

"I didn't invent it," Sears said defensively as he looked down on the valley. "They brought the technology to me. They needed a public face to keep the secret. I learned enough to keep it running, but I didn't come up with it."

"Yes, your secret," Petrovina spat. "That you did all this with technology stolen from Russia."

Remo had kept quiet on the subject for the ride up. He shook his head firmly.

"Only after Russia stole it from Japan," he insisted.

He spoke with utter certainty. Both Sears and Petrovina saw the confident cast of his face. As he looked out across the valley, Chiun nodded agreement.

"What are you talking about?" Petrovina demanded.

"Russia doesn't do complex, Petrovina," Remo explained. "Russia does clumsy. Tanks and trucks and missiles that rattle apart as soon as they're driven off the showroom floor. Russia can't build a toaster small enough to fit in your garage. If they can't build it with hammers, they can't build it. This was the Japanese. If you want specifics, it was the Nishitsu Corporation that came up with all this."

Both Sears and Petrovina knew the company well. Nishitsu was huge. Like most people in the West, they each owned several Nishitsu appliances.

"How do you know?" Petrovina asked skeptically.

"Because we've had experience with this stuff," Remo replied.

And he told them about a man both Remo and Chiun had encountered before. A man who wore a suit that could compress atoms and redirect them through telephone lines. The suit had been developed in Japan by Nishitsu and stolen by the Russians. Twice Remo and Chiun had gone up against a Russian in the suit. One time they had met a Japanese who worked for the corporation that had developed it.

Petrovina remained skeptical, but Mike Sears was nodding with growing enthusiasm.

"The suit," he said excitedly, eyes wide with interest. "You actually saw it? I mean, you saw it *work?*"

"It was a thing of evil," Chiun said coldly. He made a point of tucking his long fingernails deep inside the sleeves of his kimono.

"Wow," Sears said. "I never saw it myself. It was in the specs he brought. There were schematics and everything. We were able to reverse-engineer the technology from the data he stole and adapt it to the Vaporizer."

"You are saying this is true?" Petrovina asked.

"It's basically the same thing," Sears said, nodding. "Only on a much bigger scale. We were redirecting a lot more matter than is present in a single human being. No sweat, because the fiber-optic lines gave us much more capacity than even we needed. The only real problem was that the suit was built to protect the wearer. It reconstructed on the far end after transport because the matter was contained. Our open version couldn't reconstruct like that. Not a problem for inanimate matter, but for organic material…''

His voice trailed off. He had seen the look on Remo's face.

Remo was peering down into the valley, his expression dark with disgust. Wordlessly he left the others, taking off down the hill.

''Where are you going?'' Petrovina asked. She started after him, but Chiun held her back.

''Leave him be,'' the old Korean cautioned. ''He cleans up the mess Russian meddling has wrought.''

Remo found his way down the stone slope to the valley floor. The trash stretched up high before him.

He had spotted the deformed bundles from above. They decorated the nearer slope of the trash heap.

The Russian sailors from the *Novgorod* looked like mutated mockeries of human beings. Misshapen white bones jutted out like armor-plated spines on deformed dinosaurs. Uniforms were intermingled with flesh. Buttons were fused to the exposed radius of one man's twisted forearm.

From the mound of garbage, Remo heard a pathetic wheezing. He quickly scaled the pile.

Gennady Zhilnikov had survived the process. The Russian submarine captain was deformed almost beyond recognition. Yet there was a glimmer of human intelligence in his pleading eyes. He held his arms out in prayer.

Remo killed him gently, mercifully.

Afterward he went through the others, checking for signs of life. No more had survived.

Just to be certain he searched for the body of Jack James. He found the Mayanan executive president lying dead on a rotting heap of trash, his head haloed by his own twisted limbs.

Turning, he hiked back up the hill. The others were waiting for him in the Jeep.

"I guess they just don't make gods like they used to," Remo announced as he climbed into the passenger seat.

As seagull squawks echoed loud and shrill across the valley behind them, the Jeep turned lazily around. They headed back down the rutted ravine path.

33

They had no choice but to release him.

Ever since Nikolai Garbegtrov had been trundled through the high gates of the Russian embassy in New Briton, his Green Earth followers had been gathering outside. They set up tents, lit candles, carried signs, sang protest songs.

The mob was growing, and it was getting ugly. They were demanding the release of the former premier.

The Russians had planned to spirit their traitorous former leader back home to a prison cell and a lengthy sentence. But this was a new era. And with cameras lined up beyond the gates, the entire world was watching.

They couldn't let the world see them dragging the screeching Garbegtrov from the building, couldn't risk a riot breaking out. In the end the Russians caved to the pressure of the protesters.

When Nikolai Garbegtrov stepped out the front gate in the company of two Green Earth elders, a cheer rose up.

The former Russian leader was wearing a white cap with the green Green Earth emblem on the front.

The men with him wore identical caps. So did many in the crowd. The caps were made from 100% recycled material. Garbegtrov loved recycling. Garbegtrov loved Mother Earth.

The ex-premier raised his hands in victory.

''Hello, friends!'' Garbegtrov yelled to the crowd.

The crowd yelled back. There was love in Garbegtrov's eyes. There was love right back at him in the eyes of the protesters, his people. Everyone loved everyone.

Garbegtrov was about to speak of his confinement. To tell those gathered about the hardships and horrors he had endured during his day of captivity. Hours during which he had been warm and fed, unlike the people who had suffered years in freezing hunger in gulags while he had presided, fat and uncaring, over old Soviet Russia.

He was going to say many things, but something strange suddenly happened.

Garbegtrov saw something small and slow flying toward him from the direction of the street. So slow was it that he could clearly see that it was a small pebble.

It was an odd thing to see a pebble fly. Odder still when it seemed to abruptly pick up speed and bank upward.

The instant the pebble disappeared, the former Soviet premier felt the warm sun on his head. But that wasn't right. Sunlight had not touched his scalp in many months. It could only be doing so now if...

With sudden shock, he felt for his hat. His hand touched skin. He turned, horrified, to the crowd.

They had seen it. So had the cameras. From Europe to America, all around the world, everyone saw the tattoo emblazoned across his bald head. *U.S.A. #1.*

From the crowd there came a collective gasp of disbelief. It turned into a full-throated roar of rage.

The America-haters of the Green Earth movement were not alone. Garbegtrov's former supporters in the media who shared their opinions screamed outrage.

Placards and cameras fell. Microphones and candles were trampled underfoot. As one, the crowd charged.

Garbegtrov tried running for the gates, but the Russians had locked them behind him.

The former dictator of the Soviet Union fell whimpering to his pudgy knees, shielding the hateful slogan across his scalp even as the enraged crowd fell upon him.

No one noticed the thin man with the thick wrists who stood across the street bouncing pebbles in his hand.

As the crowd tore former Soviet Premier Nikolai Garbegtrov to shreds, Remo Williams let the stones slip from his hand, one by one. When he walked away he was whistling.

34

Two days later Remo was sitting on the kitchen counter of the Connecticut duplex he and Chiun shared. There was a dictionary on the counter next to him. It was open to the *E*s. Remo was on the phone with Smith.

"The situation is under control," the CURE director was saying. "The authorities are investigating the matter. The good news is that all world leaders have departed Mayana safely."

"Whoopie-ding," Remo said. "After seeing those guys in action up close, I think most of the world would send us a thank-you bouquet if we'd let them get turned inside out. So does all this mean we have to go to war with Nishitsu again?"

"It does not look that way," Smith replied. "While the Nishitsu Corporation did have men in Mayana, according to the information I have uncovered, they were there as saboteurs. They wanted to protect the technology that was, after all, developed by them before it was stolen by the Russians."

"Chiun will be disappointed. I think he was psyching himself up for the annual Japanese head harvest."

"About the Vaporizer. The device is being dismantled. Teams have been dispatched to the old Jamestown site to search for any more bodies among the trash."

"I still want to know how they got their hands on the Nishitsu technology," Remo said.

"Blame Alexei Aliyev," Smith replied.

Remo frowned. "Who?"

"He is a Russian who was kept at the site in the guise of a janitor. Dr. Sears took instructions from Aliyev. He was shot sometime during the confusion. You did not know?"

"No," Remo said.

"Perhaps he offended Jack James in some way. In any event Aliyev worked on the vibration-suit project years ago. When the project was canceled, he was out of a job. He offered his technical know-how to the highest bidder, which wound up being the Mayanan government. He adapted the old technology to the Vaporizer. As I explained to you before, it is basically the same way the *krahseevah* could travel through phone lines, albeit on a much grander scale."

"I'll say. You should have seen the size of that dump, Smitty. They'll be cleaning it for years."

"Perhaps," Smith said. "Or perhaps they will just leave it as is and close down the area. An abandoned garbage dump would be a fitting monument to Jack James."

"I still can't get over that one," Remo said. "I'm amazed he got as far as he did."

"It is not so surprising," Smith said. "While insane, James was always a charismatic individual. That quality would not have been altered by plastic surgery. The world thought he was dead so no one would think to look for him among the living. And he emerged back in the public eye enough years after his false death that memory had faded.''

"I guess," Remo said. "The harder thing for me to figure out is why the Russians let that Aloha guy get away."

"Actually that has been a serious problem ever since the collapse of the Soviet Union. Many former government scientists have decided to offer their services to the highest bidder. This is a real threat to the world as far as biological, chemical and nuclear weapons are concerned. Unfortunately Aliyev is just one of many."

"As usual you're a regular Little Mary Sunshine, Smitty. If there isn't anything else, let's end on that happy note."

Remo hung up the phone.

Hopping down from the counter, he snatched up the dictionary. Book in hand, he went out into the living room.

Chiun sat in front of the big-screen TV. The old Korean was watching the news.

"I looked that thing up," Remo announced.

Chiun didn't turn. "What are you braying about now?"

"That thing you said you want to be called. Reigning Master Emeritus. I looked it up." He read from the dictionary. "Emeritus. It means 'holding after retirement an honorary title corresponding to that held last during active service.'" Snapping the book shut, he glanced at his teacher, a look of triumphant expectation on his face.

"You move your lips when you read," Chiun said blandly.

"Honorary shmonorary, this means you're still Reigning Master, doesn't it?" Remo accused. "Even while I'm the Master of Sinanju *you're* the Master of Sinanju, too. And not *a* Master or *retired* Master or *former* Master, but *the* Master."

"I suppose it could be interpreted that way," said the Master of Sinanju.

"But I'm still Reigning Master, right? Or have the last three decades just been about jerking me around?"

Chiun waved an impatient hand. "Yes, you are Reigning Master. So say the histories, so you are. Free to make mistakes and embarrass me in the eyes of my ancestors in whatever stupid or depraved ways your heart desires."

"Great. I just want to know one thing," Remo said. "Will I still be able to pick whoever I want as my pupil?"

"That is your prerogative as Master."

"And you won't get on my case if you think I've picked wrong or if I don't train him exactly like you would or if I don't toe every little line like your idealized version of the perfect little Master of Sinanju?"

The old Korean gave him a baleful look. "And where exactly, Remo, did you find it written that I must scoop out my brain and cut out my tongue so that I do not notice and cannot comment on the egregious mistakes and humiliations you will inevitably commit in your vulgarized American version of Sinanju Reigning Masterhood?''

''Wishful thinking I guess,'' Remo said.

On the television a reporter for one of the major networks was standing at the edge of a smoking crater that seemed to go on forever behind her.

''The death toll here stands at eight so far, with a loss of property estimated at forty-seven million dollars,'' the reporter said in pinched, nasal tones.

At first Remo thought a bomb had gone off. He learned that a gas main had exploded. The explosion had been caused by a sinkhole that had opened up and swallowed most of a California neighborhood. The hole had created a mudslide that had wiped out another neighborhood in a canyon below. Four dozen houses were lost, three times as many people were homeless and many fire trucks and rescue vehicles had been crushed, swallowed up or washed away.

Remo learned that all the destruction and carnage had been the result of a weeklong attempt to save three kittens caught down a storm drain. The cats had apparently been pulled up to safety using nylon fishing line and a twenty-five-cent Easter basket earlier that evening.

The story of the attempted murder in Mayana of every world leader was bumped to a fifteen-second blurb at the end of the newscast after weather, sports and entertainment news. After that, images of wet kitties being toweled off were played under the closing credits.

Remo considered the events of the past few months and days. He didn't realize his silence had drawn attention until a squeaky singsong broke his private thoughts.

"Now what are you grinning at?" the Master of Sinanju asked.

Remo looked down into the wrinkled face of his teacher. When he saw Chiun, his smile of contentment stretched wider.

He couldn't help it. The world was good, everything was right and Remo Williams was happy.

"Dorothy was right, Little Father," Remo said, his smile threatening to spill off his beaming face. "There's no place like home."

James Axler
Outlanders®

TALON AND FANG

Kane finds himself thrown twenty-five years into a parallel future, a world where the mysterious Imperator has seemingly restored civilization to America. In this alternate reality, only Kane and Grant have survived, and the spilled blood has left them estranged. Yet Kane is certain that somewhere in time lies a different path to tomorrow's reality—and his obsession may give humanity their last chance to battle past and future as a sinister madman controls the secret heart of the world.

In the Outlands, the shocking truth is humanity's last hope.

Stony Man is deployed against an armed
invasion on American soil...

FREEDOM WATCH

An unidentified stealth craft takes out two U.S. satellites before
making a forced landing in the dangerous border region of
Afghanistan and China. White House advisers claim the mystery
machine originated in Siberia and urge the President to retaliate
with a nuclear strike. Stony Man deploys Phoenix Force and
Able Team to find the enemy who's using technology linked
to Area 51 and who are prepared to unleash its devastating
power to attack the free world....

STONY MAN

*Available in
February 2003
at your favorite
retail outlet.*

Take
2 explosive books
plus a
mystery bonus
FREE

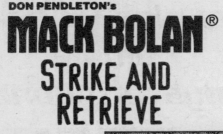

DEATH LANDS®

Skydark Spawn

**Available in
March 2003
at your favorite retail outlet.**

In the relatively untouched area of what was once Niagara Falls, Ryan and his fellow wayfarers find the pastoral farmland under the despotic control of a twisted baron and his slave-breeding farm. Ryan, Mildred and Krysty are captured by the baron's sec men and pawned into the cruel frenzy of their leader's grotesque desires. JB, Jak and Doc enlist the aid of outlanders to organize a counterstrike—but rescue may come too late for them all.

Or order your copy now by sending your name, address, zip or postal code, along with a check or money order (please do not send cash) for $6.50 for each book ordered ($7.99 in Canada), plus 75¢ postage and handling ($1.00 in Canada), payable to Gold Eagle Books, to:

In the U.S.	In Canada
Gold Eagle Books	Gold Eagle Books
3010 Walden Ave.	P.O. Box 636
P.O. Box 9077	Fort Erie, Ontario
Buffalo, NY 14269-9077	L2A 5X3

Please specify book title with order.
Canadian residents add applicable federal and provincial taxes.

GDL61

James Axler
Outlanders
EQUINOX ZERO

As magistrate-turned-rebel Kane, fellow warrior Grant and archivist Brigid Baptiste face uncertainty in their own ranks, an ancient foe resurfaces in the company of Viking warriors— harnessing ancient prophecies of Ragnarok, the final conflict of fire and ice, to bring his own mad vision of a new apocalypse. To save what's left of the future, Kane's new battlefield is the kingdom of Antarctica, where legend and lore have taken on mythic and deadly proportions.

In the Outlands, the shocking truth is humanity's last hope.